dangerous lover

dangerous lover

LISA MARIE RICE

An Imprint of HarperCollins*Publishers*

HarperCollins books may be purchased for educational, business, or sales promotional use. For information please write: Special Markets Department, HarperCollins Publishers, 10 East 53rd Street, New York, NY 10022.

FIRST EDITION

Interior text designed by Diahann Sturge

Library of Congress Cataloging-in-Publication Data

Rice, Lisa Marie.
Dangerous lover / Lisa Marie Rice—1st ed.
p. cm.
ISBN: 978–0–06–120859–1
ISBN–10: 0–06–120859–0
1. Women booksellers—Fiction. 2. Landlord and tenant—Fiction. 3. First loves—Fiction. 4. Soldiers—Fiction. 5. Murderers—Fiction. 6. Conflict diamonds—Fiction. I. Title.

PS3618.I2998D36 2007
813'.6—dc222 2007005008

07 08 09 10 11 ID/RRD 10 9 8 7 6 5 4 3

This book is dedicated to
all those who have impossible dreams.
May they all come true.

Many thanks to my agent, Ethan Ellenberg,
and to my editor, May Chen.

Summerville, Washington
St. Jude Homeless Shelter
Christmas Eve

He needed Caroline like he needed light and air. More.

The tall, emaciated boy dressed in rags rose from his father's lifeless body sprawled bonelessly on the icy, concrete floor of the shelter.

His father had been dying for a long time—most of his life, in fact. There had always been something in him that didn't want to live. The boy couldn't remember the last time he'd seen his father clean and sober. He had no mother. All his life, it had been just the two of them, father and son, drifting from shelter to shelter, staying until they were kicked out.

The boy stood for a moment, looking down at his only blood relation in this world, dead in a pool of vomit and shit. Nobody had noticed his father's dead body yet. Nobody ever noticed them or even looked their way if they could help it. Even the other lost, hopeless souls in the shelter recognized someone worse off than they were and shunned them.

The boy looked around at the averted faces, eyes cast to the floor.

Nobody cared that the drunk wasn't getting up again. Nobody cared what happened to his son.

There was nothing for the boy here. Nothing.

He had to get to Caroline.

He had to move fast before they discovered that his father was dead. If they found the body here, the police and social workers and administrators would come for him. He was eighteen, but he couldn't prove it. And he knew enough about the way things worked to know that he'd become a ward of the state. He'd be locked up in some prisonlike orphanage.

No. No way. He'd rather die.

The boy moved toward the stairs that would take him up out of the shelter into the gelid, sleety afternoon.

An old woman looked up as he passed by, cloudy eyes flickering with recognition. Susie. Ancient, toothless Susie. She wasn't lost in alcohol like his father. She was lost in the smoky depths of her own mind.

"Ben, chocolate chocolate?" she cackled and smacked her wrinkled, rubbery lips. He'd once shared a chocolate bar Caroline had brought him, and Susie had looked to him for sweets ever since.

Here he was known as Ben. In the last shelter—Portland, was it?—his father had called him Dick. Naming him after the man-

ager of the shelter always bought them some time. Not enough. Eventually, the shelters got sick of his father's drunken rages and found a way to kick them out.

Susie's hands, with their long, black, ragged nails, grasped at him. Ben stopped and held her hand a moment. "No chocolate, Susie," he said gently.

Like a child, her eyes filled with tears. Ben stooped to give her grimy wrinkled cheek a kiss, then rushed up the stairs and out into the open air.

No hesitation as he turned into Morrison Street. He knew exactly where he was going. To Greenbriars. To Caroline.

To the one person on the face of the earth who cared about him. To the only person who treated him as a human being and not some half-wild animal who smelled of dirty clothes and rotting food.

Ben hadn't eaten in two days, and he had only a too-short cotton jacket on to keep the cold away. His big, bony wrists stuck out of the jacket's sleeves, and he had to tuck his hands into his armpits to keep them warm.

No matter. He'd been cold and hungry before.

The only warm thing he wanted right now was Caroline's smile.

Like the arrow of a compass to a lodestar, he leaned into the wind to walk the mile and a half to Greenbriars.

No one looked his way as he trudged by. He was invisible, a lone, tall figure dressed in rags. It didn't bother him. He'd always been invisible. Being invisible had helped him survive.

The weather worsened. The wind blew icy needles of sleet directly into his eyes until he had to close them into slits.

Didn't matter. He had an excellent sense of direction and could make his way to Greenbriars blindfolded.

Head down, arms wrapped around himself to conserve what little warmth he'd been able to absorb at the shelter, Ben slowly left behind the dark, sullen buildings of the part of the city that housed the shelter. Soon the roads opened up into tree-lined avenues. Ancient brick buildings gave way to graceful, modern buildings of glass and steel.

No cars passed—the weather was too severe for that. There was nobody on the streets. Under his feet, the icy buildup crackled.

He was almost there. The houses were big here, in this wealthy part of town. Large, well built, with sloping green lawns that were now covered in ice and snow.

He usually made his way through the back streets, invisible as always. Someone like him in this place of rich and powerful people would be immediately stopped by the police, so he always took the back streets on a normal day. But today the streets were deserted, and he walked openly on the broad sidewalks.

It usually took him half an hour to walk to Greenbriars but today the ice-slick sidewalks and hard wind dragged at him. An hour after leaving the shelter, he was still walking. He was strong, but hunger and cold started to wear him down. His feet, in their cracked shoes, were numb.

Music sounded, so lightly at first that he wondered whether he was hallucinating from cold and hunger. Notes floated in the air, as if borne by the snow.

He rounded a corner and there it was—Greenbriars. Caroline's home. His heart pounded as it loomed out of the sleety mist. It always pounded when he came here, just as it pounded whenever she was near.

He usually came in through the back entrance, when her parents were at work and Caroline and her brother in school. The maid left at noon and from noon to one the house was his to explore. He could move in and out like a ghost. The back door lock was flimsy, and he'd been picking locks since he was five.

He'd wander from room to room, soaking up the rich, scented atmosphere of Caroline's home.

The shelter rarely had hot water, but still he took care to wash as well as he could whenever he headed out to Greenbriars. The stench of the shelter had no place in Caroline's home.

Greenbriars was so far beyond what he could ever hope to have that there was no jealousy, no envy in him as he touched the backs of the thousands of books in the library, walked into sweet-smelling closets full of new clothes, opened the huge refrigerator to see fresh fruits and vegetables. Caroline's family was rich in a way he couldn't comprehend, as if they belonged to a different species living on another planet.

To him, it was simply Caroline's world. And living in it for an hour a day was like touching the sky.

Today nobody could see him approach in the storm. He walked right up the driveway, feeling the gravel through the thin soles of his shoes. The snow intensified, the wind whipping painful icy particles through the air. Ben knew how to move quietly, stealthily when he had to. But it wasn't necessary now. There was no one to see him or hear him as he crunched his way to the window.

The music was louder now, the source a yellow glow. It wasn't until he had reached the end of the driveway that Ben realized that the yellow glow was the big twelve-pane window of the living room, and the music was someone playing the piano.

He knew that living room well, as he knew all the rooms of the big mansion. He'd wandered them all, for hours. He knew that the huge living room always smelled faintly of woodsmoke from the big fireplace. He knew that the couches were deep and comfortable and the rugs soft and thick.

He walked straight up to the window. The snow was already filling in the tracks his shoes made. No one could see him, no one could hear him.

He was tall, and could see over the windowsill if he stood on tiptoe. Light had drained from the sky, and he knew no one in the room could see him outside.

The living room was like something out of a painting. Hundreds of candles flickered everywhere—on the mantelpiece, on all the tables. The coffee table held the remains of a feast—half a ham on a carving board, a huge loaf of bread, a big platter of cheeses, several cakes, and two pies. A teapot, cups, glasses, an open bottle of wine, a bottle of whiskey.

Water pooled in his mouth. He hadn't eaten for two days. His empty stomach ached. He could almost smell the food in the room through the windowpane.

Then food completely disappeared from his mind.

A lovely voice rang out, clear and pure, singing a Christmas carol he'd heard in a shopping mall once while he helped his dad panhandle. Something about a shepherd boy.

It was Caroline's voice. He'd recognize it anywhere.

A frigid gust of wind buffeted the garden, raking his face with sleet. He didn't even feel it as he edged his head farther up over the windowsill.

There she was! As always, his breath caught when he saw her.

She was so beautiful, it sometimes hurt him to look at her. When she visited him in the shelter, he'd refuse to look at her for the first few minutes. It was like looking into the sun.

He watched her hungrily, committing each second to memory. He remembered every word she'd ever spoken to him, he'd read and reread every book she'd ever brought him, he remembered every item of clothing he'd ever seen her in.

She was at the piano, playing. He'd never seen anyone actually play the piano, and it seemed like magic to him. Her fingers moved gracefully over the black and white keys, and music poured out like water in a stream. His head filled with the wonder of it.

She was in profile. Her eyes were closed as she played, a slight smile on her face, as if she and the music shared a secret understanding. She was singing another song even he recognized. "Silent Night." Her voice rose, pure and light.

The piano was tall and black, with lit candles held in shiny brass holders along the sides.

Though the entire room was filled with candles, Caroline glowed more brightly than any of them. She was lit with light, her pale skin gleaming in the glowing candlelight as she sang and played.

The song came to an end, and her hands dropped to her lap. She looked up, smiling, at the applause, then started another carol, her voice rising pure and high.

The whole family was there. Mr. Lake, a big-shot businessman, tall, blond, looking like the king of the world. Mrs. Lake, impossi-

bly beautiful and elegant. Toby, Caroline's seven-year-old brother. There was another person in the room, a handsome young man. He was elegantly dressed, his dark blond hair combed straight back. His fingers were beating time with the carol on the piano top. When Caroline stopped playing, he leaned down and gave her a kiss on the mouth.

Caroline's parents laughed, and Toby did a somersault on the big rug.

Caroline smiled up at the handsome young man and said something that made him laugh. He bent to kiss her hair.

Ben watched, his heart nearly stopping.

This was Caroline's boyfriend. Of course. They shared a look—blond, poised, privileged. Good-looking, rich, educated. They belonged to the same species. They were meant to be together, it was so clear.

His heart slowed in his chest. For the first time, he felt the danger from the cold. He felt its icy fingers reaching out to him to drag him down to where his father had gone.

Maybe he should just let it take him.

There was nothing for him here, in this lovely candlelit room. He would never be a part of this world. He belonged to the darkness and the cold.

Ben dropped back down on his heels, backing slowly away from the house until the yellow light of the window was lost in the sleet and mist. He was shaking with the cold as he trudged back down the driveway, the wet snow seeping through the holes in his shoes to soak his feet.

Half an hour later, he came to the interstate junction and stopped, swaying on his feet.

The human in him wanted to sink to the ground, curl up in a ball, and wait for despair and then death to take him, as they had taken his father. It wouldn't take long.

But the animal in him was strong and wanted, fiercely, to live.

To the right, the road stretched northward, right up into Canada. To the left, it went south.

If he went north, he would die. It was as simple as that.

Turning left, Ben shuffled forward, head low, into the icy wind.

One

Summerville, Washington
Christmas Eve
Twelve years later

She was here.

He could feel her, he could *smell* her.

Walking into the small bookshop with the old-fashioned bell over the door, the man now known as Jack Prescott knew he'd found her.

He was exhausted, having traveled for forty-eight hours straight, on a pirogue from Obuja to Freetown, via Air Afrique from Lungi Airport to Paris, Air France from Paris to Atlanta, Delta from Atlanta to Seattle, then a rickety puddle jumper he could have flown better himself to Summerville.

Even through his exhaustion, though, his senses were keen. Twelve years later, he could still recognize her touches. The candles on the windowsill, the gentle harp music playing faintly in the background, a smell of cinnamon, vanilla, roses and *her.* Unmistakable, unforgettable.

Coming in from the airport, the news that she was still in Summerville and, astonishingly, still single had blown him away. He hadn't been expecting that. He hadn't been expecting anything but difficulty and frustration in tracking her down.

He had all the time in the world to do it in, now.

Colonel Eugene Prescott's death had freed him from bonds of loyalty and love. The day after the Colonel's death, Jack had sold ENP Security and flown to Sierra Leone to take care of the last of his responsibility to the man who'd become his father.

It had cost gunfire and bloodshed, pain and violence, but he'd taken care of the mess as his father had asked on his deathbed. Jack had done what had to be done, salvaged his father's reputation, punished the fuckers who'd mounted a rogue operation, and was finally, finally free from all responsibility for the first time in twelve years.

His life as a Ranger and his duty to the Colonel and his company had kept him busy. As long as the Colonel was alive, Jack had tried to keep Caroline out of his head, and he was successful, mostly—except at night. She had her life, wherever it was, and he had the Colonel to serve. But after stopping Vince Deaver, he was free. He'd turned straight around and flown as fast as modern aviation could take him from Africa to Summerville.

It was crazy, he knew it was crazy to look for her here,

twelve years later. Why would Caroline stay in Summerville? She was beautiful, talented, smart, rich. She'd end up where all beautiful, smart, talented, rich women go—some big city on a coast. Maybe even abroad.

And no way could she be single, not someone who looked like Caroline. She'd be married with kids. Any man in his right mind would snatch her right up and keep her pregnant to be sure she stayed.

He had no illusions. Caroline wasn't for him. She was probably happy and fulfilled, with a family of her own. Jack knew he'd never have a family, it wasn't in his destiny.

He was going to keep out of Caroline's life because he had no place in it.

But Jack had to see her. *Needed* to see her, like he needed to breathe. Just one more look before starting the next stage of his life, whatever that would be. He'd closed the door on ENP Security when he'd buried his father. The company was gone, the house sold. Everything he needed was in his duffel bag and suitcase. He was ready to turn the page, right after one last look at her.

So he'd come here to start his quest, to the last place he'd been before becoming Jack Prescott, to the last place he'd seen Caroline. Her family was established here, there was bound to be a way to track her down.

He didn't care where she'd gone—whether she was still in the U.S. or had settled abroad or had gone to the moon. He was an excellent tracker—the best there was. He'd find her, eventually, however long it took. He had the rest of his life to do it in, and he certainly wasn't hurting for money.

Just one look, and he'd disappear forever.

In the end, he didn't have to track her down, though. The taxi driver in from the airport knew where she was.

Here. Right here, where she'd been all along. In Summerville.

Single.

Jack had been planning on checking into a hotel, cleaning up, having a nice meal in a restaurant, then sleeping for twenty-four hours. He'd been in a firefight, and he'd been traveling for two days straight. He was exhausted.

It was Christmas Eve. Everything would be closed on Christmas Day and the next day, Sunday. On Monday, he planned to start his search for Caroline.

But then the taxi driver said Caroline Lake—*his* Caroline Lake—was still in Summerville and ran a small bookshop, and so there was no question where he'd go.

Straight to her.

Quick, light footsteps on the hardwood floor and *shit*, before he was ready, there she was.

"Oh!" Caroline Lake stopped suddenly, the welcoming smile dying on her face as she saw him. "He-hello."

He knew what she saw.

She saw a tall, heavily muscled man with long black hair tied back carelessly, dressed in cheap, rough, dirty, crumpled clothes. He hadn't showered or shaved in three days, and he knew that lines of exhaustion creased his stubbled face.

He knew what she felt, too.

Scared.

She was alone with him. He had unusually sharp hearing,

and he heard no other human sounds in the small shop. The icy sleet storm outside was so severe that the streets outside were deserted, as well. If he turned out to be violent, there would be no one to hear her cries for help.

There was nothing he could do about the way he looked—dangerous. The truth was, he was every inch as dangerous as he looked.

Though Caroline couldn't possibly see the Glock in the shoulder holster, or the tactical folder in the boot or the .22 in the ankle holster, an armed man carries himself differently than an unarmed man. He'd killed four men two days and two continents ago. At some subliminal level, she was picking up on this.

She was standing very still, nostrils slightly flared, instinctively pulling in oxygen in case she had to run. She wouldn't know that was what she was doing, but he did.

He was an expert on human prey and how it reacted to danger.

First, defuse her fears.

He stood utterly still, watching her carefully. He would rather rip his own throat out than hurt her in any way, but she couldn't know that. All she knew was she was all alone with a big, potentially violent man.

"Good evening." He kept his voice low and without inflection. Calm. He kept his body language utterly nonthreatening, moving only his lungs to breathe. Not smiling, not frowning.

It was the only way he knew to reassure her. Words wouldn't do it. Stillness would. If he were crazy, he couldn't stay so still. Agitated minds make for agitated bodies.

It worked. She relaxed slightly, nodded, smiled.

He couldn't smile back. For a second, he couldn't breathe.

Christ, she is so fucking beautiful. She'd somehow become even more beautiful than his memory. How could that be?

Slender yet curvy. Not tall, yet long-limbed. Her hair was the richest color he'd ever seen—a wild mix of reds and golds, with pale champagne streaks running through it. Her coloring was so vivid the eye naturally gravitated to where she was. Jack couldn't imagine looking at another woman while Caroline was in the room.

She stepped back slightly.

He was staring at her. Worse, he was scaring her.

"Terrible weather," he rumbled. His voice was deep, unusually so, but he kept his tone even and low.

It took a huge effort, one of the hardest things he'd ever done in a hard life, but he took his eyes off her. Hungry as he was for the sight of her, he couldn't keep staring, or she'd freak.

So he looked around him, at what she'd created.

It was a pretty bookshop, with a high, beamed ceiling, hardwood floor with what looked like expensive rugs scattered around, pinewood shelves and tables with bestsellers on them. The harp music had given way to an a cappella choir of women's voices singing madrigals. Over the smell of her—soap, shampoo, and the scent of roses that haunted his nights—he could smell potpourri, candle wax and resin from the small Christmas tree decorated with miniature books standing in a big red ceramic pot in the corner.

The entire shop was warm and welcoming, a delight to all the senses.

Jack had good peripheral vision and kept looking around until she visibly relaxed. He turned back to her. "Very nice bookshop. My compliments."

Her lips turned up in a slight smile. "Thank you. And it's not usually so deserted. I was expecting a Christmas Eve rush for all the lazybones who haven't bought their presents yet, but the weather has kept everyone indoors."

Jack tried not to frown and look disapproving. What was the matter with her? Jesus, the last thing she should do when alone with a man was point out just *how* alone they were.

She'd always been like that, too trusting.

Once, in the shelter, old man McMurty, doped up on God knows what shit he'd scored on the streets, had sidled up to her when she'd smiled at him.

Jack knew what McMurty was like when he was high. The filthy fucker would have put his hands on Caroline if Jack hadn't blocked him. After Caroline left, Jack had shoved McMurty up against the wall, showed him the Bowie knife he'd shoplifted and promised McMurty that if he even so much as breathed in Caroline's direction, ever again, he could kiss his balls good-bye.

Jack had meant every word.

Pretty, slender ringless hands opened wide. "Can I help you with something? We have a fairly good selection, and I can order anything you want if we don't stock it. It takes about a week to arrive." She smiled up at him.

She was a woman now. A stunningly beautiful woman, whose face showed the sorrows she'd suffered. The chatty taxicab driver had told him all about Caroline and the downfall of the Lakes. Jack had heard all about the car accident that had killed her parents and injured her little brother. The discovery at their death that Mr. Lake had been making bad investments, that there was no money to cover the hospital bills, with barely enough to pay for the double funeral. Then six years of caring for an invalid brother, only to lose him two months ago, saddling her with even more debts.

All of that showed in her face. Faint lines starred her eyes, though they were still that haunting silver-gray color. She'd slimmed down even more. The young Caroline had had a lovely, open face with a perpetually sunny smile. This Caroline showed sorrow and serenity, the sunniness gone.

And yet, Jack could still see the young Caroline, the heart of her—the lovely, gentle girl who'd befriended an outcast inside the beautiful woman who'd known heartache and grief.

The young girl had haunted his days and nights. The woman in front of him nearly brought him to his knees.

Christ, he was staring again, lost. She'd said something—something about books. He didn't want books.

"The sign," he said.

"I beg your pardon?" She swirled a lock of shiny red-gold hair behind a small ear. He'd seen her do it a hundred times.

"You've got a sign at the front of the shop. ROOMS TO LET. Do you still have a room available?"

It had been the motor-mouth taxi driver who'd told him that Caroline rented rooms to boarders to boost her income from the bookshop.

Caroline looked at him for a long moment, clearly sizing him up. He couldn't shrink and he couldn't take a shower and shave and he couldn't change his clothes right then. All he could do was remain motionless and keep his expression neutral. There was nothing he could say or do to convince her if she didn't trust him enough to want him in her home. The only thing he could do was wait.

And hope.

Finally, Caroline sighed. "Yes, as it happens, my boarders just left, so I do have a room. But let's discuss it sitting down, why don't we? You can leave those behind my desk if you'd like." "Those" were his ancient duffel bag with the brand-new luggage lock and a suitcase.

No way was he leaving them out of his sight. "Thanks, I'll just put them down next to me so no one will trip over them," he said casually, hefting the duffel bag over his shoulder and picking up the suitcase.

She nodded and turned to walk between the rows of books to the back corner of the shop, where a small sitting area had been set up.

Though she was more slender than when she was a girl, she was also curvier. She had a tiny waist that begged for his hands to span, rounding out to a perfect ass. He had to work hard to keep his eyes off it, in case she turned around and found him ogling her. That would have got him tossed out on his ass, PDQ.

Jack recognized a couch and two small armchairs that had once been in her father's study. They were old and worn but still looked comfortable. Jack put his duffel bag behind one of the small armchairs and sat down in it, hoping it would take his weight. He wasn't built for old, delicate furniture, but he needn't have worried. The armchair might be shabby, but it was of good quality.

"Would you like me to take your jacket, Mr.—?" Caroline held out a hand.

"Prescott. Jack Prescott. And no, thanks. I'm still a little chilled from the weather outside."

"I can imagine," she murmured, withdrawing her hand.

Jesus, he couldn't take his jacket off. Out of reflex, and because he hated being unarmed, he'd grabbed his bag off the carousel and ducked into the nearest men's room to slip his Glock into his shoulder rig. And then he'd completely forgotten about it. He'd had no idea whatsoever that an hour after landing, he'd actually be sitting down, with Caroline, who wanted him to take his jacket off.

Jack was very very good at strategic planning. He'd been born with it. Then Colonel Prescott and the Army had taken that and refined it. Jack had been an outstanding operative, always able to think several moves ahead.

The fact that he hadn't thought to hide his weapon before entering the bookshop, where he might be expected to take his jacket off, was off his own personal radar. That was exactly the kind of mistake that could have gotten him killed on the job.

But even without the weapon, he couldn't take his jacket off. No way. Besides his weapon, he had a hard-on. A huge blue-steeler that felt like a club between his legs, and his pants were just loose enough to show it.

Walking behind Caroline, watching the sway of her hips and the way her hair bounced on her shoulders, sniffing the air in her wake—every hormone in his body woke up and smelled her roses. All the blood in his body had streamed straight to his cock.

Well, *that* was guaranteed to keep him off her list of possible boarders. No woman in the world would agree to have a man in the house who swelled erect just by looking at her.

This was insane.

Jack's body was his to command. It did his bidding, always. If he needed to go without food or water or sleep, his body obeyed. Extremes of heat and cold didn't bother him. Sex was never a problem. When he wanted to fuck, he got a hard-on and when he didn't, his dick stayed right down between his legs.

But watching Caroline's graceful walk to the back of the shop, hips gently swaying, he got massively aroused with each step she took.

All he'd wanted was a glimpse of her. Getting to live with her in Greenbriars within an hour of landing at the airport was something he hadn't even thought to hope for. And yet here he was, maybe five or ten minutes away from actually living with Caroline, in Greenbriars, and he was about to blow it. He couldn't think of anything more likely to disqualify himself as a potential boarder than his dick flying in her face.

She was the only person on the face of the earth who could mess with his mind and his dick that way. Nothing ever got in the way of what he wanted. Certainly not sex. Sex was fun and sometimes necessary to blow off steam, but it wasn't something he allowed to interfere with his life, ever.

Jack was intensely mission-oriented. He focused narrowly

on the mission, whatever it was, to the exclusion of everything else. The mission now was to move into Caroline's house, and he shouldn't have allowed anything to cloud his mind, let alone stiffen his cock.

His boner shocked the shit out of him. That wasn't how he worked. He was in control, always.

Not now, though. All thoughts fled from his mind as he walked behind Caroline. She was wearing pretty pointy-toed shoes with high heels, impossible shoes for the sleety afternoon but perfect to showcase long, slender calves and delicate ankles. There was a slight, rhythmic hiss of stocking as she walked, and he had felt the pulses of it through his skin. The rhythm of her heels tapping on the wood matched his heartbeat exactly, the little flutter of a silk blouse as she walked echoing the flutter of blood rippling through his veins.

"Here," she said and, looking around, he thought, *yes, here. Great.*

On the couch, on the rug, on the hardwood floor. Against the wall, bent over the counter. Anywhere, just as long as he could get in her and stay there for hours.

It was only when she cocked her head to one side, a slight frown between auburn eyebrows, and said, "Mr. Prescott?" in a light, inquisitive tone, that Jack realized with a jolt to his system what he was doing.

Fucking it up, that's what he was doing.

He *never* fucked up.

So he gritted his teeth, managed a quiet "Thank you" through clenched jaws and sat, forcing himself to think of Sierra Leone, Obuja and Vince Deaver. Of blood and betrayal, torture and the screaming of women. So much blood the ground was soaked with it, running in red rivulets. Women bayoneted to death. Highly trained soldiers using children as target practice. The sniper's red mist around kids' heads as the shot went home . . .

That did it. The images cooled his blood and sickened his heart. His cock went straight back down.

His teeth were clenching so tightly it was a miracle he didn't have shards of enamel coming out his ears.

Caroline must have felt something wrong in the air, because she sat gingerly on the edge of the armchair, knees and calves and feet aligned, arms crossed tightly across her midriff, body language tight. Unconsciously ready to stand up or even leap up if he made her any more uncomfortable than he already had.

He was a man who kept his cool in armed combat, but seeing her change her body language scared the shit out of him. *He'd* done that. He'd made her feel edgy and wary, when he should have done everything in his power to reassure her.

Maybe it was the exhaustion and jet lag. Nine time zones, a total of thirty-six hours in the air and maybe six hours' sleep in all.

Whatever it was that was making him groggy and horny and a dumb-ass, he had to shape up fast or he'd be tossed out on his ear.

He cleared his throat. "So, ma'am." He looked her straight in the eyes, heroically never allowing his gaze to drop to her breasts or legs, and made his expression impassive. "As I said, I understand you have a room to let. I'm looking for a place to stay, and a room sounds just fine for now until I find my feet. You said you have a room free?"

Caroline breathed in and out. Jack knew what her head was saying—*no, no way. Are you crazy? This guy's scary-looking and could be nuts.*

But Caroline also thought with her heart. Her eyes dropped and fixed on his boots. They were his combat boots and were ancient and cracked and stained. The heels were worn.

A soldier always looks after his feet. In the field, a blister can get infected and turn a foot gangrenous in twenty-four hours. His combat boots were comfortable and waterproof and had served him well. He hadn't even thought about changing into better shoes when making his way back.

What Caroline saw was a man with worn clothes, stubble on his chin and down-at-heel boots. A man who looked like he'd traveled hard and long and was down on his luck. He could see the softening in her eyes. She lifted her gaze to his and uncrossed her arms and sat back slightly.

His heart thudded.

Yes. Oh shit, *yes!* It was a done deal. It was going to be okay. Bless her soft heart. She'd made the decision. Now it was just a question of finding the right words, the ones to convince her head to take a chance on him because her heart already had. He could still fuck it up, but not if he paid attention and said the right things.

Caroline had relaxed a bit, but she wasn't smiling. "Um, yes, I do. I have two rooms, actually, a single and a double and they are both free. One boarder left two weeks ago, and the other two boarders left four days ago."

"So I'm in luck." He tried on a small smile. "I'll take it. The double, because I like my space."

She sighed and dropped her eyes to where a long, pink-tipped finger was playing with a loose thread. She bit her lips, clearly struggling with something. She sighed, a light exhalation of breath. When she lifted her eyes to his, she'd come to a decision.

"The double room I have is spacious and comfortable, Mr. Prescott, and in a beautiful old home about a mile and a half from the city center. The price includes meals and"—she smiled—"I assure you I am a very good cook."

Oh, Jesus. Caroline and *food*. Jack nearly fell to his knees weeping. He hadn't had a decent meal in . . . shit. Since before Afghanistan.

He dipped his head. "Sounds wonderful, ma'am. Exactly what I need, since I can't boil water myself. I'll—"

"Wait." She put up a slender hand and took a deep breath, as if to brace herself. She looked him straight in the eyes. "That's the good news. The bad news is that the house comes with the Boiler from Hell, which unfortunately has been going on the blink every other day, even after having been fixed by the Repairman from Hell." She glanced at the whiteout outside the window. In the sudden silence, they could hear the icy needles pinging against the windowpane. "And in this weather . . . well, let's just say it can get uncomfortable. And the lighting is sometimes erratic, there's some wire crossed somewhere, and no one can find it. If you work on a computer, it makes it hard, and my last boarder lost several important files. And since I seem to be in confession mode, two treads of the staircase are broken, so if you forget and walk down the stairs at night to get a glass of milk, you're fairly likely to break your neck." She let out her breath with a whoosh, tensely watching his face to see his reaction to her words. "So there you have it. And I understand completely if you decide you don't want the room after all."

It was hard to keep from snorting. Jack had been waiting for *twelve fucking years* to see her again, never actually believing it would ever happen. He'd dreamed of it on the cold, stony ground while undergoing weeklong training exercises. It had kept him awake in the jungles of Indonesia and for six long, freezing months in a winter barracks in Afghanistan.

And she thought a little cold, some flickering lights and broken treads could keep him away?

The hounds of hell couldn't keep him away.

"I'm used to discomfort, ma'am," he said. "A little cold won't bother me, believe me. I have a laptop with good batteries and I'll be careful on the stairs. And I'm pretty handy with my hands. Let me see if I can do some repairs around the house for you."

"Oh." Caroline blinked. "Wow. That—that's very kind of you. And incredibly useful. I can only hope you're better than Mack the Jerk, which is what I call the man who comes and fumbles around in my house and takes my money." She swallowed, her pretty pale throat convulsing. "And of course, you can deduct any repairs you make from the rent. I insist."

Something clenched tightly in Jack's chest. She clearly needed the money. Even the cab driver knew she needed money, probably all of Summerville knew she needed money, but here she was, willing to give him a break on the rent for his help. It was literally impossible for Caroline to take advantage of someone.

Whatever else happened, whatever went down between them, Jack vowed she'd never have money problems again for the rest of her life.

"No problem, ma'am," he said gently. "I like to work. I'm not used to being idle. I don't mind making repairs, fixing things up. It'll give me something to do while I settle in."

She tilted her head to one side. "Were you in the military, Mr. Prescott?"

"Yes, ma'am. Army. A Ranger, for seven years. And my father was career military. Army, too. Retired a full colonel. He built up a security company afterwards, and I quit the military to help him run it. He died last week." A spasm of grief—uncontrollable, unstoppable—crossed his face.

"Oh, my," she said softly, reaching across to touch his hand. The touch was brief, meant to be consoling, and burned. It was all he could do to keep from snatching at her hand. "I am so sorry. I know perfectly well what it is to lose a parent. It's incredibly painful. You have my condolences."

He inclined his head, unable to speak.

Silence. So thick it was a presence in the room. The only sound was the wind rattling the window in its casing.

Jack had got his dick down, but in the meantime something had happened to his throat. It was tight, and hot. A wild tangle of emotions warred in his chest, emotions he didn't dare let out, but that felt like hot knives slicing away inside him.

Grief. Lust. Sorrow. Joy. He'd lost his father, and he'd found Caroline.

She watched him, saying nothing, as if she understood what was going on inside him. Finally, she broke the silence. "Well, Mr. Prescott, I guess I have a new boarder."

He lifted his eyes to hers and coughed to loosen his throat. "Guess you do, ma'am. And please call me Jack."

"All right, Jack. And I'm Caroline. Caroline Lake." Jack nearly smiled. The one and only time he ever got drunk was the day the Colonel received news that he had inoperable stomach cancer. Jack accompanied the Colonel home, saw him into bed, then went right back out again. That night he got hammered and woke up two days later in some bimbo's bed with a big ornate 'C' tattooed on his right biceps.

He knew who she was, all right.

Jack asked, because he knew she was expecting it. "How much is the rent?"

"Five hundred dollars a month." She said it sorrowfully, watching his eyes again. "I know that sounds like a lot, but really—"

He held his hand up, palm out. "That's fine. Sounds reasonable. Particularly with meals, not to mention meals prepared by a good cook. I'll save a lot on restaurants. So . . . how do I get out there?" He knew perfectly well how to get to Greenbriars, but it would sound weird if he didn't ask.

"Do you have a car, Mr. Prescott?"

"No, not yet. I came in straight from the airport in a taxi. I'll rent something on Monday."

Caroline stood, and he stood, too, catching the handle of his bag. He was too close to her and stepped back immediately. It was an instinctive reaction. He was so tall he had to be careful not to loom over people. He particularly didn't want to make Caroline uneasy.

"Well, no one else will be coming in today, not in this weather." She gave a rueful shrug. "I think I'll just close up the shop. You can ride home with me, Mr. Prescott."

"Thank you, ma'am. I appreciate it."

"Okay, Jack, and do please call me Caroline."

"Caroline," he said, the word passing his lips for the first time in twelve years.

She was staring up at him and seemed lost in thought.

He waited a beat, then—"Caroline? Ma'am?"

Caroline shook herself slightly. "Yes, um . . . Why don't you wait for me at the front door? I need to close down my computer and change my shoes."

She looked down at her pretty shoes, guaranteed to melt in the snow. Jack looked down, too. Their feet made an almost shocking contrast, as if they belonged to two different species instead of two sexes—Caroline's in the pretty, small, pointy beige heels and Jack's in his huge, ancient, battered combat boots. Their heads came up at the same time, and their eyes locked.

Jack clutched his bag tightly, because the temptation to reach out and touch her was almost unbearable.

He'd never touched her, not once, in all the times she'd visited the shelter. He'd thought about it endlessly, but he'd never dared.

Caroline moved to her office, behind a waist-high counter.

His knuckles tightened on the handle of the bag as he listened to the beeping sounds of a computer system closing down behind the cubicle wall. Her head disappeared as she bent to change shoes.

Caroline came out wearing lined boots, a wool cap and an eiderdown coat that reached almost to her ankles. Even bundled up so much it could have been a man or a Martian in there, she was so desirable it hurt. He watched her walk gracefully to a wall panel, switch off the lights and open the door.

Her gasp was loud even over the roar of the wind.

It was like opening a gateway to a freezing cold hell. The wind had risen and was howling like a tortured soul in the deepest reaches of the underworld, driving painful needles of sleet that stung the skin. It was so cold it stole the breath out of your lungs.

"Oh my God!" Recoiling as if someone had slapped her, Caroline stepped back straight into Jack's arms.

Jack pulled Caroline farther into the room and fought the wind for control of the door. He actually had to put some muscle into it. He leaned against it, held out his hand and put command in his voice. "Give me your car keys."

Just that brief exposure had Caroline shivering. It took her several tries to open her purse, but she made it and dropped a set of car keys in his palm. Then blinked at her obedience. "Why—"

"You'll freeze to death out there. What make is your car and where did you park it? I'll bring it around and park right out front so you don't have to walk around in this weather."

Caroline looked confused. "A green Fiat. It's parked just around the corner to the right. But listen, you're not dressed for the—"

She was talking to thin air.

Two

I am either very lucky or very crazy, Caroline thought, shivering in her coat. Just thirty seconds exposed to the swirling freezing hell out there, and it felt as if she'd spent the winter camping in the Antarctic. She was chilled to her bones.

Lucky or crazy? Which was it?

Lucky was a strong contender because she needed the $500 desperately, and it had fallen into her lap from the sky on a day when she could never have hoped to find a new boarder. Paying off Toby's medical bills had required taking out a huge loan against Greenbriars, and the money from her boarders was essential. She couldn't possibly make the mid-January payment without the $500 in rent.

She'd been heartsick four days ago when old Mr. and Mrs. Kipping had come down to breakfast to announce that *we're so sorry honey, but we're moving out*. They were supposed to stay until May, until renovation work on their home was completed. But Mr. Kipping had lost several chapters of his biography of Alexander Hamilton to a short circuit somewhere in the house and, the crowning blow, Mrs. Kipping had contracted bronchitis because of the frequent breakdowns of the boiler.

There was no money at all to pay an electrician to test the wiring to find the source of the short circuit, and Caroline could probably fly to the moon more easily than she could afford a new boiler.

She'd still be paying off debts when she was eighty. If she lived that long. So far, her family's batting average in terms of extended life expectancy wasn't too encouraging.

Mrs. Kipping had been in tears at the thought of leaving, and it had taken all of Caroline's self-control not to break into tears herself. The Kippings were a lovely couple and had been with her for almost a year. They'd been delightful company and had provided enormous comfort to her during Toby's last days. Caroline didn't know how she could have faced coming home to an empty house from the hospital. And after Toby's funeral . . . she shivered.

In the beginning, the Kippings often remarked that they could never remodel their home into anything as beautiful as Greenbriars. That was before the lost files, the constant cold showers and waking up to ice in the bathroom sink. Caroline knew that Mr. and Mrs. Kipping were very fond of her and loved her cooking and that it was only Mrs. Kipping's bout of bronchitis that forced their decision. Anna Kipping was fragile and Marcus, her husband, was afraid of losing her.

Still, he'd had tears in his eyes at leaving, too.

Finding a new boarder on Christmas Eve in this terrible weather was like a wonderful miracle.

Not to mention the biggie—not being alone on Christmas Day. The day she'd lost her parents to a hideous car accident. The day Toby was so injured he never walked again. It had taken him six pain-filled years to die.

So that was the lucky theory.

Then, of course, there was the crazy theory, which was probably the correct one. She *was* probably crazy to accept a man who looked as dangerous as Jack Prescott into her home and, as if that wasn't enough, handing him the keys to her car half an hour after meeting him.

Marcus and Anna Kipping had been the safest people on the face of the earth—two darlings in their late sixties whose worst vices were Double Chocolate Fudge ice cream and an unholy passion for Gilbert & Sullivan. Marcus could recite the lyrics to *H.M.S. Pinafore* at the drop of a hat.

Jack Prescott, on the other hand, looked anything but safe. She'd felt her heart speed up as they talked, ridiculous as that sounded. Yes, he looked rather scary. He was rough-looking, tall, with the kind of muscles you can't buy in a gym and an air of rocklike toughness.

He was also attractive as hell, which was something she'd never encountered in her boarders. Frightening, but sexy. So there might be a third theory to add to the lucky or crazy explanations—sudden hormonal overload.

When she'd briefly touched his arm, a shiver had run down her spine. She'd felt the steely muscle through his shirt and jacket, the hardest man she'd ever touched. And a flash of heat had run through her at the idea that he was probably as hard as that . . . all over.

Not that he'd done anything to make her uncomfortable, other than being so frighteningly large and . . . and dangerous-looking.

The exact opposite of Marcus Kipping, with his predilection for cardigans encasing sloped shoulders and thin arms. Jack Prescott's massive musculature was visible through a shirt and a jacket. He was the most thoroughly male man she'd ever met and sexy as hell.

And Caroline, who never lied to herself, realized that in the end, it was the reason she'd said yes. God help her, that flash of heat had been the reason she'd said yes. It had been so long since she'd felt it.

If she had the sense God gave a duck, she should have said no to him. No to him as a boarder and certainly no to handing over the car keys to a perfect stranger. Who knew who he was? Maybe he was a serial killer or . . . or a war veteran suffering from posttraumatic stress disorder and who would one day soon crack and climb a tower and start sniping at passersby. Maybe one day they'd find her lifeless body in a pool of blood, or he'd make off with what very little family silver remained.

No one took in a boarder without references. Mr. and Mrs. Kipping had been recommended by the head of her bank and had known her parents.

Who knew Jack Prescott?

But his deep voice had been so calm, that big body so still. And the look of grief that had crossed his face when he spoke of his father's death . . . that had been real, and deep. Caroline recognized true grief—she was the world's greatest expert.

He looked scruffy and tired, as if he'd been traveling for a long time. His jacket was way too light for the gelid temperature outside, and his clothes were rumpled, as if he'd slept in them. His boots were old and worn. Those old boots had been the last straw.

They were the boots of a man down on his luck.

Caroline knew all about being down on your luck.

There was something else about the man, too, besides his sexiness and steadiness. Something almost . . . familiar. Which only reinforced the crazy theory, because she'd never set eyes on him before in her life. She'd never even set eyes on anyone *like* him before.

None of the men she knew had hands that large and that strong, or shoulders that broad. None of the men she knew moved with an athletic grace and tensely coiled energy, like a blaze that was temporarily banked but could flare into life at any moment.

Not in the military anymore, he'd said, but he still had a military bearing—square-shouldered, ramrod-straight back, great economy of movement. And saying *ma'am* all the time. It was sweet, but not exactly the favored mode of address of men talking to women in the twenty-first century. Obviously, living with a colonel for a father had rubbed off on him.

The man she knew best was Sanders McCullin, and he was as far from Jack Prescott as it was possible to be. Sanders was tall, though not as tall as Jack, blond, classically handsome and impossibly elegant.

If Caroline had only half the money Sanders spent each month on clothes, her financial worries would be over. Of course her financial problems could be over tomorrow, Sanders made that clear enough, particularly now that poor Toby was gone. If she married Sanders and became Mrs. McCullin, life would go back to what it had been before her parents died. Safe, secure, comfortably wealthy.

On bad days, like this one, with the Kippings gone, the possibility of coming home to a freezing house that would stay freezing until Monday afternoon because the Jerk was the only person on earth who could coax her boiler back to temporary life, and he didn't make house calls on holidays, a Christmas Eve with no sales at all, the prospect of being alone on Christmas Day, of all the days in the year—well, on days like this, the thought of marrying Sanders made a lot of sense.

Except, of course, for the minor fact that her skin crawled at the thought of kissing him, let alone sleeping with him, which just went to show that she *was* crazy. Half the women in town wanted to sleep with Sanders, and the other half already had, putting Caroline, as always, in the minority.

And now, in a bid to shore up the crazy theory, she'd just given a man she didn't know her car keys. The only things she knew about Jack Prescott were that he was a stranger in town and had very little money. Knowing that, what did she do?

Hand him the keys, politely, because he'd asked.

How smart was that?

If he stole her car, how could she get home? She'd be stranded until the weather cleared, with only the weeks-old yogurt,

Diet Coke and wizened apple in her small fridge for food. There was no way a taxi would come out in this weather and—

A sharp rap on the window made her jump. A second later, Jack Prescott was back in the room, covered in snow. His long black hair was dusted with white. Even his black eyelashes had turned white. He gave no sign of being cold, however. He gave no sign of even being uncomfortable. He looked exactly as he had before—tough and self-contained.

"I've got the car parked right outside." He was so close Caroline had to tip her head back to meet his eyes. "It's hell out there, so we'll have to hurry. Are you warm enough in that coat?"

That was rich, coming from someone wearing a denim jacket. "Yes, I'll be fine." She shifted her heavy briefcase from one hand to another, surprised when he simply took it from her. He was already carrying his own duffel bag and a suitcase. "That's okay," she protested. "I can carry that."

He didn't even answer. "Do you need to engage the security system before we go out?"

Security system. Right. Uh-huh. As if she had $3,000 to spare for a security system to stave off wild-eyed thieves just slavering to rob her complete collection of Jane Austens and all her Nora Robertses.

"No. I—uh, I just lock the door." She held up the Yale key. "It's got a dead bolt, though."

He just looked at her, dark eyes fathomless, then nodded as he took the key. "Okay. I'll lock up. If you've got gloves, put them on. I left the engine running, so the car is warm. Let's make it quick."

He seemed to have just . . . assumed command. The Army and that colonel father had really imprinted him.

Still, the idea of having someone else in the car with her in this weather was such a relief. Bad weather terrified her, and this weather was off the charts. Her Fiat was temperamental and ornery and used to the temperate climate of Italy. It intensely disliked being taken out in the cold. Breaking down in the middle of a snowstorm was just the kind of thing her car enjoyed doing.

At least she'd have her new boarder with her if the worst happened. Jack Prescott looked strong enough to get the car to Greenbriars by looping his belt around the front fender and pulling, if it broke down on the way.

He had his hand on the door handle, watching her. "Okay?" he asked quietly. Caroline nodded, and he opened the door for her. "Let's go."

It was exactly like being punched in the face and stomach by a giant, frozen fist. A step outside the door, and Caroline couldn't see more than a few inches in front of her face. The snow was falling thickly, wildly, in great sweeping sheets, punctuated by needles of sleet blown sideways. She couldn't hear anything above the howling of the wind, and the cold penetrated so absolutely, she froze on the spot. Her muscles simply wouldn't obey her.

Something hard across her back propelled her forward. Her feet scrambled to keep up, slipping a little on the ice coating the sidewalk. She couldn't even see the car, though she knew the road was only a few feet away.

A savage gust of wind whipped sleet into her eyes, and

she lost her footing. She stumbled and would have fallen if Jack hadn't caught her. He simply picked her up one-armed, opened the door of the car, settled her into the driver's seat and closed the door. A few seconds later, the passenger door opened, and he slid in.

Caroline tried to catch her breath, pulling in the heated air of the car to warm her lungs.

Thank God it *was* warm in the car. Those few seconds outside had been enough to frighten her to death. She could hardly move except to shiver for long moments. Even through her gloves, her hands were so frozen she could barely feel the wheel.

Caroline clutched the steering wheel, shaken. "My God," she whispered. "I've never seen anything like this before." She looked across at the big man quietly watching her. He seemed to fill more than half her small car. "Thank you for getting me here. I don't know if I could have managed on my own. They would have found my dead, frozen body outside the shop door."

"No problem." He ratcheted the car seat as far back as it would go to accommodate his long legs and buckled up. "But we'd better get going. It's not getting any better."

No kidding. "Okay."

It occurred to Caroline that the instant she'd crossed the threshold, all thoughts had fled her brain—the cold had simply wiped her mind clear. She hadn't even checked to see that Jack locked up—hadn't even thought about it. He had—she remembered now hearing the snick of the lock turning behind her, but if she'd been on her own, she'd have simply slammed the door shut—or not. And the shop would have been open all weekend.

And thank God Jack had gone to get the car. She might easily have missed it, wandering up and down the sidewalk, blinded by the snow until she ended up a dead frozen lump in the street.

Her little Fiat was humming under her feet, rocking slightly from the wind. Caroline stared ahead in dismay through the snow-covered window, groping for the stick shift and switching on the windshield wipers. It took a full minute to shift the snow on the windshield. The snow was so heavy she couldn't see past the hood. There was a lamppost next to the car, she knew, but she couldn't see it.

What a nightmare.

Jack was looking at her quietly. "Do you want me to drive?" It was as if he could read her mind.

Oh God, yes! The words were there, waiting to tumble out. Caroline bit her lips to keep them back. She wanted desperately to relinquish the wheel. Bad-weather driving scared her. Bad weather led to accidents. Her parents had died in a blizzard just like this one, when their car slid into an intersection, straight into an oncoming truck . . . *don't think of that.*

"Caroline?" he said again. "I don't mind driving in the snow."

She was tempted. Oh God, was she tempted. Just dump this terrible trip into those large, capable-looking hands. He'd do a better job of it than she, Caroline was sure.

But this was her car, and it was her responsibility to take her new boarder home. Life had taught her the hard way to face up to her problems herself, without help.

"No, that's okay." Bringing the seat forward, she put the car in first and pressed on the accelerator. The wheels spun, then bit. So far, so good. "I'm fine," she lied, and eased slowly out into the street. Into what she hoped was the street.

Good thing she knew the way home blindfolded, because that's the way she was driving. Great white sheets of snow came hurling out of the sky, sometimes driven horizontal by the howling wind, driving the flakes into wild circular flurries. Sometimes it looked as if it were snowing *up*.

Caroline punched the radio on, an old habit when driving in bad weather. She spent most of her time alone in the car, and the radio made her feel connected to the rest of the human race.

"—biggest blizzard since 1957, our weather service is telling us, even worse than the one in 2001 and I, for one, don't have any trouble believing it."

Caroline smiled as she heard Roger Stott's beautifully modulated baritone on the air. He could make even horrific weather sound sexy. She'd dated him for a couple of weeks on the basis of his voice alone, before the problems with Toby drove him away.

Just one more man in a long line of potential suitors who couldn't face what she had to deal with.

"And now for some international news. UN peacekeeping forces in Sierra Leone have reported that a group of U.S. mercenaries massacred a village of women and children and made off with a fortune in blood diamonds. The head of the group is in a UN prison awaiting extradition. UN spokeswoman Elfriede Breitweiser said that the men worked for a U.S. security contracting company based in North Carolina called—"

The radio clicked off. Caroline looked over in surprise at her passenger. His dark eyes met hers. "Weather's too severe for bad news."

And how. Caroline was battling the wind buffeting her small car, trying desperately to hold the car to the road without sliding. She clutched the steering wheel with white knuckles, bending forward to peer through the windshield. She could barely see the edge of the road and was driving more by instinct and memory than by sight.

This was awful. She was crawling along at ten miles an hour. At this speed, they wouldn't get home for an hour. Caroline pressed her foot down on the accelerator.

It happened all at once.

Too late, Caroline felt the deadly absence of grip in the road. An instant later, a sharp sound shot above the noise of the howling wind. Instantly the car careened wildly as Caroline lost control, spinning dangerously to the left. Panicked, she braked hard, and the car spun horribly, completely out of control.

A dark shape suddenly loomed, two glowing lights visible high up off the ground like the eyes of a giant predator. A desperate squeal of brakes and a blast of horn as deep and as loud as a foghorn . . .

It took Caroline a full second to realize that she was about to ram head-on into a massive truck. "Oh my God!" she screamed, as they slid on the black ice, right into the path of the dark, massive oncoming shape.

"Let go of the wheel and brace yourself," a deep, calm voice said. Two strong brown hands gripped the wheel, turning the car into the slide, and Jack's left leg reached over hers as he gently tapped the brakes in a slow, regular cadence, shifting down the gears.

The slide slowed, became controlled, not that awful, sickening spinning horror. The car made a complete 360-degree turn. Jack kept it moving left until they came to a stop an inch from a lamppost on the left shoulder of the road. A second later, the massive truck barreled by, horn blaring angrily. The small car rocked with the wind displacement.

It happened so quickly. One second she was battling the wind and snow and the next they were in free fall. The adrenaline shock of a near accident raced burning through her system. If Jack hadn't taken the wheel, they'd have died in a crush of steel, in a mangle of broken bones and blood.

They'd been a second from dying.

She had her hands to her mouth, covering a scream that wanted to break out. The tickle of bitter bile trickled up her throat, and she swallowed, hoping she wouldn't vomit.

Caroline was shaking so hard she felt she would fall apart, the vision of the front of the truck bearing down on them still fresh in her eyes. She was gulping in air frantically, throat tight with panic.

Her seat belt was unlatched, massive arms pulled her to a broad chest.

Oh God, strength and safety.

She dived into him, huddling, trembling, arms tightly wound around his neck, breathing in panicked spurts, until the worst of the shaking died down.

A big hand held the back of her head, almost covering it. Caroline's face was buried in his neck, the stubble along his jawbone scratching her forehead. Her nose was right against the pulse in his neck, beating steadily and slowly, like a metronome, in contrast to her own trip-hammering one.

There was the minty scent of snow, a pleasant musky odor that must have been him and, oddly, the smell of leather. His long black hair had come loose in the wind and flowed around her face, surprisingly soft.

There was nothing soft about the body she was held against, though. It was like embracing steel. He'd pulled her tightly against himself as if he could absorb her wild trembling.

"It's okay," he murmured. She could feel the vibrations of his deep voice. "Nothing happened, it's okay."

It wasn't okay, not by a long shot.

This was exactly how her parents had died—a bad snowstorm, black ice, a truck plowing into their car. A mangle of flesh and steel so horrendous it had taken the highway patrol six hours with the Jaws of Life to get their bodies out. There had barely been enough of her father to bury.

Caroline had woken up more nights than she could count in a sweat, imagining her parents' last seconds of life. The terror as they saw the truck looming suddenly out of the snow, the heart-sickening realization that it was too late. Her father had been impaled on the steering wheel, his legs sheared off at the thighs. Her mother had lived for two weeks, in a coma.

And Toby, poor Toby. Sweet, gentle Toby. Condemned to live the next six years of his life in a wheelchair, in constant pain, only to die before he reached his twentieth birthday.

She saw that in her dreams, lived it, night after night after night. And in her nightmares was the constant presence of Death, coming to take her, too, as it had taken the rest of her family. She couldn't hope to cheat him forever.

This had the dark, metallic taste of her nightmares, only it was real. Caroline dug deep for control, found it, eased away from him.

"What was that?" Her voice was high-pitched and breathless. She looked up into Jack's face, dark and intent. The only sign of stress was white lines of tension pinching his nostrils. He was being brave, so should she. She drew in a shuddering breath and tried to keep her voice level. "What happened to the car?"

"Tire blew," he answered grimly. "Front left."

Oh God, *no*. Her tires were old and bald. Caroline had been putting off buying new tires, hoping to hang on for at least another month, knowing it was foolish and knowing she had no choice.

She'd nearly killed them because she couldn't afford new tires. And now one of them was flat.

It was just too much. Changing a tire in this weather. How on earth did you change a tire in a *blizzard*?

"Do you have a spare and a jack?" he asked.

"Yes." The spare was as old as the other tires, but she did have one, and a jack. Considering the condition of everything else in her life, it was probably rusted and would snap in two in the cold.

It was so tempting just to put her forehead down on the

steering wheel and weep out her rage and frustration, but as emotionally satisfying as it would be, it wouldn't get them home.

A vicious blast of wind rocked the car, and Caroline clutched Jack's jacket for balance. Dear God, they couldn't stay here while she dithered—they'd freeze to death. Caroline turned in her seat and put her hand on the door handle, hoping her hands would stop shaking soon.

"What do you think you're doing?" That deep voice was harsh. Caroline looked over her shoulder in surprise. His brow was furrowed, and he was frowning at her, the skin stretched tautly over his high cheekbones.

"Ah . . ." What did he think? They couldn't stay here a moment longer than necessary. "Getting out to change the tire. We need to get home soon before the weather gets even worse. In a little while we won't be able to drive in the streets."

Night had fallen. The glow from the streetlights couldn't penetrate the snow, and it was almost completely dark in the car. All she could see of him was the whites of his eyes and his white teeth. He touched her arm, briefly.

"Pop the trunk and stay in here. Don't open your door, not even for a second."

There wasn't time to protest. The passenger-side door opened briefly, and he slipped out. In that one second that the door was open, a gust of wind blew a snow flurry into the car, sucking out the heat. Caroline opened the trunk and heard metal clanging in the back.

A second later, he was at her front left fender, jacking the car up, working almost blind. Every once in a while, the fierce wind would part the curtain of snow, and she could see him, large and dark and intent, kneeling by the fender. She switched on the overhead light, hoping it could help in some small degree, though she doubted it. It probably comforted her more than helped him.

Sooner than she could have imagined possible, he was knocking at her window.

He bent to put his mouth close to the glass. "Do you want me to drive?" he shouted, his deep voice carrying above the howl of the wind.

Oh, God, yes! Yes, yes *yes!*

The hell with politically correct. The hell with duty. The thought of driving in this weather over black ice with her bald tires made her break out in a sweat. It was another accident just waiting to happen.

Caroline met his eyes through the glass and nodded.

"Scoot over and buckle up." His hands were cupped around his mouth, but even so, his words barely carried.

He wasn't going to make her get out and circle the car. Bless him. Caroline managed to make it over to the passenger seat without breaking her hip on the stick shift. Jack waited until she was in the seat and pulling the seat belt over her chest before opening the door.

He could barely fit his legs in the footwell and had to ratchet the seat back to its fullest extent, bringing it even with hers. He started the engine, letting it warm up.

Caroline turned to him, a large dark shadow in the dark. "That was quick. It would have taken me an hour in this weather, if I'd even be able to manage it at all."

He looked over at her. One corner of his mouth lifted in a half smile, just a quick flash of white teeth. "I've changed a lot of tires under enemy fire. You learn to be fast."

"I'll just bet you do. Listen—" Caroline breathed deeply. She owed him an apology. "I want to thank you for changing the tire. That was my responsibility and—oh, goodness, you're hurt!" Something dark and liquid gleamed on his right hand. "Heavens, first you change my tire for me, then my car bites the hand that feeds it. I'm so sorry." She fumbled in the glove compartment and came out with tissues, which she held against his hand. The tissue turned immediately dark red. He'd gashed his hand badly. She changed tissues. "Hold that against your hand for about five minutes until the bleeding stops. You might need stitches, that's a nasty cut. We can stop at the emergency room of the hospital on the way."

"No." The deep voice was gentle as he covered her hand with his. She'd taken her gloves off to drive and felt a jolt as his large, rough hand covered hers. His hand was hot, radiating heat not only to her hand but to the rest of her body.

It was electric, the feel of his skin against hers. In the darkness, his hot hand seemed to anchor her. His grip on her hand was light, but the effect of it was enormous. Heat zinged through her, a sharp contrast to the cold, to the panic she'd felt.

She'd been frozen with panic, and his touch sent strength and heat through her system.

He squeezed lightly, then lifted his hand away. "I heal fast, don't worry about it. We need to get going now, or we won't get home at all."

"But your hand—"

"Is fine." He switched off the overhead light, put the car in gear and stepped on the accelerator. In a moment, they had crossed back over to the right side of the road. "Don't worry about my hand. Just direct me to your house. We need to get there as quickly as possible. Where do I turn?"

He did heal quickly. The deep gash had almost stopped bleeding.

Caroline peered out the window uncertainly, though visibility was nearly zero. It was impossible to tell where the intersections were. The only way to find out would be by crashing into a car.

"Keep on straight down this road for three-quarters of a mile, then turn right. I'll try to navigate for you."

"Okay," he said calmly. He was driving much faster than she had dared to. She would have said something—fast driving scared her—but he was clearly in total command of the car, and the more quickly they got home, the happier she'd be.

She peered out the window, trying to discern landmarks. It was haphazard at best. At times, a ferocious gust of wind lifted the snow curtain for just a second. She saw the benches outside the railing along Grayson Park, then the big Christmas tree at the corner of Center Street and Fife, then—"Here," she said suddenly, relieved. "Turn right here."

He took the corner so smoothly, they might have been driving on a balmy summer evening. Caroline counted off lampposts and started to relax. Another five minutes, ten tops, and they'd be home. "The first left, the second right and it's the fourth driveway on the right."

The car pulled to a stop right in front of the garage. Caroline closed her eyes and breathed deeply for the first time since she'd gotten into the car.

Home. She was home.

Well, not quite yet. She stared ahead at the rusted garage door with near hatred.

Time for another apology. "I'm sorry," she said contritely, digging in her purse for the keys, hands still shaking. "The remote doesn't work. The door has to be opened manually. I'll do it."

"No." He reached over and took the keys from her hand. "Don't get out. I'll take care of it."

Her boiler was temperamental, but the garage door was utterly reliable. You could *count* on it not working. It took her muscle and time and many a chipped nail to turn the key in the rusty lock and lift the door.

"Are you sure? I can—"

Again, that touch from his big hand. Heat and reassurance, the punch of sensual awareness, gone when he lifted his hand. After his touch, the cold and the aftermath of panic rushed back in. "I'm sure."

Lit by the headlights, she watched him bend and lift the door as if it were brand-new, freshly oiled and weightless. A second later, they were safely in the garage.

Home. For real, now.

Caroline got out of the car and had to order her knees to stiffen. Her legs were shaking. All of her was shaking still from the near accident, a deep, almost uncontrollable tremor. The keys were rattling in her hand. She had to clench her fist closed to stop the noise.

"Thank you," she said again to the big man, over the roof of the car. She met his eyes, dark and inscrutable. "I owe you—"

He held up a huge hand and shook his head. "Please don't. Let's just get inside." He picked up his bags and her briefcase. "Lead the way. I'll follow you."

Caroline opened the door to the house, fingers crossed, tense, expecting the worst.

Thank God, the worst hadn't happened. Yet.

The air was not quite freezing, there was a low hum from somewhere under her feet and she could relax a little. The boiler hadn't gone off today. She kept it on a minimum setting so the pipes wouldn't freeze, which they did regularly when the boiler went on the blink. But today the gods of heating were smiling down at her, as well they should, considering the number they'd pulled on her last week.

The temperature was uncomfortably cool, but as long as the boiler was working, it was okay. She'd turn the thermostat up, and in half an hour the whole house would be warm.

Her heating bills were atrocious, but heating was not something she was prepared to skimp on. Not, certainly, with a new boarder. And definitely not in the middle of a blizzard.

She led Jack through the mudroom into the big, two-story atrium. Entering was always a delight. Designed by a disciple of Frank Lloyd Wright, every room of Greenbriars was light, spacious, perfectly proportioned. The atrium was simply spectacular. An old friend of the family had once said that Greenbriars was like a beautiful woman, and the atrium was her face. When her parents had been alive, there had been two Winslow Homers, a Ming vase, a Murano chandelier and an immense antique Baluchi carpet in the atrium.

All long gone.

The only thing left was the airiness and grace of the room itself, with its black-and-white-marble flooring, arches leading to the library, the living room and her study and the big, graceful, winding maple staircase leading to the bedrooms on the second floor.

Through all the tough years gone by, through Toby's long, painful decline and death, through all the sadness and hardship, entering Greenbriars never failed to lift her spirits.

Greenbriars was alive to her, and was in many ways the last family member left to her. She'd fought ferociously to keep it, even when everyone—the family lawyer who'd had to tell her that there was no money in the bank, Jenna, her best friend, who thought she was nuts to stick by Greenbriars, Sanders, who quickly grew annoyed that she had to pinch pennies and eventually dumped her—everyone said to sell.

Caroline would have sold Greenbriars only to save Toby's life, but he died before it became necessary. And now—well, now Greenbriars was her only connection with her family and her only solace. She was tied by unbreakable links of love to the place. To sell it would be to deny the people she'd loved so much. Selling was unthinkable.

As long as she had a breath in her body, Greenbriars would be hers. Cost what it might.

She watched Jack Prescott as he took in his surroundings. People reacted in different ways to the mansion. Some people's jaws dropped. Some were blasé. Some didn't even understand how beautiful it was and saw only a big house that needed painting and repair work and new furniture.

It was a litmus test.

His reaction was perfect. He stood in silence for a minute, dark eyes taking in the architectural details, then he turned to her. "What a beautiful place. Thank you for accepting me as a boarder."

Yes, perfect. Caroline smiled up at him. "I hope you'll be comfortable here. The double room is on the third floor, under the eaves. I'll show you the way."

He shook his head. "Don't go up two flights of stairs for my sake. Tell me how to get there, and I'll be fine."

Oh, God. What a relief. The worst of the trembling was over, but her legs were still shaking.

"Go up the main staircase, turn right and you'll find another staircase at the end of the hallway that will take you up to your room. It has an en suite bathroom that's yours alone. The sheets are clean, and you'll find clean towels in the big white cabinet in the bathroom. You should have enough hot water for a shower. Dinner's at seven thirty."

"Thank you." He inclined his head. "I'll be down at seven thirty," he said, then turned and took the stairs two at a time, moving fast. Caroline watched his broad back until he disappeared, hoping she'd done the right thing, knowing that she'd had no choice.

Three

The instructions, of course, hadn't been necessary. Jack knew his way up to the big airy room at the top of the house. He stood outside the door, his hand on the handle, and took in a big breath, still amazed that he was here. With her.

The house was as beautiful as in his memories, only bare and unadorned. Before, there had been paintings on the walls, big pieces of old furniture, soft rugs, elaborate vases. As a boy, he'd had no idea how valuable they could be. All he knew was that he'd never seen rooms as full of beautiful things as Caroline's home.

He was no expert, but he'd learned a lot over the years. Enough to know that there had been a fortune in paintings, rugs, sculptures, antiques. Most of which were now gone.

It didn't make any difference. The mansion was still gorgeous, like a beautiful woman without makeup. Still, it pained his heart to think of Caroline selling off her inheritance, piece by piece. It must have hurt.

The room under the eaves was exactly the same as it had been twelve years ago, only shabbier and in need of a coat of paint. The furniture was the same, too, pleasant but unexceptional. Obviously, nothing in this room had been valuable enough to sell off. The room held a big four-poster bed with a huge green-and-white quilt, an armchair in need of reupholstering, a chest of drawers and a small desk on which sat a TV set and a radio.

More than enough to make for comfortable living, particularly for a man used to roughing it. He'd do just fine here, until he moved into Caroline's bedroom, which he vowed would be just as soon as humanly possible.

The mechanics of that—getting from being a boarder to a lover—was something he'd have to work on. But he was good at strategy. Sooner or later it was going to happen. She was single, that much was clear, even though there was probably a boyfriend in the background. How could there not be? It was unthinkable that any man with a pulse and working equipment could be in the same room as Caroline and not want her.

The bathroom was the same as before, too. Large, with white fixtures and cream-and-green tiles on the walls. The sink was cracked, and a few wall tiles were missing, but for someone who'd been on shit-burning detail in Iraq, and who'd dug his own latrines in Afghanistan, it was superluxurious. As promised, there was a stack of white towels in a big white wooden cabinet. The towels were clean, but old and threadbare. Who the hell cared? In a second, his dirty, rumpled clothes were on the floor, and he was under the shower.

The shower stall was equipped with shampoo and soap in a holder. The water was only lukewarm, but it still felt good as he lathered up.

Both the soap and the shampoo were rose-scented. The smell went straight to the primitive part of his brain that associated roses with Caroline.

Damn! It was precisely the part of his brain that was connected to his cock, and had been for twelve years. Roses equaled Caroline equaled a hard-on.

Jack took his time washing up, getting rid of more than the dirt and sweat of a forty-eight-hour trip back from Africa. He was washing more than the grime of travel off—he was washing his old life out.

For twelve years, he'd been the Colonel's to command. The man who'd found a starving, half-mad mongrel behind a trash can and taken him in had had his undying loyalty. Colonel Eugene Nicholas Prescott, man of honor, the father of his heart. If the Colonel hadn't gotten ill and died, Jack wouldn't be here. He'd still be helping the Colonel run ENP Security.

He'd never allowed himself more than the vaguest kinds of daydreams of an alternative life while the Colonel was alive. He'd been as loyal to him as any feudal knight to his king. But now, in the space of a week, Jack had buried his father, sold the company and the house and shut down the rogue Sierra Leone mission. All the ties with his old life were severed.

It was all over. He was starting a new life, right here in Caroline's shower, smelling of roses.

Now his skin smelled like hers, though it sure as hell didn't *feel* like hers. Hers was so pale, so smooth. Smooth and incredibly soft to the touch, too.

Jack remembered every second she'd spent in his arms in the car. It had taken every ounce of self-control not to tilt her head back and kiss her. He'd had to clench his teeth, hard, because what he'd wanted more than his next breath was to open her mouth with his and plunge inside.

Her mouth was made for kissing, soft and pink, a little honey trap he'd wanted to fall into so badly he'd ached. Only a lifetime of self-discipline had stopped him.

They'd been in real danger out there, and not just from the truck. All her tires were basically shot and if another one blew, with no other spare, they'd have been done for. There was no way they could have lasted out the blizzard in the car. So he'd been a real good boy and held her for comfort, just long enough to let her regain control of herself.

She'd trembled in his arms. His job had been to hold her until the worst of the trembling stopped, then get them both to a warm place as soon as possible.

His imagination had run riot. In his head, he got rid of his jacket, sweater, jeans, shorts, boots. Her thick coat, sweater, bra, panties, stockings. In his head they were naked—not in a chilly car in the middle of a blizzard, but on a sunny deserted beach. A place where they had all the time in the world for him to explore her body, touch all that luscious rosy ivory skin. Run his mouth along that long, pale neck, down to the breasts he'd seen outlined by the sweater.

The adrenaline of the close encounter with death had pooled in his cock, and he'd been as hard as a club. He'd wanted to mount her, enter her, fuck her, more than he wanted his next breath.

It was an enticing thought, but dangerous as hell. They weren't on a sunny beach, they were in real danger of freezing to death.

So he'd dropped a kiss to the top of her head so light she couldn't feel it, then let her go, to concentrate on getting them to Greenbriars safely.

But now . . . now that he was in a warm, wet cabin that smelled of Caroline, his mind went wild. He imagined licking his tongue into that beautiful mouth, his nose up against her skin, the scent of roses filling his head. Biting her lips, urging her closer, closer still. Sliding his hand along that long, white neck.

Jack looked down at himself and groaned at his enormous, painful boner, red and swollen, hard as a pike. Harder than in the car.

He knew why he had a hard-on that wouldn't quit.

Part of it was that he hadn't had sex in nearly six months. Afghanistan was as close to a no-sex zone as had ever existed on earth. After Afghanistan he'd spent the past month at his father's bedside, then in Africa, cleaning up after Vince Deaver. True, six months was a long time for him to go without sex, but he'd done it before, on long missions.

Part of it was the male reaction to surviving danger. Or his, anyway. It happened every time he survived a firefight. His cock went up in celebration of life and thanksgiving that he wasn't six feet under. When he could, after combat, Jack went out hunting for a woman for relief, and when he couldn't, his fist worked just fine.

He and Caroline had been in as much danger as if they'd been on a mission in downtown Baghdad.

He hadn't said anything—Caroline had been massively freaked as it was—but they'd nearly died out there on the road. While fighting the wheel of her car, the part of his mind that was always calm and thinking ahead to the next step no matter what the emergency had appreciated the irony.

Jack had survived the worst life could throw at him, time and again. He'd cheated death a thousand times while waiting for Caroline. Being crushed beneath the wheels of a truck half an hour after finding her again would definitely come under the category of "shit happens."

But these reasons weren't really why he had such a boner.

What had set him off was being in the same house as Caroline, having talked to her, touched her, held her in his arms—that's what had his cock swollen and weeping. After so many years in which she'd haunted his dreams, he was finally with her, and it was scary as hell.

Do. Not. Fuck. This. Up, he told himself.

He couldn't count the nights lying on a cold hard cot when her face swam before him. At first, he'd been ashamed to jerk off thinking of her, but it turned out that no matter how many women he had, she was the only one who could turn him on simply by thinking of her.

Jack liked women. He liked the way they smelled, the softness of their skin, their voices. He liked sex, too. He was courteous to his sex partners, even if it was a one-night stand, which most of his encounters were. A little foreplay, in for a while, then out, then get up and go. Oh, he had stamina, that wasn't the problem. The problem was he couldn't remember much about the woman after walking out the door.

He remembered everything about Caroline. Everything. How she looked with her hair in a ponytail, or loose around her shoulders. He remembered every item of clothing he'd ever seen her in and every expression she'd ever had. He remembered every single word she'd ever said to him. It was all seared into his mind, and it would probably take a shot to the head to get rid of it all.

So naturally, when he reached for his cock to unload some stress, a generic woman with, say, one head, two tits, four limbs and a pussy simply wouldn't do. Caroline floated into his head in those moments and he'd long ago given up the fight to keep her out.

Now there was something more, something unexpected. Turned out the Caroline he'd mooned over for twelve years was long gone, vanished with the years. The beautiful girl had been replaced by an even more beautiful woman, mature and stunning, intelligent and classy, a woman who wore sadness like a shroud, utterly irresistible.

The girl had been very pretty, like a million other upper-class girls, with a sunny smile showing off ten thousand dollars of orthodontics, wearing a thousand dollars' worth of clothes. She bathed regularly and had someone to wash and iron her clothes for her. Lots of girls in those conditions look pretty.

The woman she'd turned into, though, knocked the breath right out of him. She was like some sad princess longing for her lost kingdom.

Jack remembered every second she'd been in his arms as he reached down for himself, gave one, long experimental stroke.

The hard-on had to go, right now. There was no way he could go down to dinner in this condition, she'd kick him right out. *Please God*, he thought, *let me get through the evening without embarrassing myself.*

To be really sure his dick would stay down, he should park himself in the shower under cold water and jerk off a couple of times, just to get rid of the fierce, itchy arousal he felt. His skin prickled with the desire to touch her again, only not for comfort this time and not dressed for cold weather with layers of clothes between his skin and hers.

No, he wanted to touch her and see whether he could make that smooth ivory skin turn pink with desire. He wanted to watch it happen, watch the flush cover her breasts, while he kissed them. He wanted to touch her sex, feel himself making her wet, ready for him.

Caroline was downstairs, right now. Waiting for him. She wasn't a memory, a photograph, an image in his head. She was a flesh-and-blood woman, more beautiful even than in his dreams and she was downstairs cooking a meal for him.

He'd see her every day, as much as he wanted. It was impossible to think that he wouldn't get her in his bed. His cock swelled even more at the thought.

His fist was working hard now, pumping, as the images of a naked Caroline spread out on a bed just for him filled his head. He wanted to know what sounds she made when she was turned on, feel her heels and nails digging into his back, feel her cunt pulling at him as he stroked inside her . . .

It was all so much more intense now that he'd seen her again, felt her, smelled her. Now that he had so much more sensory input as he imagined fucking her, hard. For hours.

If she were here right now, he'd take her in the shower, kissing her all over first in the steamy heat, making her ready. Entering her with his fingers first, oh so gently. He was big, and she had to be ready for him. He wanted her wet and soft and open for him. When his hand told him she was ready, he'd lift her, hold her legs apart, start pushing inside her . . .

Sometimes it took Jack a long time to climax but he'd been semiaroused since he'd seen her, and when he imagined entering her, parting her tissues with his cock, he groaned.

The image filled his head with unbearable heat—the two of them in the rose-scented cabin under the pounding water, as he pounded into her. He could see them, could almost feel her softness against him, and it set him off.

Red-hot needles pricked down his spine, and he started spurting violently, hips jerking in time with his fist. He came and came, leaning one-handed against the shower stall, until his knees were weak and it felt like he'd emptied himself of every ounce of moisture in his body.

He watched himself, the red, hugely swollen head of his cock emerging from his fist, coming in huge spurts against the glass cabin, disappearing instantly in the water streaming down the sides. His lungs ached, his skin felt too tight, his head was a balloon that could burst any moment.

For a moment, the climax wiped out all thoughts from his mind as he was reduced to his animal senses. After coming, he was usually relaxed and refreshed—a little like going for a good, sweaty run. Sex was nice physical exercise with a nice little payoff at the end.

Nothing like this. This felt like dying—as if everything he was came shooting out of his cock, leaving him weak and disoriented.

As strong as the orgasm was, though, it wasn't quite enough. When Jack's knees could support him again and he walked out of the shower stall, he was still semierect, still wanting her. Every cell in his body was turned on, damn it, attuned to the woman downstairs. He looked down at himself in disgust, big flag waving at half-mast.

His dick was so sensitized, the cooler air of the bathroom outside the shower stall felt icy cold on his skin. It missed the warmth, the fantasy that his fist was Caroline's cunt.

At that thought, his dick went straight back up into a full erection.

Fuck.

How could he go down in this condition? Well, only one thing to do—wear a chastity belt. Or his tightest black jeans, which was the same thing. A hard-on would have no place to go in those jeans, he knew from painful experience. If he started swelling, his cock would meet stiff denim, and the pain would make it go down again. That was the plan, anyway. He hoped it would work.

He couldn't stay in the shower forever, jerking off until there was nothing left in him. It would take all night and probably all day tomorrow.

Jack unlocked the padlock on his bag and dumped all his clothes out. There weren't many clothes, because he'd had to travel light. The only clean clothes he had left were a pair of sweats, the black jeans and a black turtleneck sweater. He hadn't even thought to pack an extra pair of shoes, so the boots would have to do. Monday, he'd buy some clothes.

He dumped the last of the items in the bag on the bed. Fifty thousand dollars in ten bricks of $5,000 each. His toolkit. Another Glock with five magazines of ammo, and a cloth bag. Luckily, he still had his security pass, so he'd been able to check his weapons at the airport.

He took a small screwdriver out of the toolkit and checked the baseboard until he found an air vent close to the chest of drawers. Bending, he checked it out. Perfect. Tiny flakes of rust spotted the four screws holding the vent grate to the metal plate in the wall. The grate hadn't been removed for years to judge from the buildup of soot and rust. Unscrewing the vent took time and some muscle, but eventually he had the screws lined up on the floor and the grate removed.

He checked his watch as he put the items from the bag far enough back in the vent so they wouldn't show even if you were looking for something. He had no idea who cleaned the rooms, whether it was Caroline or a cleaning lady, but he didn't want them stumbling onto the Glock, or the ammo, or—Jesus!—the contents of the cloth bag. They should be safe enough in the steel tube. It would only be until Monday.

Monday he was going to open a bank account, deposit the cash and the cashier's check for eight million dollars and register for a safe-deposit box for the contents of the cloth bag.

He checked his watch—7:25. He'd be on time for dinner.

One last thing. Crouching, he opened the cloth bag and emptied its contents onto the hardwood floor, the dull, irregular rocks rattling as they spilled out in a stream.

Jack studied the jagged mound. Except for the odd glitter as the light caught a natural facet, the rocks could have been pebbles from a riverbed.

Instead, he was looking at at least $20 million in uncut diamonds.

He knew he was looking at rocks that represented human suffering on an unimaginable scale. They'd been mined by slave labor—men and boys who toiled under the tropical sun from first to last light on a cup of rice, immediately shot in the back of the head when they grew too weak to work. An entire country was tearing itself apart because of dull rocks just like these—over eighty thousand people killed over the past year in Sierra Leone. Countless others had had their hands, lips and ears chopped off by the drugged-up baby soldiers fighting in the Revolutionary Army.

Vince Deaver and his men had been willing to massacre an entire village of women and children for them.

No wonder they called them blood diamonds.

It was a miracle that no blood oozed from the stones. But no—they were as neutral as they were inert—just rocks, for fuck's sake. Just rocks.

Jack looked down at the mound people were willing to kill

and to die for and made a small noise of disgust before putting them back in the bag. Twenty million dollars of pain and suffering and misery. Murder, rape, dismemberment—that's what the diamonds represented.

He'd taken them simply because there was no one left in the village alive to give them to, and he'd have died himself rather than let Deaver have them.

Jack put the bag behind the money, the Glock and the ammo, then carefully screwed the grate back onto its plate, thinking how crazy people were to be willing to kill and die for a bag full of rocks.

He rose and made his way swiftly down two flights of stairs toward something warm and living and beautiful. Something definitely worth killing or dying for.

Encampment of the United Nations Observer Mission in Sierra Leone near Obuja, Sierra Leone
Christmas Eve
4:58 P.M.

His name was Axel and he was Vince Deaver's new best friend.

Axel was Finnish, loved computers, American jazz, missed his fiancée Maja back in Helsinki and hated Africa and everything connected to it. Best of all, he was blond, five-ten, weighed about 170 pounds, *just like me*, Deaver thought in satisfaction.

Axel always stopped by to see him in the small detention

center of the UNOMSIL when he got off guard duty at 1700 hours. At 1703, Deaver could count on good old Axel stopping by, regular as clockwork.

The detention center itself was a joke. Deaver could have escaped at any time over the past three days. His grandmother could have escaped using her dentures and a hairpin. The UN peacekeeping force was not in the prisoner business, and it showed.

Deaver needed more than a way to break out of the detention center—he needed to get out of the encampment and out of Sierra Leone if he wanted his diamonds back. Good old Axel was his ticket out.

It was dark inside the detention center. Electricity was intermittent, the air-conditioning worked sporadically, so the shutters and the door were kept closed against the blistering heat of the tropical sun, intense even in December.

Deaver made sure the lights were turned off during the day, even when the shutters kept the room in semidarkness. Axel had to be used to a darkened room.

Deaver checked his watch. The luminescent dial showed 1700 hours, on the dot.

Axel would be punctual. Deaver had studied him the way an entomologist studied bugs. He knew how Axel reacted to stimuli, and he had his plan worked out down to the finest detail. The Army had trained him well.

17:01.

Deaver jumped up and down to make sure nothing rattled or clinked and patted himself down. There would be a moment when he would have to move fast and silently. More than one soldier had died because a knife clinked against a belt buckle and gave away a position.

He checked his pockets, his boots and flexed his arms. He'd been cooped up for three days now and his muscles were stiff. He was used to hard workouts, and confinement didn't suit him.

Neither did the thought of being extradited back home for a trial for mass murder.

When Deaver finally caught up with Jack Prescott, he was not only going to get his diamonds back but he'd make the fucker very very sorry he'd interfered, before blasting his fucking head off. Deaver had spent a couple of pleasant hours last night imagining Jack tied to a chair while he used his knife.

Deaver was very good with his knife.

17:02.

He checked his plan again, ran through it for the thousandth time. About 90 percent of good soldiering was planning and preparation. The plan was good, and he was prepared.

He turned his back to the door.

17:03.

The door opened wide, and Axel walked in, good Finnish soldier from his head to his toes. His fatigues were clean and freshly pressed. The baby blue UN helmet that was such an attraction, practically a beacon, to snipers the world over firmly on his head, boots spit-shined.

"Hello, Mr. Deaver," Axel said. His English was excellent. "How are you today?"

The light from the open door filled the room. Since his

back was to the door, Deaver's eyes were able to accommodate quickly to the light pouring into the room from behind his back. Going from darkness to tropical light could blind a man for minutes.

"Hi, Axel. Close that door, will you?"

"Certainly." Deaver heard the snick of the door closing and turned around. By now, Axel had become used to what he considered Deaver's fetish for darkness.

Floor-to-ceiling bars divided the shack in half. Deaver considered his cell a personal affront. The bars were loosely planted in the wooden planks and fixed by screws to the stucco ceiling. The lock was a joke—it would fall apart if you blew on it too hard. How the fuck did they think a cell like that could hold a man like him?

The problem wasn't getting out, the problem was what to do afterwards. They were about twenty miles from the Sele River. Even if he could make it through the jungle to the river, he'd need to steal a boat and motor his way down to Freetown. It would take three days, at least. Everyone knew there was only one place to escape to, and that was Freetown.

By the time he made it to the capital, Freetown and, worse, Lungi Airport would be crawling with UN troops with his photograph in their hands, itching to capture the American renegade.

So he needed to make sure no one would be looking for him. He needed a body that looked like Vincent Deaver they could bury.

Axel was sympathetic to him, he'd made that clear. Axel

loved America and his tidy Finnish soul had been horrified at what he'd seen in his two-year tour of duty in central Africa. "Hell on earth," he called it.

Axel had made it plain more than once that he thought it a ridiculous waste of time and effort to keep Deaver in detention.

He was right, of course. This part of the world had been on a rampage for fifteen years, tribe against tribe, with brutally ferocious massacres on a daily basis. On the Revolutionary Army scale, what Deaver'd done was the equivalent of a slap in the face.

So Axel was definitely on his side. Deaver had even thought about bribing him for travel documents. Might have worked, but he needed something else from Axel, besides documents.

His body.

Pity, because he liked the guy. But what can you do?

"Merry Christmas, Axel." Axel's head swiveled to follow the source of his voice. Deaver sat on his cot, legs spread, forearms on knees, hands clasped. Utterly, totally nonthreatening.

Axel's eyes would slowly be adjusting to the dark shed after the bright tropical light outside.

Deaver's body was a still statue slowly taking shape, like a film in the developing pan.

"Merry Christmas, Vince. I came to say good-bye." Axel walked toward Deaver and wrapped his hands around the bars.

Deaver let his gusty sigh fill the room. He lifted his head.

Axel would be able to make out his movements by now. "Man, oh man, I'm going to miss you. Miss our talks. I'm just happy you'll be out of this shithole and with Maja."

"Oh, yeah." Predictably, Axel's face creased in a smile at the mention of his girlfriend. Axel was slated to leave this afternoon for a two-month rotation back to Finland. He hadn't even tried to hide how glad he'd be to get out of Africa and back to his computer, snow and Maja, probably in that order.

Axel pulled up a stool and pulled out a little magnetized travel chess set. They had spent the past three days playing through the bars. Deaver had been letting him win two games out of three.

"Hey," Deaver said, putting on a shy, abashed expression. "You've been really good to me, here, you know?" He put a little folksiness into his voice, just two guys chewing the fat on a lazy afternoon. "And I was thinking, what with you going back home for a while and all, that I'd like to give you something. I really owe you, man. I have something for you to give Maja. You know, as a Christmas present. I bet you didn't get anything for her."

Bingo. Axel hung his head. There wasn't much but jungle within a hundred-mile radius. Jungle and soldiers and blood and misery. Nothing a Finnish woman would want.

Deaver stood and walked toward the bars, crooking his finger to bring Axel closer. Curious, Axel stood against the bars. Though they were separated by the bars, they were close enough to feel each other's breath.

"I've got something real special for Maja. Something she'll

like . . . a lot." He allowed himself a smile. "Something sparkly. Something all women like." He shrugged and winked, man to man. "Won't do me much good in here. You might as well get some use out of it, know what I mean?"

Axel nodded eagerly.

Deaver knew that everyone in the UNOMSIL encampment assumed he had the diamonds. Or rather, since he'd been frisked, knew where the diamonds were.

If only. It was a fucking fortune. Enough money to keep him happy for the rest of his life, wherever he wanted to settle down.

Away from Africa, away from Afghanistan and Uzbekistan and Kazakhstan and all the fucking 'Stans. Away from Iraq, away from all the shithole places with kids blowing themselves up just for the pleasure of gutting you while they did it and women who hid grenades under their burqas and men willing to shoot you for your fillings.

No more.

No more twelve-year-olds high on ganja or palm wine carting around AK- 47s they could barely lift, with access to unlimited ammo and just itching to bag a white man. No more roadside IEDs, no more leeches or scorpions or lice, no more MREs, no more rough sleeping.

He'd *earned* that money. It was fucking *his*. He'd been dreaming of a big hit for years, and when he'd heard the rumors of a village whose men had all gone off to war and with millions of dollars in conflict diamonds hidden in the ground, he'd instantly known that this was It. His big chance.

He'd never have to soldier again, or ever have to work at

anything, ever again. Never take orders again, never do anything but what he damned well pleased.

No more jungles, no more deserts. No more bivouacking in primitive encampments on stony ground.

Deaver planned on living in luxury for the rest of his natural life. Buy a mansion somewhere nice, somewhere sunny, somewhere OUTCONUS. In the Bahamas maybe. Or maybe Monte Carlo.

Why not? Buy a big house with a pool and servants and lots and lots of women. Not that many beautiful women wanted to fuck a soldier, but they sure as hell lined up ten deep to fuck rich men.

He could taste it, smell it, feel it, this new life.

And it was all gone. All his dreams for his future, a future he'd sweated and taken bullets for, wiped out in a second by Jack Prescott.

Deaver's fists clenched as he remembered in a white-hot rage that moment when his future was snatched away from him. He and his men had opened fire on the village, softening it up. A knife against the throat of the daughter of one of the women, and he had the location of the diamonds. He'd run into the hut, found the bag and was running toward his men, who were eliminating the villagers—no sense in leaving witnesses behind—when all of a sudden, four spaced shots rang out, followed by sudden silence.

A sniper, picking off his men, one by one.

In his scramble to get to safety, the bag slipped from Deaver's fingers as he ran to the nearest hut, leaping over the dead bodies in the central clearing. He slid into the opening and turned around, rifle to shoulder, and saw a big man disappear into the jungle with *his* diamonds.

He knew it was useless trying to follow. If Jack Prescott didn't want to be found, he could disappear like smoke.

Deaver had spent the next few hours ransacking the village, turning over bodies, in the hope that there was another stash of diamonds, but by the time he'd come to the conclusion that there was nothing left, UN soldiers had surrounded the village and taken him into custody.

For a moment the heat of rage swept through him, wiping out every other thought except that of hunting down that fucker Jack Prescott, getting his diamonds back and killing Prescott with a knife, taking a couple of days to do it.

None of this showed on his face. He bent his head forward and dropped his voice to a murmur. "Come in here, Axel. And I'll give you something that will make Maja drop to her knees in gratitude."

"Okay, Vince." Though there was no one else in the hut, Axel dropped his voice, too. As if they were about to exchange confidences.

Deacon stood up and backed away slowly. "Come inside." His voice was still low. "I'll show you what I've got for you. For her."

Axel didn't even hesitate. Deacon knew Axel thought of him as someone much like himself. Nice white boy caught up in the craziness that was West Africa.

Axel unlocked the cell door and walked inside, following Deacon, who'd reached his cot and pulled something out from under the hard mattress. A cloth bag with smooth round objects that rattled.

Axel's excited breathing was loud in the darkened room.

Deacon smiled. "Maja's going to love these. Come over and look." Deacon reached over the cot to suddenly open the shutters, flooding the room with harsh light. Axel was temporarily blinded and would remain blind for about a minute and a half. More than enough time.

Deacon had closed his eyes and turned his back to the window, and he could see just fine.

His hand dropped to his boot, where he quickly and quietly pulled out a long thin dagger with a folding handle the UN troops hadn't even noticed. He'd been briskly frisked for arms before being shut up in the detention center, but no one had thought to check his boots. Or his belt buckle with the minirevolver or the garotte wire along the inside of his belt.

The garotte was out of the question. Deaver needed Axel's clothes intact. A slow choking death would loosen his bowels and bladder. And a bullet wouldn't do—it would stain his uniform with blood.

There was only one way to do it.

Deaver dropped the bag into Axel's hands. The bag opened under Axel's eager, fumbling fingers. When the bag was open, he poured the contents in his hand. It took him a few seconds to realize that he held not diamonds but stones. His head lifted.

"What—" he began. It was his last word on this earth. Deaver hooked his left arm around Axel's chest and with his right he slipped the stiletto he kept as sharp as a scalpel straight into the brain stem. It immediately stopped all bodily functions. Axel went from sentient being to stone in a tenth of a second. He slumped into Deaver's arms, an instant corpse.

Deaver worked fast.

In five minutes he'd exchanged clothes and shoes. Axel kept his passport and airline ticket on his person at all times. He'd told Deaver he had an unholy fear of the cleaning staff stealing them. The UN peacekeeping mission had been too much for him. Well, good old Axel was getting out of Africa, in a manner of speaking. Permanently.

Deaver hitched Axel up in a fireman's lift and made for the door. He opened it slightly and waited for a moment in which no one was visible. It was 17:20, close to dinnertime, and the encampment was deserted. When Deaver was sure no one could see, he slipped out the door and made his way around the back.

The detention center backed onto the jungle. In the steamy heat, Deaver made his way carefully, disappearing immediately into the dense foliage, leaving barely anything to track. He was lucky. If he'd had to carry a man in the high deserts of Afghanistan, the sand would have kept his footprints for weeks. In the jungle, his tracks would be covered within the hour.

He walked until his instincts told him he was beyond the natural patrol point and put Axel down. Deaver looked at him, stretched out on his back. He looked peaceful, as if he were taking a nap.

You should thank me, buddy, Deaver thought. *I just gave you a great death. The best.*

It was the one thing soldiers feared above all else—a bad death. Long, lingering, painful. The RA rebels specialized in hacking deaths, where it takes a man maybe an hour to die after having his hands, then his arms, then his feet and finally his head chopped off. Sometimes it took the child-soldiers, wielding axes half their size, ten tries to separate the head from the body.

Deaver had seen men taking hours of agony to die after having been gut-shot or having their insides ripped open by a land mine. Two employees of ENP had been hacked to death by a ragtag squadron of RA thugs. It was after looking down at their bodies that Deacon vowed to get himself some real money and finally get out of the business.

That was when he heard about the diamonds.

Axel had had his own fears. Four UN peacekeepers—a Norwegian, a Pakistani, a Brazilian and a Brit—had been found tortured to death last month, their bodies having been dumped into the UN encampment during the night as a warning not to cross RA troops.

The medical examiner said they'd been raped repeatedly "with something big and wooden," then skinned alive. Axel had told him this with a shudder, and Deaver realized it was his worst fear.

It would never happen to Axel, now. He'd gone out like a light being switched off. One moment he was happy in the knowledge that he was going to give diamonds to Maja, then bam! Lights out.

Lucky guy.

Deaver was going to have to mutilate the body, but Axel

was already dead. It wouldn't make any difference to him.

When a patrol finally found him, they had to think it was Deaver's body, fallen into the hands of the RA. Deaver looked down, studying the body. Hacking off limbs is harder than it looks, unless you have a tree stump and a big axe, which most of the assholes in the RA did.

All Deaver had was his Kobun Tanto, but he kept it as sharp as a scalpel. He'd dressed enough deer growing up in Arkansas to know how to go about doing what he had to do. He bent, inserting the knife point between the tendons on the inside wrist, and quickly severed Axel's right hand. He picked it up and flung it far into the jungle. He could hear the small thud as it fell. In five minutes, the second hand was severed and flung in the opposite direction, the unclotted blood forming a red arc as it flew through the air. The hands would be eaten before nightfall.

Now came the distasteful part. Deaver bent down, knife point on the throat and in one quick, hard movement, slashed Axel open from sternum to pubic bone. There was very little bleeding, but Axel's bowels bulged out through the opening. With several more slashes, the skin on Axel's face hung in tatters.

The Revolutionary Army was known for its stoned thugs who loved torturing and mutilating their victims. There would be no doubt in anyone's mind what had happened. The story of the diamonds was well-known. RA soldiers broke into the encampment, kidnapped Deaver, tortured him for the diamonds, and left his body to rot in the jungle.

While Axel left for Finland and Maja.

Deaver straightened and stepped back to admire his handiwork. The predators of the jungle would come across the body as soon as he left. No matter when a UN patrol found the body, what would be left would be Deaver's clothes, wallet, passport, ENP Security ID and very little else. With no hands and no face, the only thing that could identify Deaver was DNA, which would have to be analyzed back in Paris, if anyone cared enough to want a positive ID.

By the time the DNA analysis results were back, Deaver would be long gone, back in the States, tracking down Prescott to get his diamonds back.

He knew just where that fucker Prescott would go. Deaver knew from the moment he set eyes on Prescott, that he was trouble. He made it his business to find out his weak spots. The fucker didn't have any. He didn't drink, he didn't do dope and he couldn't be bought. The only weakness Deaver could find was a woman. A girl. Prescott kept a photograph and a press clipping about her, hidden in a secret compartment in his rucksack. Deaver had managed to make photocopies once, while Prescott was away. He'd watched Prescott take the photo out and stare at it, endlessly.

So he knew where that fuck was going. Back to that bitch he'd mooned over forever, the one he jacked off to.

Deaver'd find him, oh yeah. He'd find them both and the diamonds, too. It would be a real pleasure killing them before he disappeared again, forever.

Four

Summerville

Oh, my, Caroline thought, watching through the wide arch as Jack quickly descended the stairs and strode through the atrium into the dining room. There was a rare, very definitely feminine flutter in her chest.

Boy, does he clean up nicely.

Gone was the scruffy, unshaved look of a man who'd been traveling hard and rough. He'd washed his hair and tied it back. It gleamed an intense, shiny black.

He had on tight black pressed jeans and a black turtleneck sweater. Though the clothes were informal, they had the odd effect of looking like elegant evening wear. The clothes also showcased his body, strong chest muscles and biceps showing under the sweater.

In the bookshop, it had been clear that Jack Prescott was

a tall, strong man, but Caroline had been too busy worrying about whether to accept him as a boarder and then about whether they'd actually make it home alive to dwell on his body.

But now they were safely home, they hadn't died, the boiler hadn't died, and he didn't seem like a serial killer. Now she could look her fill. In between setting the last of the tableware and lighting the candles, she watched him.

She'd rarely seen such a perfect specimen of a man. It was something other than being buff. Buff was normal nowadays. Even Sanders was gym-fit. This was something beyond that—it was sheer male power, unadulterated, unadorned.

His eyes met hers and held as he made his way quickly down the staircase and into the dining room. Some expression, one she couldn't pin down, passed over his face when he saw the dining table.

Had she overdone it?

She looked over the table, set with her best Villeroy & Boch tableware, which her parents had bought on their honeymoon in Paris thirty-two years ago. She still had four unbroken Waterford crystal glasses and there were still bits and pieces of the family silver. Enough, certainly, to set an elegant table for two.

She'd been lighting the last of the candles when he stopped on the threshold. They looked at each other, utter silence in the room. What incredibly magnetic eyes he had. They held her own. His gaze was so compelling, she could scarcely look away . . . with an exclamation of pain, Caroline blew out the match that had singed her fingers. It stung. She glanced down at the angry red spot on her index finger.

In a second, he was by her side, a deep frown between his eyebrows. He picked up her hand and examined it carefully.

"It's nothing," she said, tugging at her hand to free it. It didn't work. He was holding her in a perfectly painless yet unbreakable grip. How stupid, to burn her finger on a match staring at a man. You'd think she'd never seen a man before, the way she'd been staring at him.

A flush of embarrassment rose from deep inside her. She was cursed with the skin of a redhead, and she knew that her cheeks would be flushed and that the flush would extend down to her breasts.

He was standing very close, close enough for her to smell him. He'd used the soap she left for all the guests, but *his* smell—the one that had been imprinted on her brain, on her very nerve endings in the car—overrode the attar of roses. Maybe it was the combination of such female and masculine scents blended together that made her slightly dizzy.

For a moment she felt light-headed and would have swayed if he hadn't been holding on to her hand so tightly.

"You've got delicate skin. You wouldn't want that to blister." He reached past her and picked up an ice cube from a water glass. "Here. Hold that against the burn for a few minutes." He held the cube against her finger and curled his hand around hers.

He didn't step back, as she would have expected, but watched her in silence, his hand around hers. Caroline was aware of her heart beating, slow and hard, and of the incredible warmth of his hand. She didn't know what to do. Of course, she should withdraw her hand from his, but somehow her muscles wouldn't obey, so she simply stood quietly, watching him. His irises were a dark, deep brown, almost indistinguishable from the pupils.

A drop of melted water fell through her closed fist to plop onto the marble floor, sounding loud in the hush. It was as if that small splash awoke her from a deep slumber. She took in a deep breath and flexed her fingers under his.

He opened his hand immediately, and she looked down. The ice had done the trick. The redness was almost all gone.

"Thanks," she murmured, stepping back. Stepping away from him was harder than it should have been, as if that big body exerted a gravity of its own, a small planet made of heat and bone and muscle.

"You're welcome. Here." He dug into his jeans pocket and came away with a plain white envelope. "We should get this over with right away."

She held it, looking up at him. Though he wasn't in any way handsome or even good-looking, he had an oddly . . . elegant face, long and lean, with a strong bone structure no longer blurred by the stubble. Deep grooves bracketed his mouth.

The paper crackled under her fingers. "What is this?"

"The five hundred dollars for the first month of rent, plus a five-hundred-dollar deposit. If you'll have me, I plan on staying a while. I'll pay on the twenty-fourth of each month if that's okay by you."

Wow. That was wonderful by her. The thousand dollars was going straight into the bank on Monday morning. Caroline pulled out a drawer of the secretaire where she kept her bank statements, dropped the envelope in, and nudged it closed with her hip.

She'd been incredibly low all day, alone in the bookshop, with only an empty house to come home to and a long, long lonely Christmas weekend to look forward to. But now it appeared things were looking up.

She smiled as she walked to the kitchen. She'd outdone herself with dinner, maybe to celebrate no longer being quite so *alone*. Jack Prescott was a boarder, it was true, but he was turning into a good one. Who knew? Maybe he even had conversation in him. Maybe—

"Caroline?" His deep voice was low, a questioning note in it. She turned. In the kitchen a bell pinged. The roast was ready. "Yes?"

He pointed a long finger at the secretaire. "Aren't you going to count that?"

She stared at him. "Count what?"

"The money. I want you to count it."

Caroline looked at him, then at the drawer. She gave a half laugh. "But—but I trust you."

He inclined his head gravely. "That's reassuring to hear. And to know. But you should count it, just the same."

"But the roast—"

"Won't burn in the minute it will take you to check to see that the money is all there. Humor me. Please." That harsh face didn't seem to have pleading in its repertory. The word had been said softly enough, but something in his face said it wasn't a word he used often. And it definitely wasn't a face you would say no to.

Well, someone as big and strong as he was, an ex-soldier to boot, probably didn't need to say pretty please very often. He probably just took what he wanted.

It was, after all, the way of the world.

Caroline had butted her head time and time again against those more powerful than she was, and she'd lost, every single time. Power in her world was usually money and connections, not physical strength, but since she didn't have any of them—money or connections or physical power—she always came out the worse for wear.

He didn't move, and he didn't say anything else, so on a sigh, she turned back and pulled open the drawer. The envelope wasn't sealed—the flap was tucked into the envelope like a Christmas card.

Inside were ten very new, very crisp hundred-dollar bills. She counted them, one by one, laying each bill on the surface of the table with a little slap, then when she'd done counting, tucked them back into the envelope and placed the envelope back in the drawer.

It had been a charade, but maybe he'd been right to force her to check. The crisp feel of the notes was so reassuring. The month of January was going to be okay, money-wise. The boiler hadn't conked out yet. She had an attractive man over for dinner.

Man, she was on a roll.

Caroline turned back to him. He hadn't budged an inch, it seemed. She'd never met anyone, man or woman, who could keep so still. "Now, unless that money is counterfeit, and if it is, I'll know it on Monday morning when I deposit it in the bank, I suggest you sit down and pour us a glass of wine. I'll be right back."

When she walked back into the dining room, he was already seated and had poured them both half a glass of wine. He stood immediately as soon as she crossed the threshold.

Caroline put down the roast beef and sat, noting that he didn't sit down until she did. That rule had gone out with the dinosaurs, though apparently Jack Prescott hadn't heard about it.

Jack's dark gaze took in the table, then shifted to her. "This looks absolutely wonderful. Thank you. I didn't dream when I landed that I'd be having such an elegant meal tonight. I thought I'd check into a hotel and try to find a diner somewhere."

Caroline smiled, pleased, as she served him. Yes, she had set a good table. And tonight she'd outdone herself with the cooking. It was an old trick. When depressed—slap on more makeup, slip on your prettiest blouse, put on some great music. Just as long as it didn't cost money she didn't have, Caroline knew all the tricks.

The dining room was beautiful in its own right. When her parents had been alive, it had been painted a light canary yellow that went wonderfully well with the warm cherrywood Art Deco dining set. A year after the accident, on one of the few occasions he'd actually managed to stand upright, Toby had slipped and banged his head against the sharp corner of the buffet, then against the wall, leaving a bright red track of blood.

Caroline had been so appalled and heartbroken at seeing her brother's blood on the wall, the next weekend she'd painted the walls an uninspiring, flat mint green that was just one shade off hospital khaki. It had been the only color on sale the day she'd stopped by the local hardware store.

Other than that, the room was as it had been in its heyday, when the Lakes entertained senators and judges and famous writers and artists. So far, she hadn't had the heart to sell off the dining room set, though if Toby had lived much longer, the dining room set would have had to go, together with the last of the artwork and, eventually, the house.

The cherrywood table was polished to a high gloss. The candle flames were reflected deep into the wood, as were the crystal glasses, almost as sharply as if the tabletop were a mirror.

The candle flames were reflected in Jack's dark eyes, too, tiny flickers of light in darkness. There was another kind of light in his eyes, too, unmistakable.

There was no doubt that he was appreciating more than the dinner. He hadn't said an untoward word, but the male interest was evident and potent. He didn't do anything as crass as look her up and down—his eyes remained riveted on her face—but Caroline had been on the receiving end of enough male attention to know quite well when it was directed at her. Jack Prescott was definitely interested.

She was looking good, she knew that. She'd showered and taken special care with her makeup and put her hair up, with a few tendrils left down to caress her shoulders.

She had on one of her mother's Armanis. There was no way on this earth she could afford a cocktail gown like the one she had on, never in a million years. But she still had her mother's wardrobe, and a rich and varied one it was, too. Monica Lake had had excellent taste, with a wealthy and indulgent husband who loved to shower her with gifts and show her off.

In an effort to raise her spirits, Caroline had decided to dress up for the evening. Damn it, it was Christmas Eve, and instead of spending it alone in a cold house, she was spending it with a very attractive man and—wonder of wonders—the boiler hadn't broken down yet so she could wear the black off-the-shoulder cocktail gown without feeling like an idiot.

It almost felt like a date.

When was the last time she had been on a date? Long before Toby's last collapse. September, maybe?

She'd gone to Jenna's bank to pick her up for lunch and Jenna had introduced her to the new vice president, George Bowen. He was blond, handsome, thirtysomething, and he was immediately smitten. He got her number from Jenna and called that very evening for a date.

George took her to an upscale Japanese restaurant, cool and elegant. It was a wonderful September evening, warm and ripe with promise. George was smart, funny, romantic. Charming company. Sexy in a low-key way. Caroline was seriously thinking of sleeping with him after a couple of dates, wondering how it would be, when her cell phone rang. Toby's nurse. Toby was having an attack.

George insisted on accompanying her home and watched, horrified, as she dealt with Toby.

She never heard from George again. She never even *saw* him again. It was embarrassing the way he avoided her.

He managed never to be around when she picked Jenna up for lunch, and he never responded to the one message she left on his answering machine. Caroline didn't need to be hit over the head to understand that he didn't want to be part of her life in any way. Her life was way too harsh for him.

After that, she and Jenna had lunch at her bookstore, First Page, taking turns paying for the Chinese takeout. It was easier on everyone that way.

Jack put down his fork and took a sip of wine. "Wow. I can't remember a better meal. Actually I can't remember my last good meal at all. It was definitely before Afghanistan."

Caroline watched Jack eating. He had excellent table manners, though she quavered every time he picked up his wineglass. His hands were large and rough-looking. They were capable of delicacy, though. His movements were precise and controlled. Maybe her wineglass was safe, after all.

George had had small, soft, white hands. She tried to imagine him as a soldier in Afghanistan and failed miserably.

"What exactly were you doing in Afghanistan?" she asked, piling more food on Jack's plate and smiling inwardly at his grateful nod.

"I went twice, once for the government, once for the company. The first time was a six-month rotation right after I got my Ranger Tab. We were on winter patrol in the Hindu Kush. The second time was after I resigned my commission to help my dad run his company. We landed the contract to protect Habib Munib. I just got back a couple of weeks ago."

Caroline blinked, fork halfway to her mouth. "Habib Munib? Isn't he—heavens, isn't he the president of Afghanistan?"

"Yeah. Sort of. That's the theory, anyway." Jack's hard mouth lifted in a half smile. It didn't soften his features but it softened her a little. "Truth is, Habib isn't president of much these days beyond the Presidential Palace in Kabul and about a ten-block radius around it. Any warlord up in the mountains has more real power—and certainly more firepower—than Habib does. And every warlord in the country—and believe me there are a lot of them—is gunning for him. Keeping him alive is . . . a challenge. We managed mainly by creating the sandbag capital of the world around him."

She'd seen photographs of Jack! She must have. Habib Munib was often in the news and the pictures showed him surrounded by his American bodyguards. Big beefy guys, mostly, with beards and sunglasses, cradling alarmingly large black guns. She'd imagined them to be U.S. officers, but apparently they weren't.

"Did you enjoy the challenge?"

He paused to think. "Yeah, I did. A lot. We had to outthink some pretty inventive and seriously nasty bad guys. It helped that Habib's one of the good guys. Studied at CalTech, got himself an engineering degree that he doesn't use and solid poker skills, which he does. The man's got a good head on his shoulders. He's his country's best hope for a future that isn't grinding poverty and crazed fanatics out on the streets killing people to keep the country safe from women who wear lipstick and nail polish. We worked really hard to keep him alive."

Caroline watched his face as he talked. She'd forgotten to turn the overhead chandelier on, so most of the light came from candlelight. It turned his darkly tanned skin a deep bronze, the flickering flames alive in his dark eyes.

The house was lukewarm at best, but Caroline wasn't cold. He was sitting at right angles to her, their elbows almost touching, and he seemed to be radiating heat. She felt enveloped by it, the very molecules of air between them speeded up and hot.

"If you liked the work so much, why did you leave?"

"I got word that my dad was sick. He didn't tell me he was feeling bad—didn't want to worry me. It was his secretary who told me. She called and said that Dad was vomiting blood. I flew straight back. I bullied him until he went to the doctor." A faint smile creased his face—a second and it was gone, like a shadow of a smile instead of the real thing. "He was stubborn, my dad. Hated doctors. It took some doing to get him to one. And when I finally dragged him in for tests, we found out he had stomach cancer. I couldn't leave him while he was sick. The cancer was very advanced. He only lasted a few weeks. After he died, I decided to do something else."

Caroline rested her chin on her fist as she looked at him. "Why?"

He put his fork down, thoughtful. He took his time answering. That was something Caroline liked. She disliked glib quips, ready-made answers. He was clearly struggling to find the right words. It was entirely possible that words weren't his medium. He was a soldier, after all.

Finally, he spoke, his deep voice quiet. "My father was a soldier all his life. When he retired, he founded a company where he could use his special skills. I loved my time in the Army, but I know now that, in a way, I enlisted in the Army to please him. When he needed me for the company, I resigned my commission to help him. I was happy to do it. If he were alive, I'd still be in Afghanistan, still with the company. But after he died, I realized"—he stopped and struggled for words—"I—I realized that the company was *his* dream. Not mine. I have another dream, another plan for my life. And much as I miss him, my father's death set me free to pursue it."

There was silence in the big room. Through an archway was the living room where she'd lit the fire. It crackled and popped.

He was comfortable with silence. Caroline liked that. "So tell me, what is this dream?"

He hesitated. "I have—some special skills. Some the Army gave me, some I was born with. They were useful to my father, and I was happy to place them at his service and at the service of the company's clients. But he's gone now. I think I want to use my skills for other kinds of people. The kinds of people who can't go to a security company and have their problems solved by buying what they need." His teeth clenched, the strong jaw muscles flexing under the dark skin. "Security companies protect the kind of people who already have the means to protect themselves. They're usually rich or at least have enough money to buy themselves the protection of a whole company. A lot of them have companies of their own, with employees to stand between them and danger. Hiring extra security is sometimes just icing on the cake, and sometimes, frankly, a status symbol. I think what

I'd really like to do is teach people who need it self-defense skills. People who need to know how to defend themselves but can't afford professional security staff."

"And is that what you want to do here? Start a—a what? Self-defense school? Here in Summerville?"

He nodded. "I wanted a fresh start. I . . . passed through here with my father when I was a child. I liked the place. I just always had it in the back of my mind that I'd like to settle here."

"There are worse places to live." A huge gust of wind rattled the windowpanes, and Caroline gave a wry smile. "And then, of course, there's the delightful, balmy weather."

He gave another half smile. "I'll confess I didn't plan on arriving in the middle of a blizzard."

"I'll bet you didn't. Summerville's a nice enough town, but I have to warn you that sometimes the winters can be vicious. The weather forecasters are predicting a particularly cold and long one this year. Is that going to scare you off?" It wasn't entirely an idle question. It would be a pity if he went. He was going to make a nice boarder, and the steady money would be very welcome.

He froze, as if she'd said something of unusual importance. "No, ma'am," he said softly, watching her eyes. "A little bit of cold weather isn't going to scare me off, believe me. I've been thinking about this for a long, long time."

Caroline was silent, watching him as he bent his head and finished off the last of his third helping of roast potatoes. Steadily, neatly, he'd tucked away an astonishing amount of food. Apparently what he'd said was true—he hadn't had a good meal in months. "This meal was delicious, thank you."

"I'm glad you enjoyed it. I think a little extra effort is called for on Christmas Eve, don't you? And I've got a nice meal planned for tomorrow." She dabbed her mouth with one of the heavy linen Pratesi napkins she only took out on special occasions. "But I warn you, you won't be getting fed like this every day."

He took in a deep breath, clearly searching for the right words. Caroline was distracted for a moment by the sight of his massive chest wall expanding with the breath. She could see his pectorals through the sweater. He probably had thick chest hair, judging from the wiry black hairs on his forearms. A sudden image of that chest without the sweater bloomed in her mind, and a surge of pure heat shot through her.

It was so unlike her, she almost looked around to see if it was someone else who had turned hot at the thought of a man's naked chest instead of her, Caroline Lake, Ms. Cool.

"I won't be complaining, ma'am," he said finally. "I spent seven years eating MREs, and they taste like year-old dog food mixed with rubber. 'Bout as chewy, too."

"Well," she answered, amused, "I'm not too sure what MREs are—sounds like some kind of a weapon, actually—but they must be dreadful. I'll treat you better than the Army did, that's for sure."

"Yes, ma'am." His dark eyes bored into hers. "I'll just bet you will. I'm looking forward to it."

His words were completely neutral, polite, even. There was nothing suggestive in either his tone or body language. He kept his gaze strictly above her neck. But there was no mistaking the undertone of his words. Sex hormones suddenly swirled in the air, a little flurry of them, so powerful she was not only at a loss for words but could feel the air leave her lungs.

Potent, dark, utterly male desire flared in the room, so powerfully she could practically see the waves of desire coming at her from across the shiny surface of the table. Caroline had been desired before, but she'd never felt this dark magnetic pull before.

She should say something, something lighthearted to dissipate the tension in the air. But for the life of her nothing came to mind. She couldn't even look away from him, his dark gaze so compelling it was like a punch to the stomach. Her chest felt tight, and she found it hard to breathe.

It took Caroline a full minute to realize that it wasn't just him. She was feeling desire *back*. It had been so long since she'd felt it she hadn't even recognized it. Jack Prescott was so unlike the men she'd been attracted to in the past that it hadn't even occurred to her that she could desire him.

Caroline was attracted to men who were witty and sophisticated and worldly. Men who enjoyed books and the theater and had an ironic take on life. The little she'd seen of Jack Prescott showed that he was almost the exact opposite. She hadn't seen wit—indeed, he'd been serious to the point of grimness. He didn't look sophisticated, or worldly. True, he'd traveled, but to outposts of civilization, where an ability to wield a gun was more useful than a knowledge of the local museums.

That was her head talking. The rest of her body simply

wasn't listening. It was completely taken over with hormonal overload, a reaction to the sheer . . . *maleness* of Jack Prescott. It was humbling to think that her body wasn't paying any attention at all to what he was saying, what books he might have read, what his politics might be.

No, her heart rate and breathing speeded up because he had the most magnificent male body she'd ever seen. Her knees trembled at the sight of his hands—large, elegant, rough, strong. His deep voice set off vibrations in the pit of her stomach.

Oh, this was bad. Jack Prescott was her boarder. He was paying her an above-market price for life in her very beautiful but at times fiercely uncomfortable home. She couldn't afford to be breathless when she spoke to him, or for him to catch her sneaking admiring glances at the breadth of his shoulders or the size of his biceps.

Caroline had to get a grip on herself *now.*

She had to put this back on a landlady-tenant basis. Cordial and impersonal.

She pasted a polite smile on her face and made polite landlady-talk. "Would you like some more roast beef?"

"No, ma'am," he said, unsmiling. "I'm fine." His eyes never wavered from hers.

They were so dark. She'd rarely seen eyes that dark, with only a hint of a distinction between the pupil and the iris . . .

She shook herself.

"I hope you saved some room for dessert. I made chocolate mousse. We can take it in the living room with the coffee, if you'd like."

He became, if possible, even more still. His eyes probed hers, as if she'd said something compelling.

"Yes, ma'am. I'd like that very much." He rose before she did, in a smooth, graceful motion, and pulled her chair out as she stood up. When was the last time a man had done that?

Caroline pointed at the living room. "Go on ahead, I'll bring in the coffee and the mousse."

When she walked into the living room carrying a tray with two bowls of mousse and two cups of coffee, she saw him crouching beside the fire, feeding a log, stoking the wood with the poker. Sparks flew up the flue. A log fell, bursting into red-hot flames, outlining his broad back in a rim of fiery red. The tight black jeans showed the long, massive muscles of his thighs, flexed in the crouch. He rose easily and turned.

"Here, let me get that." He took the tray from her hands and put it on the coffee table.

The fire rose, renewed, great rolling flames greedily licking at the wood, filling the room with heat and the friendly crackle of the flames. It was like a third person in the room with them.

Caroline sat back on the sofa, sipping her coffee. As so often in difficult times, she tried to count her blessings. She was in good health. January's bank payment would be made. February's—well, that was in the future, wasn't it? Jack said he was staying. He didn't look like the kind of man who'd run screaming from a temperamental boiler. She might make it through February. She might not. One thing the last six years had taught her was not to sweat the things she couldn't influence or change. And to make the most of things, thinking resolutely positively. She'd trained herself to do it.

Unfortunately, frantically thinking happy thoughts didn't always work as well as she wanted. Tomorrow was Christmas Day, when the world as she knew it had come to a crashing end. Christmases were always so hard.

There were so many memories of happy Christmas Eves in this room. Mom and Dad and Toby, music and laughter and firelight. She remembered a Christmas Eve with Sanders, before the accident. Toby'd been, what? Seven? She'd started dating Sanders—the first of their many stop-and-go affairs—and she'd invited him over for Christmas Eve. Her parents had been charmed by Sanders's good manners and adult conversation. That was before they got to know him. Later, her father had grown to despise him. But that first evening they were all smiles.

She—well, she'd been blindly infatuated. So blind that she lost her virginity to him a couple of months later.

That evening, Mom had filled the living room with candlelight. Her mother had loved candles. She lit them on every possible occasion and sometimes just because she felt like it.

The memory of that evening could warm her still. She could even remember the sharp smells of that evening melding together—Mom's Diorissimo, hot candle wax, woodsmoke, the cook's cakes and scones, Earl Grey tea and Dad's bourbon. A heady scent of joy and celebration.

She'd played the piano and they'd sung Christmas carols. She'd played—

". . . play?"

With a wrench, Caroline brought her mind back to the present. Her boarder was sitting next to her. Not so close it made her uncomfortable, but close enough so that she could feel his body heat and feel the air move and the sofa dip as he leaned forward to put his cup on the coffee table. Seeing him this close, she felt slightly overwhelmed by the sheer size of him. It seemed his shoulders took up half the sofa.

Her perfectly normal-sized coffee cup looked tiny in his hands. His hands were compelling, unlike any other male hands she'd ever seen. Though they were huge, the skin visibly rough, as if he worked with them a lot outdoors, they were also naturally well shaped, long-fingered, elegant and strong, with a light dusting of black hairs on the backs. The nails were clean but clearly unmanicured, so very unlike Sanders's hands, which were pale and soft, with perfect, buffed nails.

Oh my God. She was doing it again—drifting with her thoughts. He'd said something. "I beg your pardon?"

Jack inclined his head toward the piano. His voice was patient. He was a strong guy—a soldier. Presumably that gave him extra patience not to roll his eyes and shout at the crazy lady who drifted away in her head at the drop of a hat. "I see you have a piano. I imagine you play. I'd love to hear you play something."

No, absolutely not was her first instinct, and she had to clench her jaws tightly closed to keep from saying the words.

No way could she play. She hadn't played since before Toby died. Not enough time had passed. Her feelings were too close to the surface, the memories too bright, the pain still razor-sharp . . .

"Please," he said and waited, watching her patiently.

Her chest was so tight it was hard to breathe. The thought

of playing the piano made her slightly ill, but how could she say no? He couldn't possibly understand what he'd asked of her. Saying no would sound as if she were insane. Or maybe even worse for a landlady—rude.

She glanced up at Jack. He was watching her quietly, his gaze dark and penetrating. She met his eyes for a moment, then looked down at her hands, hands that itched to touch the keys for comfort, hands that at the same time never wanted to play the piano again.

This was so scary.

Caroline felt she was poised on the edge of some deep, deep precipice from which there would be no return. She could either step forward and fall into the abyss of perpetual grief, a ghost of a woman with only ghosts to keep her company, forever mourning the past. Or she could step back and somehow reclaim her life and have something resembling a future.

She had to stop living in the past. She had to stop grieving. She had to stop thinking incessantly of Toby and her parents. She had to stop *now*.

This was so hard. But it had to be done. She could do it. Over the past six years, she'd learned how to do the hard things. Over and over again.

She drummed up a smile, upturned lips and a flash of teeth, hoping he wouldn't notice how false it was. "All right," she said, her throat tight. "Of course I'll play for you."

Resolutely, she got up and went to the piano. There was an off chance that over the past two months the piano had gone out of tune. God knows there'd been enough changes in temperature with her temperamental boiler to warp the wood. If the piano wasn't in tune, well then, that would be a perfect excuse not to play, and it wouldn't be her fault at all.

She stopped by the big black upright and played a quick scale. The notes rang out true and clear in the big room. The piano was perfectly in tune.

This was something she was simply going to have to face.

Clenching her teeth, she sat down. She turned, surprised, when Jack lit the candles in the brass holders on either side of the upright with one of the long matches kept by the hearth.

"Looks so pretty like this," he said, and blew the match out.

Caroline sighed. Yes, it was very pretty.

She looked up at him. "What would you like for me to play? Do you have a favorite Christmas carol? I have a pretty good repertoire of carols."

"No, no carols, please. I've been listening to way too much Muzak in airports lately." He tapped the score in front of her. "How about this? It must have been the last thing you played."

Caroline froze. "This" was the score to *Phantom of the Opera*. She'd played it incessantly for Toby the last two weeks of his life. Please God, not this.

A Christmas carol would have been easy. She could choose one with no particular memories attached. "Silent Night," maybe. Or "Hark the Herald Angels Sing." The only thing they reminded her of was school.

But the *Phantom of the Opera* . . .

Oh dear sweet God. Anything but that.

This was going to be so *hard*. Caroline touched the keys, stroking them, familiarizing herself with the touch of the ivory and wood all over again. Music had always been her refuge, her place of peace. It was a sign of how deep her grief had been that she'd stayed away from music for so long.

She looked up uncertainly and met his gaze. Dark and steady and penetrating, as if he could reach inside her mind and read all the painful emotions swirling around inside, including her panic and fear. This was a man who'd faced gunfire. How could someone like that possibly understand a fear of a keyboard?

He couldn't.

Do it *now.*

Taking a deep breath, Caroline slowly started playing a few, halting notes with her right hand. The notes were discordant, too slow, but the song was recognizable.

The opening bars of "Think of Me"—the haunting melody Christine sang to the Phantom—came out. The song was forever branded in her heart as a hymn to pain and loss.

Her hand faltered, and she kept her index finger down on F for a long moment, wondering if she could go on.

She had to. She had to not only out of courtesy to her boarder but for herself. And for her own sanity.

You must do this, Caroline ordered herself, her spine stiffening.

Her right hand picked out the notes of the opening again, faster, smoother, more melodic. The left hand came up, reluctantly, to provide the counterpoint to the lush melody. Muscle memory took over. The notes started flowing as her hands moved lightly over the keys, the song as familiar to her as her own name.

Think of me . . .

Mom and Dad and Toby had flown from Seattle to meet with her in New York for Thanksgiving. She'd taken the Amtrak down from Boston, where she was studying music and men, having a great time with both. Dad had booked a two-room suite at the Waldorf. The Lake family had four magical days together, taking in the sights by day and going to plays and musicals by night. Their last night in New York they'd all gone to see *Phantom* at the Majestic Theater. She'd been just old enough to sigh at the romanticism of the love triangle. The doomed, scarred lover banished forever to the shadows, the handsome young viscount and the beautiful young woman loved by both men.

Remember me . . .

Toby'd been just young enough to get jazzed at swirling capes, chandeliers crashing to the stage, candles rising from the water, a mysterious boat on a lake under the Opera. Toby'd been still hopping with excitement the next morning when they accompanied her to the station. She remembered boarding the train back to Boston, looking through the window at Mom and Dad blowing kisses and Toby excitedly waving good-bye. A happy family with their whole lives in front of them.

It was the last time she saw her parents.

It was the last time she saw Toby walk.

For years, he refused to listen to the CD of the musical. Caroline understood completely. It reminded him too much of what he'd lost, of the carefree boy he'd been, a boy with a whole lifetime ahead that had been cruelly snatched from him.

Then, suddenly, a couple of months ago, he started insisting that she play the music for him, over and over as he grew weaker and weaker.

Toby knew he was dying, Caroline thought suddenly, the hairs rising on the nape of her neck. That was why he asked her to play the music so often. Toby felt his death approaching and he wanted to hear the music that reminded him of the last time the family had been together, the last time he'd been a healthy boy.

She bent her head, her hands moving on their own, without her having to think of the notes.

The delicate, romantic music filled the room, filled her head, filled her heart. Her hands floated over the keyboard, the music coming from the deepest reaches of her being.

. . . please promise me . . .

She forgot where she was, she forgot about the large, dark-eyed man by her side watching her, as she was swept up in the haunting melody. A song of yearning and the promise of love when the hope is gone.

. . . that sometimes you will think of me . . .

Softly, softly the song ended on one last lingering note that echoed, then died away. Her hands slipped from the keys to lie in her lap.

Caroline bowed her head, a loose tendril of hair falling forward to lie on her shoulder.

A sudden current of ice-cold air swept through the room, ruffling the pages of the score, chilling her to the bone. Goose bumps rose on her skin. She looked up, startled, as the candles in their brass holders guttered, then died. The heavy curtains fluttered briefly, then stilled.

It was over almost before it began. The air was suddenly still once more. Wisps of smoke from the smoldering wicks rose straight up. Nothing moved.

Something had come—and gone—from the room.

To her dying day, Caroline believed that it was at that precise instant that her brother's soul departed from this life, finally, finally breaking free from the broken cage of flesh he hated so.

He'd heard her play one last time and had left the world.

Caroline had just played Toby's requiem.

Now he was finally, truly gone. And she was alone.

One large tear slipped down her cheek and fell on the keyboard, plopping so heavily that the key made a ghost of a sound.

Jack hadn't moved, but something in the very stillness of the air to her side made her turn. He was standing next to her, one big hand on the top of the piano, watching her steadily. She had no idea what he could be thinking.

Probably what a crazy, crazy woman she was.

Suddenly, Caroline was so very weary of her grief and loneliness. Something had to happen to break her out of this icy shell of sorrow that encased her. She needed human warmth and connection. She needed to touch someone. She needed for someone to touch her. Other than an occasional handshake, she hadn't touched another human being since Toby's death.

She looked up into the dark eyes of a perfect stranger and spoke the truest words she knew out of a painfully tight throat.

"I don't want to be alone tonight," she whispered.

Five

Sierra Leone

The human eye sees what it expects to see. Deaver knew that. Like all soldiers he used that fact often. Half of military tactics is deception and evasion.

So when a five-ten, 180-pound blond man wearing dark sunglasses strode confidently through the UN camp, dressed in well-pressed fatigues with the UN badge on his shirtfront and wearing the distinctive bright blue helmet of the UN peacekeeping force, nobody gave him a second glance. He was just another of the five hundred UN soldiers in the encampment.

It was evening. Half the troops were on routine patrols—unarmed, the idiots.

Deaver still found it hard to believe that soldiers would allow themselves to go unarmed. Orders from on high. Military observers and peacekeepers had to show their neutrality at all costs. Axel had thought it stupid, too. Deaver had a sudden pang of sympathy for the guy.

He felt like an incredible asshole walking around unarmed in West Africa, a place where it was as if some giant hole had opened up and sucked in everyone who was human, leaving only deranged monsters. He'd only been unarmed for a couple of days, but it felt like forever.

Deaver could only imagine what a whole tour of duty here unarmed would feel like, where if you fell into the wrong hands, you could have your hands and feet chopped off by teenagers, be staked out in the broiling equatorial sun with your bowels slashed open for the insects to eat or be skinned alive, without any weapons whatsoever to defend yourself with.

Well, the hell with that, he was getting the fuck out. Right now. Just as Axel would have.

The evening air was suddenly filled with the familiar *whump whump whump* of a helicopter. Deaver walked fast in the direction of the sound. He wanted to break into a run, but he didn't dare.

In the twilight, he could make out the familiar outline of a Huey, landing in an improvised helipad carved out of the surrounding forest. The pilot landed gently, smack in the center of the circle, and stayed in the cockpit, his hands on the controls. He clearly wanted to be out of there as soon as possible. He was landing at last light to increase his chances of survival. The route from Freetown took them over rebel-held territory. RPGs needed daylight to take planes and helicopters down.

Men dressed in jeans and sweatshirts with the sleeves cut off jumped down nimbly and started unloading boxes. They worked silently and efficiently. Within ten minutes, there was a neat stack of boxes lined up on the ground.

Deaver walked straight up to one of the men. He shouted over the noise of the rotors and the engine. "May I ask where you're going next?" He was a good mimic, and he'd talked enough with Axel to be able to imitate his slight Finnish accent perfectly.

One of the men stopped for a second to look at him curiously. "Back to Lungi," he shouted back, then took another box from the man behind him, passing it on to the man in front of him.

Perfect. Lungi International Airport, his way out. If they left immediately, he could make the 9:00 P.M. flight to Paris, then on to the States. He'd be back in the U.S. before anyone even thought to question whether Axel had made it back home.

"I'm on leave," he shouted over the thumping whine of the main rotors. "My flight departs early tomorrow morning from Lungi. I was supposed to hitch a ride with the convoy, but I missed it. My commanding officer made me go over some paperwork, the bastard." Deacon rolled his eyes. The man looked like an NCO. NCOs throughout the world are familiar with dipshit officers. "Can you give me a lift to the airport? Otherwise, I will lose my flight."

The man stopped and looked back. "We're off-loading four hundred pounds of supplies, so we've got plenty of room. I don't see why not. Wait here." He leaped into the cockpit, and Deaver saw him confer with the pilot. The pilot turned his head sharply and stared at Deaver, looking vaguely insectoid with his deep black pilot's sunglasses. It was impossible to tell his expression. Finally, after a long scrutiny he said something, and the man he'd been talking to jumped back down. He jerked a thumb toward the pilot and put his mouth close to Deaver's ear.

"Pilot said sure," he shouted. "We'll be back at Lungi in an hour. Hop on in."

Fucking A!

Deaver quickly climbed into the cabin and settled himself in for the first leg of his journey back to his diamonds and his new life.

Summerville

I don't want to be alone tonight.

The words lingered in the quiet of the room. A log broke apart, the pieces falling to the hearth with a hiss and a flurry of sparks.

Jack reached out, hesitated a moment, then used his thumb to gently wipe the tear away from Caroline's cheek. She didn't move, she didn't even blink, watching him to see how he'd react to her words. Her skin felt like satin, so tempting he lifted his hand away.

It trembled. His hand fucking *trembled*.

Jack had been team sniper for three years. Snipers are made—forged in the fire of ceaseless, pitiless training. But snipers are also born—with a rare combination of natural-born eye-and-hand coordination and the kind of nature that can wait, endlessly, for the right moment to explode into action.

Jack never lost his cool, ever. He'd hunkered behind a rock in the prone position, finger on the trigger, eye on and off the scope in half-hour intervals, for three days and three nights for the chance of catching Mohammed Khan, drinking only a liter of water and never crapping. His hand had never once wavered, and when he'd finally made the shot, it was a perfect kill. Khan had dropped like a stone with a .50 caliber bullet through the bridge of the nose, one of the few shots guaranteed to kill instantly. One shot one kill. The sniper's mantra.

He was in control of himself, always. His life had depended more times than he could count on that control.

The fact that his hands trembled scared the shit out of him. He couldn't lose control, not tonight. He daren't. If he lost control, who knew what he would do to Caroline? Fuck her too hard? Ending up hurting her? Jesus, maybe *biting* her?

He shuddered at the thought.

Right now, *right now*, he was shaking with lust, clenching his hands into fists because he was afraid he'd grab her and throw her to the floor. Every cell in his body was slick with lust, aching to have her. It wasn't just a six-month dry spell. It was as if he'd never had sex before. It felt like a lifetime of dammed-up desire was raging through his system, burning up his veins.

Touch was too difficult just right now. *Use words,* he told himself.

I don't want to be alone tonight.

"I won't let you be alone tonight, Caroline. Come with me." Cupping a hand under her elbow, safely covered by black silk, Jack lifted her from the piano stool. She rose, huge gray-silver eyes fixed on his.

Do not fuck this up, he repeated to himself. His new mantra.

He had to get a grip. When he'd come down the stairs a few hours ago, it was as if someone had reached deep inside his head and pulled out the most compelling image he could imagine, one he didn't even know he'd had in his head, something guaranteed to touch all his buttons and get his blood up.

The Lake dining room in candlelight, and Caroline standing there, lighting the last of the candles, the warm glow turning her skin the palest of ivories. She was beautiful beyond his wildest dreams, shiny golden red hair up so he could admire the long curve of her white neck, dressed in some elegant black dress that seemed designed specifically to show off her small waist and pale shoulders. Jack had never dared even dream that one day he'd be in Greenbriars with Caroline waiting for him with a smile—yet here he was, and there she was.

And when she'd invited him into the living room—Jesus. It was like some magnificent wheel of fortune turning full circle. Life had been incredibly brutal to him his first eighteen years of life. The lowest point of his life had been when he'd stood on the other side of that window, the one right there behind Caroline. The one he was close enough to touch.

He'd been a starving, homeless half boy, half beast in rags, staring hungrily at a life he couldn't even begin to fathom. He could barely imagine being on the same planet as the otherworldly creatures he had watched through the glass while shivering in the snow. Such beautiful people in such a beautiful room.

And then the wheel of fortune had turned. He'd been found by the Colonel, adopted and given everything his hungry soul ached for—love, discipline, purpose. He, the penniless boy had even, in the end, turned into a wealthy man.

And now that wheel of fortune had turned again, richly, plunging him straight into the land of his dreams.

He was on the other side of that window, now. Not the beggar boy with his nose pressed against the glass, but the man inside the room with Caroline.

Carefully, touching her only by her material-clad elbow, he nudged her closer to him. He himself didn't dare move. He felt like a big bar of C4 with the detonator cap in place. One wrong move, and he'd ignite and explode.

No, she had to come to him. And she was, too. Carefully watching him out of huge, troubled eyes, she obeyed his touch and stepped forward until her feet stood between his, and the tips of her breasts touched his chest.

Jack had no idea what she was thinking. She didn't look consumed with desire for him. If anything she looked sad and lost. Something would have to be done to change that because that wasn't what he wanted from her in bed.

Slowly, carefully, he bent down to her and brushed her lips with his. Her mouth was cold—she was like a beautiful marble statue. He lifted his head, let his eyes roam over that lovely face, then fit his mouth over hers again, a little more firmly. She watched him, gaze troubled, until the very last second, then her eyes finally fluttered closed.

Beneath the light eye shadow, he could see the thin tracery of delicate blue veins under the pale skin. He touched his lips to her eyelids, then moved over to kiss the soft skin of her temple, feeling the silky strands of hair tickling his cheek.

Her skin was a little warmer now. That marble statue was slowly turning into a human woman. He touched his lips to hers once more, a little more firmly, opening her mouth with his just enough to get one quick, heady taste of her with his tongue.

She tasted like heaven—chocolate and coffee and the wine they'd had for dinner. He could easily get drunk on her taste. He dipped his tongue in her mouth again briefly, then withdrew and lifted his head.

"Oh!" Caroline breathed, looking slightly surprised, as if a kiss were an unexpected thing. The tip of her tongue appeared and touched her lower lip, as if to taste him.

His cock throbbed at the sight, lifting and lengthening at each pass of her small tongue over that softly pink, luscious mouth. His hard-on had no place to go, trying uselessly to rise beneath the heavy denim. It fucking hurt. Jack wondered if he was doing himself some lasting damage. Could cocks break?

Every cell in his body was screaming at him to get inside her as fast as possible, but he couldn't. Not yet. There was too great a difference in their levels of desire. He was over the top, more excited than he'd ever been in his life, and Caroline—Caroline was clearly still unsure, though she was the one who'd spoken the words that had put things in motion.

Jack had to remember that what she'd actually said was *I don't want to be alone tonight.*

What she *hadn't* said was—*I want you to tear all my clothes off me, pin me to the ground, open my legs, and fuck me half to death.*

No, that wasn't at all what she'd said, and it was a real pity because that's what he felt like doing.

He had one shot at this—*one*. If he fucked up tonight, he'd never get another chance. If he got too rough, if he scared her, hurt her in any way, she'd toss him out on his ass. The one thing that shone through in Caroline was a weary, wary pride. She hadn't let any of the circumstances of her life beat her down. She wasn't going to put up with someone who scared her, or treated her roughly, not even if she desperately needed the money from a boarder.

Watching her eyes carefully, he bent his head again. This time the kiss was warmer, and her pretty mouth was already open for him. At the touch of her tongue to his, he jerked away as his cock surged. God, he'd nearly come in his pants.

He had to cool himself down a little; otherwise, this wasn't going to work.

He ran the back of his forefinger down her cheek, marveling at the satiny smoothness.

A deep breath, then he said what had to be said. "Caroline—I don't want to sound unromantic, but I don't have protection for us. I haven't had sex for over half a year and I don't have anything with me. Please tell me you've got something here."

Shit, it hadn't even occurred to him on the flights over. Normally, Jack always had rubbers with him. Most of his sex life was one-night stands—or maybe two- or even three-night stands when he liked the woman enough—so he was always prepared. But he'd come home straight from that hellhole, Afghanistan, the world's largest no-sex zone. Even if he managed to get turned on by women covered with rugs, the certain knowledge that any sex partner of his would likely be stoned to death in retaliation was a real turnoff. Sex never even crossed his mind in Afghanistan.

He'd come home to the dying Colonel, who'd sent him on his last mission, to Africa. Jack never fucked in Africa. Never.

So here he was, with literally the woman of his dreams asking *him* for sex—or at least that's what he hoped she'd asked for—and he was without rubbers, for the first time in his adult life.

Fuck. If he'd known this could happen, he'd have come equipped with ten boxes.

Caroline blinked, as if coming out of a trance. "Protection? What do you—oh!" Her hand covered her mouth. "How stupid of me. Of course—condoms! Oh my gosh, no, I don't have any condoms in the house. It's been way longer than six months for me. More like six years. In fact, it's been so long I've probably forgotten how. In fact," she continued stepping slightly back, watching his eyes, "if you decide to change your mind, I totally understand."

"No!" It came out almost a shout and she winced. Jack felt sweat trickle down his back. "No," he said again, more softly, working to make his tone normal through the sudden tight-

ness in his chest. "Look, we can do without a rub—a condom. I can be careful." *I hope*, he thought.

He'd always had complete control over his cock, though right now he was holding on to that control by his fingernails.

Caroline was silent, looking him up and down. She was struggling with something, and he gave her the time to do it. "You look healthy," she said finally.

He blinked. "Absolutely."

Healthy? Well, yeah. He couldn't be more healthy. Right now, in fact, his rude good health was practically bursting through his pants. "Outside of injuries, I've never been sick a day in my life."

She had turned a light shade of pink. "Because, um . . . well, the story's this. I was under a lot of stress this fall. My brother was very ill, and I was so worried I sometimes forgot to eat and—" She stopped suddenly, her pretty mouth closing with a snap, as if realizing she was babbling. "Well, the upshot is that my doctor put me on the pill," she said finally. "So we could—"

Whatever else she was going to say was lost in his mouth. Jack plunged both hands into her hair, to cradle her skull and hold her still for his kiss. Deeper, hotter than before. He licked his tongue inside her, dying for her taste, holding her head tightly as he angled his head for a deeper taste of her.

Her hands came up to curl around his wrists as he continued kissing her, almost desperately. He dropped a hand down to her narrow waist and pulled her tightly against him, widening his stance to bring her closer. She jerked a little as she came flat up against his rigid cock. Jack broke the kiss though he didn't want to. He wanted to stay here forever, his tongue in her mouth.

If it were up to him, they'd drop where they were, right onto the hardwood floor. He wouldn't even strip her. Just rip a hole in her stockings and panties and shove his cock right into a cunt that would be as warm and wet as her mouth . . .

Jack groaned. He opened his eyes to look down at her lovely face. Her mouth was wet and slightly swollen from his, a light flush along her cheekbones. His hands had torn her hairdo apart, and her hair lay in gleaming ringlets along her shoulders. Her hair was the color of the red-gold flames in the hearth. He was vaguely surprised that her hair felt cool to the touch, the color was so like bright golden flames. The skull beneath the hair was warm, though. The rest of her was warm, too, now—finally. His arms were full of warm, willing woman.

His arms were full of Caroline.

He had to fight to keep his breathing under control.

They were going to fuck. It was official. He was going to fuck Caroline. *Bareback,* no less. He'd never had sex without a rubber in his life. The way he felt right now, he was probably going to die of sensory overload the instant he entered her.

"I think we'd better take this into the bedroom." His voice sounded hoarse, as if he hadn't spoken in days.

Her eyes searched his. "Okay," she whispered. "The bedroom."

Oh, yeah.

The quickest way to get her to bed was to carry her. He

swung her easily up in his arms and tried not to run for the stairs.

He had the instincts of a cat. He'd done a lot of mountaineering with the Colonel and in the Rangers, and he had superb balance. But when he held her in his arms, he felt his knees nearly buckle. It was insane. She couldn't weigh more than 115 pounds. Going into battle he'd carried more weight than that in gear. Hell, he'd jumped out of planes carrying more weight than that. But it was as if a fever affected his system, making him weak and shaky.

He needed to get them to bed, fast, before he toppled to the floor with her and made a fool of himself.

Jack took the stairs two at a time and turned right at the landing. Lucky thing her bedroom door was open because he would have kicked it down if it wasn't.

Putting a boot through her door was probably not a good way to start this.

Jack stopped by the bed and let her slide slowly down his body. She had to feel his hard-on, quivering with eagerness, leaping at the contact with her body. Probably people across town could feel his hard-on. He was probably interrupting radio reception with the waves of lust emanating from his cock.

What was she feeling? He couldn't tell. Caroline stood quietly, passively, like a beautiful little doll, not moving from where he put her down.

For the very first time in his life, Jack wished women could be more like men. He wished Caroline had the female equivalent of a cock that would show him what she was feeling, show him how much she desired him. *If* she desired him.

He wanted something big and obvious like a stiff dick, to signal clearly what was going on inside her—like maybe a red light on her forehead that blinked on and off.

But women weren't like that. Their bodies were secretive, the arousal tucked away inside where you couldn't see, hidden away in the recesses of their bodies.

The only way he could know what point she was at would be to touch her cunt, run his fingers around her opening, probe her.

Jesus, what if she wasn't turned on? What if she wasn't very wet? What would he do then? He already knew she'd be tight. A woman who hadn't had sex for six years would be small.

It might be a problem. God, he hoped not.

He had a big cock. It wasn't anything he was particularly proud of, it just was. Since he wasn't the kind of man to compare dicks in locker rooms, he didn't get any bragging rights about it. He just took it as a physical fact that pertained to him, like being tall. But his size and the fact that he was as turned on as he'd ever been in his life meant he'd have to be careful with her, though his self-control was shredding, turning more insubstantial by the minute.

Like right now, looking at her in the dim light of the bedroom. He'd left the lights in the corridor on, but hadn't turned on any lights in the bedroom, so it was as if they were underwater in a faraway ocean.

The first thing anyone noticed about Caroline was her coloring, which was exquisite—from the ivory rose of her skin to the golden fire of her hair and the silver-blue of her eyes. Now she was leached of all color, a vision in shades of gray in the soft, dim light. It didn't detract from her beauty. If anything, it highlighted her pale, smooth skin and delicate bone structure. Her eyes were pale, almost colorless, as she watched him.

What was she thinking? He couldn't tell. Her features were still, like a portrait of a beautiful woman instead of the living woman herself.

He was holding her by the shoulders, feeling the delicate bone structure beneath the soft silk of her dress. He moved his hand to the back of her dress, tugging on the tab of the zipper, pulling it down. It sounded loud in the silence of the room. He unzipped slowly, trying to gauge from her expression what she was feeling. The zipper ran to below the waist. Caroline stood as still as a doll while he opened the back of her dress.

With a slight movement of his hand, Jack had his palm inside the parted material, resting against the small of her back, where the skin was smooth and warm. Exerting a little pressure with his hand, he urged her forward.

Watching him, she obeyed the silent touch and stepped forward. She had to tilt her head back and as he looked down, he marveled at what life had brought him. Her eyes weren't blue but silver in this light, wide moons he could drown in. Her mouth was slightly open, and her breathing was fast. He could feel the little puffs of air of her breath against his throat. She moved an inch closer to him, without his having to press against her back.

Yes!

He bent his head to her, stopping when she put a small hand to his chest.

"What?" he whispered, nearly in a panic. She wasn't stopping him, was she? If this was a no, he was going to howl at the moon. He was swollen with longing for her. Not being inside her as quickly as possible was unthinkable. If he couldn't slake his lust for her right now, it would probably cause him a permanent injury, leaving him hobbled for life.

"How did you know which room was my bedroom?" she asked softly.

Oh *fuck*.

This was precisely the kind of mistake that could get you killed in the field. Jack had been undercover in dangerous places and with dangerous people. Keeping your cover story straight was a life or death necessity. Fuck it up and you die.

He controlled his breathing and gently removed her hand from his chest. His heart had given a huge leap at her words. He hoped she hadn't felt it. He was thinking frantically, trying to will some blood back up into his head so he could reason it out. He brought her hand to his mouth and kissed the back of it. Each time he touched her skin, it was a little shock to feel how incredibly soft it was.

She was looking up at him, unsmiling, waiting.

Jack pasted a sheepish smile on his face. "By smell."

Caroline blinked. "By . . . I beg your pardon?"

"I have a very keen sense of smell." It was true. He could smell explosives almost as well as the Labradors the service used. He ran his thumb over her cheekbone, down over the long line of her neck. He bent his head and kissed her under her ear, sniffing loudly, like a dog. "You smell wonderful," he whispered. "Like roses and heaven. I just followed my nose. The whole house smells a little like you, though there are food smells in the kitchen and dining room and the living room smells of lemon polish and woodsmoke.

"But this room—it smells like you and only you. I stopped where the smell was strongest."

He'd pleased her. She smiled uncertainly. "That's nice. I wonder whether maybe soldiers should use smell to orient themselves instead of compasses."

He ran the back of his forefinger down her cheek, along the delicate jawbone, then fingered the neckline of her dress. "We do. Soldiers use their sense of smell a lot. I wouldn't let my men smoke for two days before going on a mission, for example." He bent and nuzzled his nose against the soft skin under her ear. "Though I must admit, I've never smelled anything half as nice in the Army as you."

He could feel her lips turn up in a real smile against his cheek.

She was more relaxed now and tilted her head slightly so he could touch his lips to her neck. Jack realized she must have sensed his intense lust and been a little fearful. The fact that he could make a little joke, however lame, reassured her. Made her think he wouldn't lose control.

He hoped to God she was right.

If this hadn't been his own personal fantasy, if she were less beautiful, less desirable, it would be better. As it was, Jack knew his self-control wouldn't last much longer. If he were a gentleman, he'd take his time with her. Sit on the bed with her, talk to her, make sure she was relaxed. Calm her down. Spend a long time on foreplay. Make slow, careful love. That's what a gentleman would do.

Pity he wasn't a gentleman. The Colonel had drummed manners in him, and they'd stuck, but it was a thin veneer. He was by nature a predator, designed by blood to prevail no matter what.

Added to that was the fact that his biological father had been a nasty, brutal drunk and, knowing his father's tastes in women, his mother had probably been a whore. The Colonel's courtly ideas swirled in his head, but his father's blood ran in his veins.

Jack had no experience holding back with women. He had no idea how to woo a lady. Actually, he had no experience bedding a lady, either. If this had been anyone but Caroline, he'd have been in her, fucking her, by now.

Jack ran his hand up the line of her back, sliding upward and around to cup her bra-clad breast. Caroline jolted.

His mouth was so close to hers he could feel her breath in little spurts, the uneven breathing of someone under stress. "Are you nervous?" he whispered.

She cleared her throat. "A little," she confessed.

"Don't be." In a second, he had her bra undone, and his hand was cupping the soft roundness of her breast, his thumb rubbing the nipple gently. He could feel her heartbeat, fast and light. He had to ask. "Are you scared?"

"Of you?" Caroline pulled back a little to look him in the eyes. "No."

His breath came out in a whoosh of relief. "That's good. Because I won't hurt you. I promise you that."

"No." Her eyes watched his, mouth uptilted in a faint smile. "I believe you."

Jack ran his hands up her back and moved to her shoulders. Slowly, he pushed the open dress off her shoulders and watched it drop to the floor, together with her bra.

She was almost naked, with only black panties and black lace-topped thigh highs and black heels. It was like some fantasy vision. Jack thought he'd built up his memories of Caroline over the years into a woman too beautiful to be true. As it turned out, his memories didn't do her justice.

Jesus, she was so beautiful it hurt the heart. Pale, perfect, so delicately built he was almost afraid to touch her. Something about his expression must have worried her because the anxious look was back in her eyes. Though she didn't raise her hands to cover herself, her shoulders hunched, as if to somehow hide her breasts. He needed to say something to reassure her.

"You're so fucking beautiful," he whispered, then winced. "Ouch. That wasn't quite how I wanted to say it, sorry."

Somehow it worked. He had made Caroline smile. "Thanks. It's not the most elegant of phrasing but . . . thanks."

What point was she at? He needed to know.

Jack knelt before her, placed one delicate foot on his thigh and slowly rolled the stocking down her leg. God, this was a fantasy scene, too, calculated to drive any male out of his mind with lust.

Her legs were long, slender without being skinny, with the

smallest most delicate ankles he'd ever seen. In a moment, he'd removed shoes and stockings.

Jesus, even her feet were gorgeous. Small, pale with an elegant arch.

Jack had never been adventurous in bed. Once he got the woman in bed, his usual style was to climb on top and put it in. Once he was in, he could stay for hours, but he wasn't much for the fancy stuff. He rarely went down, rarely was on the bottom. Meat and potatoes sex, that was his style.

But right now, running his hands along the long, elegant, soft length of Caroline's legs, he had a sudden urge to kiss her toes, one by one. Suck them. Run his mouth along the delicate arch of her foot. Lightly bite his way up to her narrow ankle.

His breathing was ragged as he contemplated her pretty feet. No, he finally decided. No way could he start at her toes. He'd come before he reached the knees.

He ran his hand up her leg, leaning forward, mouth level with her belly button. He nuzzled her flat little belly while cupping her slender calves, running a finger behind her knees, around to the inner thigh and up until he was cupping her mound, moving his hand gently back and forth in a silent signal to widen her stance.

"Open for me," he breathed against her belly. Unsteadily, Caroline took her foot off his thigh and stood with her legs slightly apart. He kept an arm braced around her back so she wouldn't fall.

Rose-scented musk rose from her, Caroline's perfume mixed with arousal. He could clearly smell it, coming from the thatch of soft, light-colored hair between her thighs. Never had a smell been so welcome. Gently, Jack pressed a finger into her and nearly wept with relief and fear.

She was wet, all right. His finger was coated with moisture as he penetrated her carefully. But not wet enough to take him, not yet. And she was god-awful tight. Her little cunt closed around his finger like a wet, soft vise. He probed gently with his finger, withdrawing so he could spread some of the moisture around her opening. Jack was operating by touch alone, carefully watching her face. When his finger brushed against her clitoris, she gave a sudden exhalation of breath, her mouth rounding in an O.

"Do you like that?" he murmured, stroking her carefully, hoping the calluses on his skin weren't hurting her. Everything about her little cunt seemed so delicate to him, the tissues incredibly soft. He ran his finger over the clitoris again, and her legs trembled. If he hadn't had his hands on her, he wouldn't have felt it.

"Yes," she whispered in the darkness. "I like that."

Jack rose slowly from his crouch, wincing against the pain in his crotch as his dick rubbed against the tight, stiff denim, and kissed his way up the center of her chest, up her neck, along her jawline. Soft, reassuring little kisses. Pecks, really.

With his finger still inside her, he could literally *feel* what turned her on, and it was just his sheer rotten luck that gentleness did it. With each soft kiss, she turned a little wetter, and his finger could slide into her with greater ease. When he nuzzled the skin under her ear, she sighed and moved against his hand, her opening softer now, and warmer.

Jack moved his other hand from her waist to cup her neck, his fingers moving in the rose-scented silken strands of her hair. Locks fell over his wrist in a soft cascade. He kissed her softly, gently, and she sighed into his mouth, moving under his hands, coming closer to him, her mouth shifting under his. She showed no signs of actually wanting to get on the bed and get it on. She was enjoying the kissing, the gentle touches, the stroking.

Was this what gentlemen did? Kiss forever? Didn't they ever get to fuck? Jack felt like steam was coming out of his groin, and his dick hurt. It hurt to breathe, too. He felt tight bands around his chest, squeezing the air from his lungs.

The only good thing was that the kisses were working. Jack stroked her tongue with his, and she actually clenched around his finger in a little ripple.

Yes!

Would it work with her breasts? Jesus, why didn't he have three hands? One to keep touching the soft, wet folds of her sex, one to cup her neck, leaving one free to touch those delicate, firm breasts. He only had two hands, though, so he was going to have to take one away. Removing his hand from between her thighs was unthinkable, it would have to be the hand cupping her head.

Only he loved the feel of her hair spilling over his hand, fingers gently holding her still for his kiss. He pressed her harder against him, as if to say—*stay.*

She did, and didn't pull away even when he probed more deeply in her mouth with his tongue.

Jack cupped her breast, loving the silky firmness. She was

small, and fit perfectly in the palm of his cupped hand. At that precise moment, Jack Prescott stopped being a man who was turned on by big breasts and switched forever to small, dainty, perfectly shaped breasts topped by delicate pink nipples.

Were they hard yet? Only one way to find out. He gently circled the nipple with his thumb, the velvety texture a soft delight against his rough skin. When he touched her nipple, she clenched tightly against the finger deeply embedded inside her and moaned gently in his mouth. A drop of moisture collected in his palm.

Shaking, he pulled his hand out of her and lifted his head. It took Caroline a second for her eyes to open, and she looked, dazed, into his own.

"Undress me," he whispered.

"Okay," she whispered back. He had no idea why they were whispering. Maybe it was the semidark room or the idea of being secluded in the middle of a snowstorm, or just the intensity of feeling that seemed to fill the room.

Hesitantly, Caroline reached out and touched his stomach. Jack had to stop himself from groaning as she fumbled her way to where his sweater disappeared beneath the waistband of his jeans. In pulling it out, the backs of her fingers brushed against his hard-on, and they both jumped. Her hands flew away, as if they'd touched something scalding hot.

Jesus, he had to clench his groin muscles tightly so he wouldn't go off.

"Sorry," she said breathlessly, looking up at him wide-eyed.

Jack couldn't answer. He knew he was a second from coming. If she touched him there again, he'd spill and embarrass himself forever.

"Maybe I should do this." Breathing heavily, his skin coated with sweat, he stepped back and crossed his arms to pull the sweater off. A second later, his hands were at the button of his jeans and he was shucking them off, together with his briefs, socks and boots.

His cock sprang free. Her eyes widened, and Jack looked down.

He couldn't blame her for the wary look on her face. Fuck, his cock almost scared *him*.

It was dark red and swollen, hard as a club, big veins visible, weeping at the tip. He didn't let her get more than a glimpse of him. Cupping both hands around her head, he stepped forward and kissed her, more deeply than before, a complete possession of her mouth, while walking her backwards the few steps to the bed. When the backs of her knees met the mattress, he picked her up and laid her gently in the middle of the bed, following her down.

The feel of her under him was mind-blowing. He was operating on blind instinct now, unable to strategize, unable to think in any way. In a second, he'd opened her thighs with his own, hands cupping her head as he kissed her deeply.

There was no waiting possible. Spreading her thighs wider to open her fully, his cock slid along the folds of her sex, then he entered her in one hard thrust, his cock parting the tight tissues, the heat and pressure unbearably exciting. It felt like he'd stuck his dick into a plug. Prickles erupted all over his body, an explosion of heat and light went off inside his head, an electric wire raced along his spine, and with the next beat of his heart he was coming in long, hard streams that made him shake.

It was totally unstoppable, there was absolutely nothing he could do about it. Every muscle in his body clenched, and he shook and groaned as he exploded inside her. Though he was incapable of thinking clearly, at some deep level he realized he could bite her in his excitement, so he took his mouth from hers and buried his face in the cloud of hair, the smell of roses prolonging his spasms. It felt like he came forever, shuddering and groaning, as every drop of liquid in his body came spurting out of his cock. He was holding on to her hips in a death grip, pushing with his toes, grinding into her so he could be as deep in her as he could, and simply hung on while he exploded, heart beating double time, breath pumping in and out of his lungs like at the end of a fifteen-mile run.

Sweat poured out of him and plastered her to him.

It took ages before he was able to settle. When he got his breath—and his brains—back, and took stock, his heart sank.

Jack lay sprawled on Caroline, making no effort to keep some of his weight off her, though he outweighed her by a hundred pounds. She was sticky everywhere from his sweat and the gallons of come it felt like he'd poured into her. Their groins were wet, and he knew come had seeped down to stain the pretty flowered sheets.

He was known for his stamina but tonight it was as if he was fifteen again and green. He hadn't even lasted a minute—

he'd come the instant he'd entered her. The explosive climax had wiped out most of his memory, but he knew one incontrovertible fact.

Caroline hadn't come.

Man, he'd fucked this up, but good.

Six

Summerville

Well, she'd asked for it.

Caroline lay under Jack's heavy weight and tried hard to breathe without wheezing. The man weighed a ton. She tried to quietly expand her lungs and contemplated the etiquette of the situation. She needed oxygen and some space. How could she do this? Would it be okay to push at his shoulders to hint that he should get off her? Would it be rude?

How soon after sex was it okay to cuddle? And of course, the big question—was he a cuddler?

He actually didn't look like much of a cuddler. He'd been grim and mainly quiet all evening. Most cuddlers were warm and chatty. Maybe he was the kind of man who had sex, rolled off the woman, then got up, the saddest kind of lover there was. The kind who left solitude and melancholy behind in the bed. She'd known a few of those.

What Caroline liked most about sex was the sense of closeness. The feeling that, for this small moment in time, she wasn't alone. She liked touching and being touched, affectionate words whispered in the ear, even if they were only true for the moment. Even a little human warmth was better than none.

That was basically what she had wanted from Jack, though she knew sex would have to come before. She'd never really enjoyed sex all that much—though the last time she'd slept with a man had been so long ago she almost didn't remember what it was like. But she did enjoy the afterwards. Quietly lying in the darkness with a man's arms around her, listening to the comforting thump of another human heart.

Right now, his was thumping triple time. It must have been a doozy of a climax because he'd shaken and groaned and panted, almost as if he were in pain. He was also as hot as a radiator. If nothing else, the quickie sex had rid her of the deep chill she'd felt. Jack Prescott was like a huge, heavy, hairy electric blanket.

Hesitantly, Caroline lifted her hand and placed it on his shoulder, wondering if she'd have the nerve to push at it.

She was instantly distracted by the feel of him under her fingers. There didn't seem to be any give in him at all. The shoulder muscle was dense, ridged, hard as steel. She stroked the heavy muscle uncertainly, and was surprised when he took her hand off his shoulder and pressed it to his mouth. He kissed her palm first, then the back of her hand, as if they were at a ball instead of lying together, his penis still inside her.

She shifted slightly and—

"You're still, um . . ."

"Hard?" he supplied. He was lying with his cheek on her hair, close enough that the hot puffs of breath against her temple ruffled her hair. His mouth was an inch from her ear, and the deep voice, so close it felt as if he were speaking inside her head, sent shivers down her spine. "Yeah. Oh yeah. I haven't begun to be finished with you."

He levered himself up on his muscled forearms and looked down at her. His features were blurry in the dim light, the whites of his eyes and his teeth light against his dark skin. His big hands clasped the sides of her head and he bent to kiss her, lightly, mouth moving gently on hers.

He lifted his mouth for a moment and tilted her head slightly so he could kiss her from another angle. Sweet kisses. First-date kisses. A postsex cuddling kiss except it wasn't post sex. They were still having sex. Sort of.

He was still iron-hard inside her, but he wasn't moving. The only thing he was moving was his mouth on hers. His kisses were warm, deep, a soft gliding of his mouth on hers. It was easy to lose herself in them, particularly now that she could breathe again.

He lifted his head once more, his gaze piercing in the dimness. "Are you okay?" he whispered, mouth an inch from hers. "Did I hurt you?"

Caroline smiled at that, pushing back a lock of black hair that had fallen over his face. "You seem to think I'm some kind of cream puff." She shook her head, her hair rasping faintly against the pillowcase. "I can assure you that I'm not."

He blinked. In an instant his expression changed utterly. The faint lines of kindness and anxiety around his eyes disappeared and his face tightened, nostrils flaring. The heat in his eyes was visible even in the semidarkness. "Oh, but you are." His voice was husky, pure sex. "You're a beautiful little cream puff, and I could eat you right up. All over."

There was no mistaking his meaning. Unbidden, an image shot straight to the most primitive part of Caroline's brain. She saw herself spread out on a bed, Jack's dark head between her thighs, big hands holding her thighs apart. The image was unsettling. No, not unsettling—arousing. Unmistakably. Her vagina tightened around his penis at the thought. Immediately, he thickened and lengthened inside her.

Her startled eyes met his. "You like that thought," he said, voice deep and low. Deep grooves bracketed his mouth. "It turns you on."

"Yes, well . . . I—I must like it." Her voice was breathless. She was completely distracted by what was going on in her body. Each pulse of his penis brought a little tug of her inner muscles tightening around him.

Amazing. That had never happened to her before—that intimate link so intense she could feel the changes in the man's body inside hers.

Caroline was not only turned on by the thought of Jack Prescott going down on her, she was turned on by *him*. While her head had whirled with her neurotic, grief-stricken thoughts, and she'd been reticent and hesitant—her body had raced right on ahead without her and become aroused all on its own. There was no question of it. Now that she was really paying attention, and her head had caught up with her body, she realized she was more turned-on than she'd ever been in her entire life.

Jack Prescott might be grim-faced and not the world's greatest conversationalist, but her body didn't give a damn because he was perhaps the sexiest man alive. The most . . . *male* man she'd ever seen.

Everything about his body was a source of intense, bewildering pleasure. The sheer size of him, the hard muscles, the thick mat of dark, wiry chest hair brushing her nipples with each breath they took, the thick, iron-hard penis buried inside her . . .

God, just the feel of him . . .

"I'd love to go down on you, honey," he said in that dark, smoky voice, "but I'd have to pull out first, and they'd have to hold a gun to my head to make me do that right now." His big hands slid down her sides to hold her hips as he began moving inside her. Long, slow, deep glides that filled her with heat. "No way," he whispered. "That's for later, when I can think of something besides *this.*" He lunged into her, a heavy thrust that took him even more deeply inside her.

Caroline's arms had to stretch to hold him. Her hands slid over the sleek hard muscles of his arms without finding a grip. Frustrated, she hooked her hands under his arms, palms flat against his massive deltoids, and held on. She could feel the intense play of muscles as he moved on her, in her.

His long, hard body was one huge erogenous zone, from

the hair-roughened legs holding her own legs open to the big hands holding her head still for his kiss. Everything about him was so utterly different from her that every touch, every kiss was new territory.

The kiss deepened, turned biting and hard. She gasped for breath as her vagina fluttered again. He felt it. He felt everything that was happening to her. He knew what was happening to her body almost before she did.

Jack levered himself up on his arms, lifting his upper body away from her completely. His chest was so wide it seemed to fill her entire field of vision, the pectoral muscles sharply delineated. Caroline stared hungrily at the massive biceps, hard and perfect. Her hands itched to touch him—touch all that hard, sculpted muscle. She reached out tentatively to stroke his chest, and his entire long frame shuddered. His eyes burned into hers.

"Look at us, Caroline," he commanded softly. "Watch what we are together."

Startled, Caroline looked down at their bodies. The hair rose along the nape of her neck and along her forearms. She'd never seen anything as erotic as their bodies joined together by their sexes. Her hands were clutching his biceps, her skin very pale against his darker skin. She watched the hard muscles of his stomach clench with his long, slow thrusts. Their pubic hairs intermingled at the deepest point of his glide into her, when she felt every inch of him inside her, black hairs intermingling with her pale ones. When he pulled his penis out, it glistened from the semen he'd jetted into her and her own juices.

With each glide into her, Caroline's arousal increased. She watched them making love, the room silent and hushed, his thrusts slow and regular. Any thought of cold was completely banished from her system. Heat rose from her groin as if she'd stepped in front of a furnace. The heat was intense, inside and out, prickles of heat and arousal running through her system. Her very veins felt incandescent.

Caroline was beginning that long, luscious slide into climax when a drop of sweat fell from his temple onto her chest.

It electrified her.

This slow, controlled lovemaking was exacting a price. His stomach muscles were so tight she could see each ridge of muscle. Caroline slid a hand from his biceps—held so tautly the sinews were visible—to his back and felt his control even there, in the hard, tightly clenched muscles. He looked as if he were a statue carved of dark marble rather than a man of flesh and bone.

The knowledge of how tightly he was hanging on to his self-control pushed her right over the edge. With a sharp cry, Caroline erupted into contractions, clenching tightly around him, shaking with the force of her climax.

"God," he muttered, as a shudder went through him. He lowered himself to her with a groan, dropping his hands to her thighs. He lifted them high and pushed them wide apart, so she was completely open to him and began thrusting hard and fast. His movements kept her on that knife's edge of climax way longer than was normal for her as pulses of red-hot pleasure coursed through her system. She was holding on to him as tightly as a person lost in a storm holds on to a tree trunk. Just as her climax was winding down, and she could breathe again, he turned his head on the pillow, moving his lips to her ear.

"More," he whispered. "I want more, Caroline." Goose bumps rose along her flesh as he inserted his hand into the small of her back and lifted her even more into his thrusts. He changed the angle of his movements, and somehow the base of his penis was rubbing directly against her clitoris. Electric shocks ran through her system as waves of intense pleasure almost too great to be borne coursed through her.

For the first time in her life, Caroline became a purely physical being, all her senses turned inward to the pleasurable tumult happening inside her body.

It seemed as if she came with her entire body, not just her sex. All her limbs shook as she held on to him, feeling with her thighs and arms the dense play of muscles as he moved inside her. Eyes closed, head tilted back, she rode out the waves of pleasure until there was no more left. There was nothing left in her, not even the strength to hold on to Jack.

Her arms and legs fell open, and her breathing slowed.

Jack stopped. "Caroline?"

Oh God, he was still iron-hard inside her, but there was no way she could participate. Every single muscle had gone limp. It was even hard to keep her eyes open.

Dimly, she realized he'd pulled out of her. He turned with her in his arms, and using his hard shoulder as a pillow, she dropped into a dreamless sleep.

Air France Flight 1240
Mid-Atlantic en route to Kennedy

Axel's VISA was good for a first-class flight across the Atlantic with Air France. *L'Espace Premiere*. The name alone was classy.

Deaver relaxed in the comfortable extralarge seat that tipped back into a bed and sipped a flute of excellent chilled dry champagne. The real thing, not the warm carbonated piss served back in cattle class.

Good old Axel. His credit card and name would fly to Atlanta, where he would disappear from the face of the earth. Deaver lifted his glass in a salute. *Here's to you, old boy.*

Deaver looked around the first-class cabin, with its plush carpeting and jewel-like colors. It was the first time he'd ever flown first class, but by *God* it wouldn't be the last.

For the first time since Obuja, Deaver relaxed and started planning the next few days. His head was clear, and he could see what had to be done with unusual clarity.

He was spectacularly comfortable, well fed, a soft pure new wool blanket spread over his knees. The first-class cabin was like a little sanctuary of soft colors, soft voices, pretty women. Even the air smelled of luxury. No stench of diesel and unwashed carpet that he'd always associated with flying. In the air was the expensive colognes of the other passengers, the heady smell of the *boeuf en croute* they'd had for dinner, the Burgundy and lemon tart, topped off by the Napoleon brandy served in crystal snifters.

No wonder the rich made all the smart moves. Who couldn't think smart with pretty stewardesses vying to serve you fabulous food and wine, slipping perfumed pillows under your head, wrapping you in the softest of blankets? Even the noise of the engines was muted up here in first class.

Deaver had flown the world, mainly in cargo planes, which was as far from first class as it gets. He remembered being airlifted from Ramstein to Jakarta. Fifteen bone-breaking, freezing hours strapped into metal benches against the bulkhead, pissing into jars.

Never again. Fuck no.

Deaver drained the flute.

"Encore du champagne, monsieur?" A stewardess appeared immediately and topped his flute again with a wink and a smile. She was tall, blonde, with uptilted brown eyes. He was on a mission, but when he got his diamonds back, he'd follow up the next time he got a smile like that.

There were only five other passengers in first class, all businessmen, and they were finally settling in for the night. The sky outside the portholes had long ago turned dark, then black. They'd been wined and dined, and now they put away their laptops, folded their newspapers, took their shoes off and, one by one, converted the seats into beds.

Deaver waited until the lights dimmed, the stewardesses retired behind the curtains and his fellow passengers were asleep.

Only then did he take out of his pocket three sheets of paper—photocopies of a smudged photograph, a wrinkled press clipping and a digital photograph. The first two had been folded and unfolded thousands of times, and the images weren't clear, but still they gave Deaver all the information he needed.

He looked first at the digital photograph, taken by one of his men, Sam Dupont, in Freetown. Sam had stayed behind in the capital to stock up on ammo, and was just ready to get back to their base camp when he saw Jack Prescott, making the rounds, asking about them. He took Prescott's photo and headed out to Obuja, where Deaver and the rest of the team were waiting for him. Prescott in Sierra Leone was bad news, and Deaver had pushed the raid on the village forward. He hadn't been expecting Prescott to make it inland as fast as he had.

His fists clenched around the crystal glass of Glenfiddich. Damn! If Prescott hadn't found a way to get upriver so fast, he'd have come across smoking ruins in Obuja, and Deaver's men would still be alive and rich.

Deaver touched the smooth sheet, circling Prescott's head with the tip of his forefinger, letting the hatred and rage run through his system. Prescott had taken what was Deaver's, and he was going to pay. But first, Deaver had to find him.

He opened the other two sheets of paper and smoothed them out. The photocopy on the right was a press clipping, the paper yellowed with age. It had been cut so that only the photograph and a portion of the caption showed. The only indication of the newspaper's name was . . . *ville Gazette.* The date was October 12, 1995.

The photo showed a young girl at the piano in a concert hall. The caption read: CAROLINE LAKE GAVE A PIANO RECITAL AT WILLIAMS HALL THURSDAY EVENING.

The other was a standard high-school portrait. There were millions of photos like this floating around the U.S. The girl was the same as the girl in the news photo.

She was a looker, that was for sure. The clipping showed a profile almost hidden by long pale hair. It could have been anyone. But the high-school picture was full-face, and you had to blink to make sure she was real.

Red-gold hair, gorgeous. A younger, softer Nicole Kidman.

That was in 1995. Twelve years ago. Of course in twelve years the girl could have gained fifty pounds, lost her hair, lost her teeth. Died of cancer. Had a kid a year. Started turning tricks. A lot of stuff could happen in twelve years.

Deaver didn't care one way or another. But that fucker Prescott cared. Oh yeah, he cared. It was the first thing he brought out to look at in the morning and the last thing he looked at before turning in. You don't do that for anything less than an obsession.

Deaver had watched women trip in and out of Prescott's bed and leave nothing behind. Prescott sure didn't keep their photographs as a keepsake. Didn't keep anything, as far as Deaver could see.

He was careful not to get caught staring at the photographs, but Deaver knew how to wire a webcam as well as anyone else. He'd even caught Prescott jerking off twice, one hand holding a photograph, the other beating his dick.

Photocopying the two photographs had been insurance. Deaver had had a sixth sense that one day he'd need something to hold over Prescott, and as usual, his hunch was right.

Prescott had his diamonds, and Deaver wanted them back. They were *his*. He'd fought for them, he'd bled for them, they were fucking his.

He was perfectly willing to put the knife to Prescott to find out where he'd stashed them. But Prescott, like all Special Forces soldiers, had been inoculated against torture. Not only that—he was a tough son of a bitch. It was entirely possible his heart would give out first.

But everyone has a weak spot, and Deaver was holding Jack's. A man who jerked off to a woman's photograph for twelve years probably had feelings for that woman. And might be willing to exchange $20 million in diamonds for her.

Seven

Summerville

Every Christmas morning for six years, Caroline had woken up with tears drying on her face. She didn't remember crying during the night, but she would wake up with wet cheeks, swollen eyes and a feeling of oppression so great it was as if a giant boulder were sitting on her chest.

Not this Christmas morning. She'd slept deeply and well, completely warm in her bed, though she kept the temperature in the house low at night.

Most mornings she woke up slightly chilled, but not now.

Right now, even though she was naked, she was warm down to her bones.

She came awake in low, swooping stages, a degree of consciousness at a time. By the time she realized that she had had fabulous sex last night with an amazing lover, that he was the source of the glow of heat under the covers and that her pillow was an undeniably hard but somehow comfortable shoulder, she was smiling.

She never thought it would be possible to smile on a Christmas morning, but she definitely was.

Her situation hadn't changed at all. She'd lost the last of her family two months ago. She had a mountain of debt so crushing it would take her twenty years just to start to get out from under it. Her house was falling down around her ears.

It was all still there, but she didn't care. Somehow, she was able to let those thoughts recede, far far away, like a long, dark cloud low on the horizon on a sunny day.

Right now, she was happy.

"I heard that," a voice rumbled under her ear. One big hand moved in her hair, long fingers delicately massaging her scalp. The other lay in the small of her back, heavy, an intense source of heat.

"You heard me smile?" she asked, charmed at the thought.

"Uh-huh." That big hand moved from the small of her back to smooth over her bottom. Nerve endings sparkled to life as he lazily moved his palm over her buttock.

There was utter silence. Caroline didn't know what time it was and didn't care, but judging from the quality of the stone gray light outside the window, it was probably early morning on a blustery, snowy day. It must have snowed again during the night. Snow lay heavy on the branches of the big oak outside her window and was inches thick on the windowsill. It absorbed all sounds. There was utter silence outside, not even a car passing.

They could have been the last humans in the world.

Caroline didn't care about that, either.

"Merry Christmas," Jack said, his voice so low she didn't know whether she'd heard him talking above her head or whether she'd heard the words rumbled deep in his chest.

"Merry Christmas," she answered, the words muffled against his chest.

Yes, indeed, it was the best Christmas morning in many many years, and it was getting merrier by the second.

His hand was covering both buttocks now, smoothing slowly, warmly over her skin. Such a simple thing—a strong male hand caressing her gently, and yet the effect was incredible. Caroline could actually feel blood rushing to her sex. She could feel herself growing moist and slightly swollen.

Oh, God! His hand was gently probing between her thighs from behind, his fingers touching her moist nether parts. Soft pressure and her legs just naturally opened. He inserted a hairy thigh between hers and opened her right leg so far he had unimpeded access to her with his hand.

He used it, too. A long finger touched her opening softly, spreading moisture around, moving so slowly she had ample time to object if she wanted to. The thought crossed her mind briefly, and she dismissed it as insane.

Jack was causing sensual whiplash. His hand between her thighs was exciting her, arousing her fully. His hand against the back of her head lowered slightly and began lazily massaging her from her shoulders to the sensitive skin of her nape. He must have had some wizardlike knowledge of human—or at least female—anatomy because she could feel herself relaxing by the second under his ministering hand.

Though the touch was light and soothing, he seemed to be able to reach deep into her muscles, unkink the knots, finding exactly where the stress points were and kneading them into oblivion. All the while igniting a fire between her legs.

She nearly whimpered when he entered her with one finger and started thrusting slowly, gently.

He somehow kept his cool, too. How did he do it?

She was melting by the second, her heart tripping a fast beat, breath speeding up and he was relaxed and calm. She could hear his heartbeat beneath her ear—slow, steady, reassuring.

His hand between her thighs somehow followed the beat of his heart. The total excitement generated by the hand between her thighs was starting to edge out the deeply relaxing movements of the other hand when he gripped her neck lightly and raised her up farther on his chest. His mouth covered hers in a slow, deep kiss that turned the blood in her veins to warm honey.

A shift of his legs, and she was somehow straddling him, fully open to the broad head of his penis, which she could feel against her sex, hot and hard.

He pulled his mouth away slightly, though she could still feel the heat of his breath as he spoke. "Stop me if you don't want this."

He had nudged his penis into her opening. He hadn't entered fully yet, the huge bulbous head was stretching the tissues of her opening. Even penetrating her that small amount was exciting.

Not want this?

He circled his penis, stretching her even more. "Don't . . . stop," Caroline gasped.

"Good," he murmured, covering her mouth again with his.

The kiss was as long and languid as his entry of her. As if he had all the time in the world, his tongue stroked hers while he entered her slowly, slowly. God, it seemed to last forever. She'd almost forgotten how incredibly big he was. It should have hurt—there'd been very little foreplay—but, incredibly, her body was ready for him.

She'd slept half-on, half-off Jack, enclosed in his arms. While she slept, her body had been readying itself for his.

Finally, he slid into her fully, down to the thick base of his penis, stretching her completely. He didn't move, he simply kept kissing her, exploring her mouth leisurely.

Caroline sighed into his mouth, shifting so that he was somehow closer, one hand in the warmth of his long hair, the other flat against his broad chest. His hand tightened on her neck as he explored her mouth in rough, deep strokes of his tongue. Inside a minute, his penis was echoing the strokes of his tongue, long and deep and slow.

Being on top usually gave a woman control over the love-making, but Caroline wasn't controlling anything. She didn't have to do anything, think anything at all. All she had to do was lie in his arms and let herself be ravished, let the slow strokes of his tongue and his penis in her spread honeyed warmth throughout her system.

One large hand pressed down on her backside as he lifted himself up into her, driving slowly, deeply, as steady as a metronome, like a warm, steel machine. Time spun out in the quiet room, the only sounds their breathing and the slight creak of the bedsprings.

After a time that could have been ten minutes or an hour, the angle of his strokes changed, deepened, speeded up. The hot pleasure that had spread throughout her body pooled in her groin and turned in a flash into blinding heat. His grip on her backside tightened as the strokes became sharper, faster, nudging upward at an angle that hit all her pleasure spots.

The creaking increased, the rhythm became faster. He wasn't withdrawing almost all the way out to slide back in, as he had in the beginning. Now they were short, hard strokes that created a heat so intense it prickled in her veins. A moan made it past Caroline's throat and came out into his mouth as she gently bit his tongue.

It was as if she'd kicked him into another gear. He jolted and made a noise deep in his chest. The thrusts were faster now, harder than before, and she was burning up from the inside with them. She could feel the steely muscles of his belly and thighs rippling as he worked her.

She could barely breathe, the heat was so intense, boiling up from where they were joined to spread throughout her entire body. She lifted away from his kiss and opened her eyes briefly, then closed them again, little sparks of light moving against her inner eyelids. He had been watching her so intently through slitted eyes she couldn't bear it, his gaze seemed to sear her soul.

Jack bent his head to kiss her neck and nipped her lightly with his teeth. The tiny pinprick of pain set her off.

"Oh!" she cried, holding on to him tightly as her vagina convulsed sharply. Somehow Jack found the rhythm of her contractions and prolonged the orgasm—forever it seemed. Just as they started dying down, his motions became rougher, less controlled, faster and, impossibly, he swelled even more inside her. With a huge groan, he locked her to him with a strong arm across her back, embedded as deeply as he could go and exploded.

Caroline opened her eyes again to find his face contracted, almost in pain, teeth clenched tightly against the sounds that wanted to escape. Inside her, she could feel the jets of semen as he came in huge spurts. She'd never felt anything like that before—as if his climax were hers, too. The jets were so strong that she had another little climax on the wings of her first.

He felt that, too. His jaw muscles clenched as he tried to hold still for her.

Finally, it was over. Caroline's head sank back down to Jack's shoulder, and all her muscles loosened. His hands loosened their hold on her and began caressing again, lightly. More to relax than to arouse.

Arousal was impossible anyway. There was nothing left in her to excite, all her cells had turned into little puddles of protoplasm.

Slowly, Jack withdrew from her. Amazingly, he was still semierect, though Caroline had no idea where he could go with it. He could forget about her. She was already starting that long, luscious free fall back into sleep.

"Caroline? Honey?"

"Mmmmff." Caroline had no desire to talk or do anything other than lie bonelessly on him, feeling his hand moving gently through her hair. She might never get out of bed again.

"It snowed all night. I need to shovel the snow on your drive and the paving; otherwise, it'll turn to ice."

"No," she mumbled. He wanted to get out of bed? Caroline held him more tightly. "Later."

"Believe me, honey, I'd rather stay in bed with you, but it needs to be done." She felt him kiss her hair and move out of her grasp. He threw the covers back just long enough to get out of bed, then covered her back up immediately.

The instant Jack left the bed, it turned cold under the covers. For the first time, Caroline was aware of how wet her groin was with her juices and his. Jack tucked the comforter around her shoulders, his hand lingering for a moment, then she heard him go into the bathroom.

He came out and a few moments later, the door closed quietly behind him. He must have dressed though she hadn't heard. He was the quietest man she'd ever known.

Caroline wanted to watch him dress, she wanted to see him naked in the daylight, but her eyes simply wouldn't open. Her breathing slowed, and she drifted into sleep as if into the arms of a beloved friend.

When she woke again, the quality of the light outside the window had changed. Even through the overcast she could tell it wasn't early-morning light anymore. Caroline lay in bed, thoroughly relaxed. The extra little nap had done her good, and she felt refreshed, almost . . . happy.

Let's not go overboard, she thought wryly. Some would even say she'd made a huge mistake and was headed for trouble. Sleeping with your boarder was not a good idea on so many levels it wasn't funny. When the affair ended, it was possible that he'd look for quarters somewhere else, and she'd have lost a very good boarder in exchange for some sex. *Very good sex,* it was true, but still.

Something impinged at the edge of consciousness, and suddenly she was aware of a regular noise that had been in the background a long time, coming from outside. Even while she'd napped there'd been the noise, she realized.

What was it? A regular, scraping noise. Caroline threw back the covers and dived for her dressing gown hanging from a hook on the bathroom door, hopping barefoot gingerly to her slippers. It was *cold*!

Pulling on the dressing gown, she made for the window but stopped in her tracks when she passed the mirror on the chest of drawers.

Caroline hardly recognized herself. Her hair was a wild reddish mass around her face, flying in every direction. She looked rumpled and unkempt and . . . incredibly satisfied. Her cheeks were flushed, her mouth looked slightly swollen from Jack's endless kisses. There was a tiny mark on her throat that could only be—a hickey. My God, she hadn't had one of those since high school. She was sure Jack hadn't meant to give her one, but she distinctly remembered him sucking at her skin while he was coming.

The memory of that moment, of feeling him swell inside her, then explode, brought a bright flush to her face and neck and had her clenching her thighs. She could still feel him inside her. Seeing her face in the mirror, Caroline thought she looked like a woman still making love.

She would have been appalled if it weren't for the fact that it had been so long since she'd seen her own face as anything but pale and pinched with worry. Now all she needed was a flower behind her ear, and she could have been a carefree tourist on vacation in Hawaii with her lover.

The swishing sound continued. Curious, Caroline glanced outside the window and saw him, methodically shoveling snow and doing a superb job of it. Somehow he'd found where she kept the shovel in the garage and had cleared a path almost to the street. It was a long path and the snow was deep. He must have shifted several tons of snow.

He'd not only cleared the walkway to the street, but he'd also cleared the driveway and found the bag of rock salt in the garage and strewn it over the paving stones so it wouldn't ice over.

It would have taken Randy, Jenna's nephew, five hours to do that job half as well, and it would have cost her $30.

As if there was an invisible thread connecting them, he suddenly stopped and looked up. Meeting his dark gaze was like a punch to the stomach.

She raised a hand in greeting.

He deserved more than that. He'd done a hard and disagreeable task for her without her even asking. Caroline threw up the window sash and stuck her head out into the freezing air.

"Thank you! Come in now, and I'll fix you a warm breakfast,

you must be freezing!" Her breath formed a cloud around her.

He only had that light denim jacket on, no match for the bitter cold. He didn't even have gloves! Caroline made a mental note to buy him warm winter gloves as a thank-you for shoveling the snow. She'd love to buy him a jacket, but her budget wouldn't stretch that far, and he probably wouldn't accept it. He seemed like a proud man who wouldn't like to be reminded that he couldn't afford a winter wardrobe. He might accept gloves, though.

Jack waved his hand at her to get back. "Close that window! Don't catch cold! I'll be finished in a little while."

He waited until she pushed the sash down, then bent to his task again. Caroline watched through the pane for a moment, admiring his economy of movement. He seemed to apply exactly the right effort for the job, movements regular and smooth.

Suddenly, she flashed on the memory of another moment when his movements were regular and smooth—inside her, pumping with the regularity of a machine. The memory sent a heat wave through her so intense her skin tingled, and she knew she was blushing furiously.

This was something Caroline was simply going to have to control. The man was no fool. He was observant and perceptive. Her skin was like a beacon signaling what she was thinking and feeling. She was remembering the sex, and it was out of her control. Amazing. Normally, Caroline had massive amounts of self-control and was always very cool and in command, the complete mistress of herself with men.

Jack, apparently, was the exception.

Well, she was going to have to learn fast how to deal with her wayward thoughts because Jack was going to be coming in very soon, and she had to be able to deal with him without turning red every other second.

Half an hour later, Caroline had showered quickly and cleaned up after last night's dinner.

In the shower, she had resolutely thought of her bank account, the boiler, and the last payment for Toby's funeral, which was due and would wipe her out financially for a couple of months. All things guaranteed to depress her spirits.

She needed that, because when she started washing herself, she was constantly reminded of how she'd spent the night. Washing herself between the legs had required particularly disheartening thoughts because before she soaped up, she could smell Jack and sex in the steamy cabinet and could still *feel* him between her legs, where she was slightly sore.

So while she dressed, went downstairs and proceeded to clean up, she was giving herself little pep talks about how she could remain cool when Jack walked back in. She could, she definitely could, why—

"Hello."

Oh God, all it took was one word in that deep voice, and her stomach muscles clenched and every ounce of blood that wasn't pooling between her thighs was rushing to her face. He'd come in so quietly she hadn't even heard him, which was a miracle considering that the garage door's hinges needed oiling.

"Hi." Caroline winced inwardly. Her voice sounded strangled, and her face could probably substitute for a stoplight.

Jack was standing very still, just inside the door, the accumulated snow on his clothes starting to melt and drip onto the floor. They stared at each other, Caroline feeling flushed and awkward.

What was this? What kind of morning after were they having? A thank-you-for-the-bang-ma'am-and-I'll-be-moseying-on-up-to-my-room-after-breakfast kind of morning? Was it a one-night stand, what they'd had? Were they starting a . . . a *relationship*, and how awkward would that be with a boarder?

It was only when Caroline saw that his hands were almost blue from the cold that she flushed even more deeply, only this time with shame.

Manners and concern for others had been drummed into her from childhood, and here she was, dithering about how she should react to Jack, while he waited patiently, hungry and tired. He must be freezing, he hadn't had breakfast yet, he'd done her an enormous favor, and she was obsessed with what to call what they were doing

Caroline held out a hand. "Let me take your jacket, it's dripping. You must be freezing! Go on up and take a shower and when you come down, I'll have a nice hot breakfast waiting for you."

He walked up to her, calmly, so close she started to take an instinctive step back before she stopped herself.

He looked down at her, smiling slightly. He'd noticed her instinctive movement. Damn the man, he noticed everything.

"Sounds great. I'll look forward to that, but first—" He bent down and covered her mouth with his. He didn't touch her anywhere but with his mouth, a source of infinite pleasure and warmth. Cold was coming off him and his clothes in waves, but he seemed to be able to infuse warmth in her through his mouth alone. His tongue stroked hers lazily, as if he had all the time in the world.

Kisses have a development, just like novels or movies. They usually start out slow and rise to a crescendo, usually becoming harder, more penetrating, involving the body and not just the mouth. In Caroline's experience, kisses led to sex or at least the promise of sex.

This was the first kiss she'd ever had that didn't seem to be going anywhere. It just sort of meandered pleasantly all on its own. His tongue and lips plucked at hers, over and over, as if he'd be perfectly content to stay there all day, kissing her gently, touching her only with his mouth. It was a summer's day by the riverbanks kind of kiss, completely different from the intense sex of last night.

It was easy to drift with a kiss like that, lightly skimming the waves of consciousness. Caroline stopped being conscious of breathing or of standing slightly on the balls of her feet to reach his mouth.

It was Caroline who bumped it up to the next level, or at least tried to. She wanted a deeper taste of him and rose even higher on her feet, clutching his jacket. The shock of encountering patches of ice on his jacket brought her back to reality with a thump. She lowered herself back on her heels and stepped back. They looked at each other. He had a slight flush along his high cheekbones, and his mouth was wet.

Caroline didn't dare look down.

Dazed, she said, "You, um, need to get out of that jacket right now."

"Here." Jack unzipped the denim jacket and handed it to her. He had a faint smile on his face, or at least the grooves in his cheeks were deeper than usual. "And at this point, I'm really looking forward to that breakfast."

She stood, holding the jacket that felt like a block of ice.

"Caroline?"

She started. "Oh! Um, go on up, now. Take your shower." She made shooing movements with her hand.

Jack inclined his head gravely, turned around, and took the stairs three at a time.

Caroline stood and watched him go up. She shouldn't. She knew that. It had been bad enough standing staring like a dummy when he'd smiled. Sort of smiled. When he lost that grim look he became incredibly attractive. Her heart had definitely thumped.

Note to self, she thought. *Never make Jack Prescott laugh.* She'd have a heart attack.

Even just watching him go up the stairs—God!

Desperately looking for something to distract her from thoughts of the wonderful view as he'd gone up the stairs, she turned the radio on, thinking to catch the news. The news was usually pretty much a downer. Today, though, all she could catch was static, so she had to concentrate really really hard on cooking breakfast.

By the time Jack came back down again, Caroline had herself in hand. She'd given herself a little pep talk—reminding herself what would happen to her bank account if he decided to leave after the first month because he couldn't deal with a slack-jawed, drooling landlady had helped a lot.

Caroline had even taken three minutes to breathe deeply from her diaphragm, repeating *ommmm* under her breath, just like her yoga teacher had taught her. So she was cool, calm and collected when Jack made his appearance in the doorway.

Except for the fact that the man messed massively with her head, Caroline was so incredibly grateful for the company. Without Jack, she knew how she'd have spent her day. Going over accounts, trying to add up the unaddupable and come out with a little profit at the end. An exercise in futility. Maybe doing the laundry. Finishing the new Janet Evanovich. Skipping lunch. Early dinner on a tray, watching TV.

In bed before nine. A bad night's sleep, full of ghosts and nightmares. Waking up to a long, lonely day.

Instead, she had company. Not just any company, either. No, she had an incredibly attractive man who said interesting things, when she could get him to talk. And when she couldn't . . . well, there was always the eye-candy aspect.

Jack sat down, and Caroline started delivering food to the table, on an industrial level. Toasted homemade bread with butter and homemade orange marmalade and blackcurrant jelly. Scones. Buckwheat pancakes, a fluffy cheese omelet, bacon, whole wheat biscuits, link sausage, fruit salad.

Jack sat, hands in lap.

"Please," Caroline said. "Dig in."

"Not until you come sit down and eat with me."

She sat and watched, pleased, as he piled food on his plate, an amazing amount, but then he was a big man who'd just done a full morning's work. "You like your coffee black, right?" At his nod, she poured the coffee, happy that she'd splurged on French roast.

"This is great. How come you're not eating?" Jack frowned.

"I'm eating," Caroline protested. "Just not . . . as much as you." Caroline nibbled on her toast, watching him down his fourth slice.

It gave her such pleasure watching him. She had out a brilliant red cotton tablecloth and her red-and-white-porcelain breakfast set. The rich smell of the coffee rose to her nostrils, melding with the smells of the toast and jam and omelet and bacon and sausage. It looked like Christmas. It *smelled* like Christmas. It *was* Christmas.

Caroline sipped her coffee, smiling. "If it's okay with you, I thought we'd have a big breakfast, then have our Christmas meal around six."

"Sounds like a plan." Jack set her delicate china cup down in its saucer without a sound and took her hand. He lifted it to his mouth, brushing his lips across the back. Caroline could feel the softness of his lips and the slight rasp of his unshaved beard. Jack's eyes held hers. "I have a few ideas about what we can do in the meantime."

Her heart gave a huge lurch in her chest. He wasn't grinning suggestively, but there could be no doubt what he meant. The heat in his eyes could have melted steel. What she saw there took her breath away.

This was so far off her radar, sitting here on Christmas morning, her hand in the hand of the sexiest man she'd ever seen, both of them thinking of the night before. Both of them thinking about sex. Both of them thinking that soon, they'd be back in bed.

He'd felt the little jolt in her hand as he'd said the words. Her hand trembled slightly in his. She couldn't think of a word to say. The silence of the house enveloped them as they watched each other.

The silence. The silence of the house. The house was *silent*. Completely, utterly still.

"Oh, God no!" Caroline jumped up, all pleasurable thoughts of lovemaking and celebrating Christmas gone, vanished from her head as if they'd never lodged there.

She knew exactly what that silence meant. The heating system gave off a constant low hum, a background noise that became white noise, something you forgot instantly, but it was always there. The utter silence in the house could only mean one thing—the boiler had died.

Tears sprang to her eyes.

"The boiler," she whispered. "Oh, Jack, the boiler's just kicked the bucket again, oh my God, I'm so *sorry*."

Caroline knew exactly what the boiler dying entailed. Mack the Jerk wouldn't come until Monday evening at the earliest, so they had three miserable, painful days to look forward to.

The house would take about two hours to lose its heat, then the icy fingers of the outside world would reach in and squeeze the house and them, hard.

All of today, all of Sunday and all of Monday would be spent in the freezing cold. It meant bundling up with every item of clothing possible, until only the fingertips and nose showed, and they would slowly chill so much it would hurt. It meant huddling around the fireplace, roasting on one side, freezing on the other. Any other part of the house would be so cold it was painful.

Once, she'd actually had to crack the ice in the toilets to relieve herself.

Foolish foolish Caroline, thinking that this Christmas would be any different from past Christmases, hard and lonely.

The light elation she'd had since waking up had vanished utterly. Things had seemed . . . so different. For the first time in a long while, there was a lot to look forward to—the zing of attraction she hadn't felt in years, a couple of days just lazing around, flirting, having fabulous sex.

Instead, a couple of grim days trying to just stay alive in the freezing cold was what she had to look forward to.

"Relax," Jack murmured, and ran a finger down her cheek.

Easy for him to say. Though, come to think of it, maybe he knew exactly what it was like to have to huddle for days seeking warmth. He'd fought in the Hindu Kush. She distinctly remembered him saying that. She knew enough geography to know exactly where the Hindu Kush was—the foothills of the Himalayas. So this was something he could do.

It's just that this wasn't a mission to some godforsaken outback, where hardship was the norm. It was a home he'd paid good money to live in, and he had the right to expect comfort.

Caroline had wanted some lightheartedness back in her life, after so many years of struggle and darkness. She'd been so looking forward to a couple of days of flirtation and lightness and . . . well, yes, sex.

She'd been planning on drowning him in good food and raiding the Lake wine cellar. What good were all those bottles of Syrah and Valpolicella doing down there in the dark?

And instead, here she was, in a repeat of the horrors of the Kippings. Cardigans pulled out, polite smiles, strangled conversation trying to avoid the stark truth of a freezing home.

Jack studied her features, then turned on his heels.

He was leaving.

Caroline didn't blame him a bit.

"Jack?" It came out a small croak.

He turned.

This was so *hard*, after all her childish yearnings. Merry Christmas, indeed. Caroline forced herself to stand upright and caught herself twisting her hands. She let them drop by her side. This was hard, yes, but she'd been doing hard for a long, long time now.

"Do you—" Shc had to swallow past the tightness in her throat. "Do you want your money back?"

She'd surprised him. He looked totally blank for a moment. There was something about his face that told her he wasn't often surprised. Then he frowned in puzzlement. "Why would I want that?"

"Because—because you're going to spend the Christmas weekend in a freezing-cold house. That wasn't what you paid for. I imagine you want to leave."

He searched her features. "You're upset," he said. "So you get a free one." He turned around again.

Caroline stood, swaying a little, blinking with surprise, holding her arms around her midriff. Already the temperature had dropped a couple of degrees. "So . . . where are you going?"

"To go get the toolkit in the garage," he said, without turning around, "so I can fix that damned boiler."

JFK Airport

"ENP Security, how may I help you?"

Deaver turned into the plastic shell of the public phone at Kennedy. "Yeah," he said in a heavy, nasal Midwestern accent. "Can I speak to Jack Prescott? This is Pat Lawrence, tell him we met at Intersec in Dubai last year."

Coming into Customs as a foreigner had been beyond weird, but it had gone smoothly. Security was primed to question Middle Eastern males, not Finns. The photo likeness had been enough for Deaver to be waved through.

First order of business, find Prescott. The Old Man had died, Prescott would be the new CEO of ENP. Deaver had to find out if he was in North Carolina still.

Axel's documents would hold for a while, but soon he'd need more.

He prepared to be put on hold. The ENP secretaries wouldn't put anyone through to Prescott immediately. They'd make him jump through hoops. Deaver had a phone card and was willing to wait it out, though.

"I'm sorry, sir," the secretary said, instead of *Hold please.* "Mr. Prescott is no longer with the company."

Deaver straightened. "*What*? That's ridiculous! Of course—"

"The company has been sold to Orion Security and Mr. Nathan Bodine is the new CEO. Have a nice day." The dial tone came on.

Fuck! Deaver stared at the phone, jaw clenched, breath coming in spurts. The son of a bitch had *sold the company*. His father barely dead in the ground, and the bastard handed over his life's work, just like that. Well, of course. Fucker had a fortune in diamonds. He wasn't going to go to work every day when he had a fucking fortune in his hand.

Deaver angrily punched out another number. Prescott's home line. Secretive bastard had never given him his home number. Deaver'd had to lift it from company files.

Eight rings. He was about to hang up when a recorded female voice answered. "The number you have dialed is no longer connected."

Son of a bitch had *run!* Simply pulled up stakes and disappeared!

Deaver hadn't factored that in at all. Prescott had thrown him to the dogs and stolen his money, but it hadn't occurred to him that he would disappear with it.

Prescott was a close-mouthed bastard and didn't have friends—or at least men he'd have confided in—in the company. Even if Deaver wanted to take the chance of showing his face in Monroe, he'd probably come up with nothing. No one would know where Prescott had run off to.

Deaver knew. Fucker had gone to his woman, this Caroline Lake. Find her, find him, find the diamonds.

He needed to regroup, and he needed ID and weapons.

There was a man in New York named Drake, lived out in Brighton Beach. Drake could get anything, anywhere, as long as you had the price. Deaver would hang out in Manhattan, get himself kitted out with new ID, while he searched the Net for Caroline Lake.

Deaver punched in a Brighton Beach number and waited.

"Drake," a smooth bass voice answered.

Eight

Summerville

"Caroline, go back upstairs. Please." Jack kept his voice gentle, but he wanted to growl in exasperation. The unheated basement was dank and damp and cold. It would take him at least another half hour to get the piece of shit Caroline laughingly called a boiler going.

She was standing next to him anxiously, eager to help though she couldn't distinguish a lug wrench from an eyebrow pencil, shaking with the cold. Her nostrils were pinched and white, and her hands were milky blue even though she surreptitiously tucked them under her armpits when he wasn't looking. He couldn't stand seeing her like this.

"No," she said, through chattering teeth. "That's okay. I want to help."

"You know what would help me?" He put down the screwdriver and pried away the backing plate. "You'd really help me if you went back upstairs where there's still some warmth left. Your teeth are distracting me. They sound like castanets."

"Sorry." She clenched her jaw.

He sighed. "That was a joke. Obviously not a very good one." He wrenched the plate open and contemplated the rusting wires and leaky pipes with disgust. "Please go up, I can't stand seeing you like this. I mean it."

"If you can stand it, I can. I mean you're a soldier. Were a soldier. Don't soldiers stick together?" She edged closer to peer past him into the bowels of the boiler, as if looking into the face of a long-despised enemy. "So that's the inside of the beast? Doesn't look like much, does it? I mean considering how much damage it causes."

Jack clenched his own jaw. No, it didn't look like much. It was the worst, oldest, crappiest boiler he'd ever seen, and he couldn't believe she was trusting this piece of shit to keep her warm. It should have been tossed onto the garbage heap ten years ago.

"You need a new filter." And a new casing and a new feed-water drum.

"Tell me about it."

"You're spending more in fixing it than a new one would cost. And you're just guzzling up electricity."

"Uh-huh."

"And you'd save even more money if you bought—"

"A condensing boiler," she finished for him. "I know. Believe me I know. I've been told all of this, repeatedly. What can I say? I don't have the money for a new filter and—trust me on this one—I certainly don't have the money for a new boiler. Maybe someday. But definitely not now."

Jack gritted his teeth. He was going to buy a brand-new filter Monday and fit it while she was out. Mack the Jerk was never going to touch her boiler again, so she'd never know. He'd give his eyeteeth to be able to buy a new boiler for her, but it would be hard to install on his own, and she'd notice.

Fuck! He *hated* this! He hated to see her pale with the cold, shaking and frightened that she'd be without heat. It was insane that Caroline had to spend even one more second without money when he had so much. What the hell did he have money for if he couldn't make her life easier?

But how to get the money to her? A sudden dump of a million dollars in her bank account two days after he showed up would raise too many red flags, though he was tempted to do just that. Fuck it. Just transfer a million, maybe two, so her money problems would be over permanently. God knows he'd have plenty left.

It was such a tempting thought that Jack gritted his teeth against it as he took apart the filter from hell, cleaned it, and reassembled it.

Caroline wasn't meant for this life. She wasn't meant to live in a shell of a home, however beautiful that shell was, without rugs and paintings, whose walls needed painting, with an unreliable heating system in the dead of winter. She wasn't meant to pinch pennies, have a continuous frown of worry between her brows, a slightly sad cast to her face.

Jack wanted to drown her in comfort. He wanted to buy her things—useful things and foolish things. Pretty baubles that would bring a smile to her face. Clothes, jewelry. Rugs, artwork for the house. He wanted her to be able to bring Greenbriars back to what it had once been.

It was going to be hard getting her to accept the money, but he'd manage. He was going to be in her life from now on. They were already having sex. He was going to keep her in bed as much as he could this weekend. There was nothing that forged a bond like sex, at least for a woman like Caroline.

She hadn't had many lovers and it had been six years since the last one. She'd been as tight as a virgin, and it had nearly blown his head off. She wasn't an easy woman. Her body had told him she was picky. And by God, she'd picked him.

Jack knew why she'd picked him. Because he'd been there, at a low moment in her life. The taxi driver had said that her parents had died on Christmas Day. Her brother had just died. It was her first Christmas completely alone, and she'd been sad and upset.

It didn't bother him that he'd caught her not because of his charm—he didn't have any charm that he knew of—but because he'd been in the right place at the right time. As a soldier, Jack had ruthlessly used any advantage he could get, even if it was only a slight elevation above an enemy soldier, the wind blowing in the right direction, or the cover of night.

He was going to press his advantage just as ruthlessly this weekend, too, bedding her until, by Monday, she'd be his.

She already was his, only she didn't know it yet. And he'd take good care of her. All his life he'd only wanted two things—to do right by his dad. And Caroline.

She was surreptitiously hopping up and down, trying to keep warm, her breath a little cloud around her face. Damn! Taking care of her did not entail her freezing that pretty tail off.

"Caroline," he began, putting down the wrench.

"Don't," she said, teeth chattering. "I'm staying here and keeping you company until you get that blasted thing going—and if you do, I'll personally nominate you for the Nobel—or you give up. Whichever comes first."

"Listen, it's fu—freaking freezing."

"Yes."

"You'll catch your death of cold."

"Yes."

"So go up."

"No." That pretty, pointed chin went up in the air a notch.

It was a real surprise enamel wasn't shooting out his ass, he was grinding his teeth so hard. Jack bent back to the boiler, trying to work double-quick, before he ended up with a gorgeous corpse.

Fifteen minutes later, he tightened the last screw and flipped a switch. A red light came on, and a second later, with a great shudder like an ocean liner taking off for a trip across the Atlantic, the boiler creaked into life.

Caroline had had her arms wrapped around herself for warmth, but her arms suddenly dropped. *"Oh my God,"* she whispered, eyes huge in her pale face. "You did it. You fixed it."

"Yeah." Jack put the tools away neatly, eyeing the boiler with loathing. He'd fixed it with the equivalent of chewing gum and duct tape, but it goddamned well better hold until

Monday when he could get a new filter in, or he'd rip the fucking thing out of the wall with his own hands. "Whoa."

Caroline had walked straight into his arms, laying her head on his chest, her arms hugging him tightly. "Thanks," she whispered. She looked up at him, tears on her eyelashes. "Oh my gosh. Thanks so much. I can't tell you how I was dreading being without heat all weekend."

His hands came up, one around her head, one around her waist, holding her tightly, looking for words, though none came.

Brand-new emotions, ones he didn't have names for, coursed through him, fierce and raw, emotions he didn't know how to handle.

No one had ever looked at him like that, certainly no woman. Women looked at him with lust, greed or indifference, never with the warmth and admiration he could clearly see on Caroline's beautiful face.

"It was nothing," he said gruffly. And it wasn't. Jesus, he wanted to shower her with pearls and diamonds. Coddle her and spoil her, take care of her problems for her. Fixing her boiler didn't even register on the scale.

In answer, she turned her head and kissed his chest. He didn't feel it through his sweatshirt, but the gesture stunned him. It was an unmistakable gesture of . . . of affection.

He'd lusted after this woman for most of his life, it seemed. The sex they'd had yesterday hadn't even begun to get her out of his head. He was okay with sex. It was what he knew, so he could deal with lust, and the thought of fucking her as long as he was physically able.

What he saw on her face nearly unmanned him. He wanted to put it back on a sexual footing, right now, so he wouldn't have to deal with all those . . . things roiling around in his chest like huge hot boulders. He was bending to kiss her when she shivered.

"Out," he said harshly. If he could have reached his own butt, he'd have kicked it. Jesus, keeping her in the cold damp basement was not a good idea. What was he thinking of? He'd actually flashed on pushing down her pants and taking her, right there, on the freezing concrete floor.

What was the *matter* with him? He wouldn't even treat a casual sex partner like that—and this was C*aroline*.

With a hand on her back, he ushered her up into the kitchen. This wasn't any good. In the half hour it had taken him to fix the boiler, the house had cooled down noticeably. He was okay with it, but Caroline would find it uncomfortably cold. Only one place to go—to bed.

Oh yeah. Get her between the sheets, start fucking. Get rid of that . . . that prickly feeling in his chest.

Jack kept his hand on the small of her back. "Keep on going up." Caroline looked up at him, startled. She blushed when she saw the heat in his eyes and smiled faintly.

"Okay."

Her bedroom had big windows, with no double glazing. The heat had simply leaked out, and it was already close to freezing. Condensation had iced the windows over, forming giant star patterns on the pane. Their breaths were making clouds around their heads. Undressing Caroline slowly like he wanted to was out of the question.

He bent down and kissed her softly, reaching past her to pull down the covers. "Don't undress, just get in."

"Okay," she whispered, toeing off her shoes and lying down. She scooted over, watching him. She'd left a big empty space on his side of the bed, an invitation as clear as if she'd engraved it on a card.

Jack undressed, watching her eyes. There was a little trepidation, a little shyness, but there was also welcome.

Naked to the waist, he unzipped his jeans and hooked his thumbs in the waistband. Hesitating, he finally just shucked them and the briefs off, taking socks and boots with him. Caroline's eyes widened when she saw him.

He didn't have to look down, he could see what condition he was in from what was in her eyes. And he could feel how swollen he was. He was hard as a club, already weeping from the tip, the drops of moisture cool against the tip of his cock. It was the only place where he felt cold. The rest of him was so hot he didn't feel the cold at all, though he was naked. All he had to do was look at Caroline and know that he was going to be inside her very soon, and a hot flush swept over his body.

"You've been thinking about this," she said faintly, when he got into bed.

"All morning." His weight made the bed dip and tip her toward him. Jack reached for her, rolled on top of her.

"All—" She gave a half laugh. "Even when you were fixing the boiler?"

Oh God, she felt so goddamned good, warm and soft, skin like satin. He rested his upper body on his forearms and looked down at her, smiling, as happy as he'd ever been in his life.

"Not then, no." Down there in the basement, his only thought had been to get the damn thing up and running and get Caroline to somewhere warm. "But before. And after. And especially now."

"Yes, I can see that."

"Feel it." Suddenly, Jack wanted her hands on him, like he wanted his next breath. He levered himself off her, to the side. He took her hand, soft, slender, long-fingered and curled it around his cock. "Feel me," he whispered. "Feel how much I want you."

Her fingers flexed under his, once, then closed around him. He hissed as a surge of blood rushed through him, straight into his cock. He'd pulled the covers up and tucked them around her shoulders, so Caroline couldn't see what she was doing. But even if she couldn't see it, she could surely *feel* what she was doing to him. Fisting her hand around him, she brought it down to the base, then slowly back up, smoothing a finger over the head of his cock. One pump of her hand, and it was weeping again. She could feel it, the little witch. The shyness was gone, and a smile of pure seduction was on her face.

She could feel everything she did to him, how his stomach muscles clenched when the back of her hand ran over them. The hand not holding his cock was on his chest, over his heart. She could feel how his breath shortened, how his heart raced.

Jack usually had a clock running in his head, and it was accurate to the minute. But now he lost all track of time in the quiet room. It was so sullen and overcast outside it was hard to tell what time of the afternoon it was, and there were no outside sounds.

There was only them, and the noises they made in the quiet room.

His rough breathing, the rustling of the sheets. The quiet slither of her clothes dropping by the side of the bed as he undressed her under the covers. The creaking of the bedsprings as he finally mounted her.

The slow *ahhh* sound she made as he rolled back on top of her and positioned himself, cock barely inside her, feeling if she was wet enough. She was, not completely primed like he was, but wet enough. More foreplay would have to come later, when he'd had her—oh, maybe a thousand more times and had cooled down a little. Right now, if he waited even a second more to enter her, he'd come over her stomach, or his head would explode, so he slowly pushed his way in. Pushed his way home.

It felt like a homecoming.

There was no mistaking it—the welcome her body gave him. Tight as she was, there was no resistance, just the wet warm sleekness of the tissues of her little cunt, parting to make way for him. He didn't have to hold her thighs open—she'd lifted her legs herself and opened them wide, heels hugging the backs of his thighs, arms tight around his neck, arching into him.

It all felt so good he stopped when he was fully embedded in her, savoring everything about being inside her. It was so luscious here, so warm, he never wanted to leave. Pulling out to start thrusting seemed insane, when she was wrapped around every inch of his cock, and he'd have to give some of that up.

No.

Jack ground his cock in her, digging his toes in the mattress to give him more leverage, and rocked in her. Tiny little movements that gave him the friction he craved but didn't require him pulling even partly out.

He circled his hips, round and round, reaching even farther inside, and with a small cry, arching her back so her perfect breasts were pressed even more tightly against him, she began coming. Sharp little contractions of her cunt, pulling at him, squeezing. She came with her whole body, arms and legs tightening around him, mouth seeking his, tongue deeply in his mouth, stroking his tongue in time with her cunt . . .

God! Without moving, just from being inside her, Jack came, in great streams of come, shaking and sweating, heart pounding, bright pinwheels of light behind his eyelids.

He couldn't move, he could barely breathe, it was so intense, so mind-blowing. Caroline was moaning in his mouth, arms and legs holding on to him tightly as if to keep him from leaving. He loved it that she was clinging to him so fiercely, but it wasn't necessary. Why would he leave? Not while every cell in his body was swamped with pleasure so acute it bordered on pain. No, leaving would be impossible.

The contractions died down, slowly. The biting, harsh, deep kisses softened, became a slow, languid meeting of lips, while Caroline's muscles relaxed, the breath leaving her on a sigh.

One last intense pulse, and his climax was over, too. Jack sprawled on her, muscles like water. He was too heavy, he knew that, but he couldn't have moved if someone had put a gun to his head. His face was buried in her hair, one golden red lock tickling his nose. It smelled of roses—that smell zinged its way to the most primitive part of his brain, the one that would always associate the smell of roses with Caroline, with sex. He hardened inside her, and she gave a shaky little laugh.

"Not yet, cowboy. I need to regain my strength."

Jack smiled. They'd have sex again, and soon. As far as he was concerned, they would have sex for the next thirty-six hours, stopping only to eat and shower. But though his cock was getting harder again by the second, he didn't move because where he was—was perfect. The feel of her, the smell of her, above all the relaxed sense of closeness. It was almost as good as the sex, and it was something he'd never had in his entire life.

It was the one perfect thing in his imperfect life.

New York
Waldorf-Astoria

If you have enough money, you can get anything you want, even on Christmas Day. Deaver took a cab to Chinatown where he bought himself an entire wardrobe from the skin out, thanks to Axel. Two excellent faux Armani suits, a gray cashmere overcoat, two khaki pants, five white dress shirts, five flannel shirts, two sweaters, ten silk boxers, ten silk undershirts, two pairs of expensive boots and a fake Vuitton suitcase. That was for Deaver's new life, just as soon as he tracked that fucker Prescott down.

For what had to be done in the meantime, he bought two cheap black suits, five white drip-dry shirts, two pairs of jeans, two sweatshirts and a forty-dollar parka. That all went into a gym bag.

He needed some walking-around money. There was $40,000 stashed away in a safe in his house in Monroe, but he had no idea if Prescott had alerted the local police, so that was out.

Right now, his staging base had to be here, in New York, where he could disappear while trying to find where Prescott had gone. Drawing cash from Axel's card on an ATM was impossible without the PIN.

But he had an ATM card on an account in the Caymans he'd opened in the name of Nicholas Clancy. The money came from a very lucrative deal in ex-military arms sold to a rebel Ossetian group, and the bank catered to people precisely like him.

It was essentially a server in a high-rise on Grand Cayman. Its customers never visited. The bank knew what it was there for and what its customers needed, so that bank gave its customers a ten-thousand-dollar-a-day limit on its ATM withdrawals.

Axel's Platinum card was enough for a suite at the Waldorf for however long it took to formulate his plan. Deaver was grateful to Axel for having made a fortune in the stock market before deciding to save the world by becoming a UN peacekeeper.

Everything about the Waldorf was pure pleasure, starting with the doorman in livery handing him out of the cab. Deaver pressed a fifty in his hand, figuring the word about big tippers would spread. The doorman, dressed like a Ruritanian general, handed the Vuitton and the bag to a bellboy and ushered Deaver into the huge marbled lobby as if Deaver might actually have some problems walking through a door all by himself.

Damn straight. He'd been living rough and hard all his life. Time to change all that, and the Waldorf was just the place to do it, to turn his life around. Ten very pleasant minutes later, he was being showed into his room, about three times the size of most of the quarters he'd lived in as a soldier, and about ten times the size of the house trailer he'd grown up in.

Plush carpeting, antique furniture polished to a high gloss, a big, high four-poster bed, a desk, deep burgundy armchairs, a bowl of shiny fruit, a tall flower arrangement. The Sun King wouldn't have felt out of place.

His suitcase and bag were neatly laid on a foldup holder. He stepped farther into the room, letting the door close behind him, breathing deeply. Christ, the place *smelled* rich! It smelled of lemon polish, freshly laundered bed linens, the sweet smells of the flowers.

Yes, this was a perfect place to set up headquarters to hunt down Jack Prescott and get his diamonds back.

In the luxurious shower, it took him half an hour to wash Africa and the long plane trip out of his system, but he had more toiletries to do it with than he'd bought in his entire lifetime.

The sullen winter sky was turning dark when he emerged

in jeans, sweatshirt and parka, exiting fast and hailing a cab a block down so the doorman wouldn't link the sleek businessman who'd arrived an hour before with the ordinary man in ordinary clothes. By the time he came back, there'd be another doorman, and after that it wouldn't be a problem.

Because Vince Deaver, roughneck soldier, was about to disappear forever.

Nine

Summerville

Caroline lay beneath Jack, still recovering from the climax and still astonished at herself that she'd been able to climax like that, without actually making love. Just the feel of him in her, just holding his penis deep inside her, had been enough to set her off. He hadn't even had to move, really.

Had Jack discovered some key to her she didn't even know herself? She was usually slow to climax, or at least slow enough that lovers complained. Well . . . lover. Sanders, actually, while they'd been having their on-again, off-again affair. Affairs.

Sanders considered himself an accomplished lover, she knew. Just like he considered himself a connoisseur of wine, a gourmet, a man with a good eye for art. The fact that she took a long time to come had been a source of friction between them, until Caroline had learned the fine feminine art of faking it.

She hadn't faked it with Jack. She'd started coming, startling herself, almost before she knew it herself. Her body had just convulsed. Just from the feel of him on her, inside her.

Amazing.

He'd been sprawled bonelessly on her after his own orgasm, but now she could feel the tension of returning consciousness in his muscles. His penis in her stirred. It was just this incredible sensation, feeling him grow hard—harder, because actually he hadn't softened much even after coming.

She ran a hand over his shoulder, down his back, reveling in the feel of him, so incredibly strong and solid. His spine was an elegantly curved indentation, dense muscles on either side. She followed the furrow down to the small of his back, where a few wiry hairs grew, and on down to his backside. She smoothed her hand over a hard buttock.

It felt so delicious, like a huge apple, and she wanted to take a bite out of it. She couldn't, so she dug her nails into the flesh of his buttock and felt an immediate response in his penis.

Positively Pavlovian! Caroline nearly laughed with delight. He was primed to respond to her, it seemed. Every movement of her hand corresponded to a movement of his penis in her. It worked for her mouth, too, she discovered as she turned her head and kissed his neck. And when she nipped him lightly, oh my, he jolted, and the penis inside her jumped!

They were carrying on a conversation with their bodies.

Her touch said—*do you like this*? And his body answered—*oh yeah!*

His big hands moved in her hair, and he angled his head closer to hers. When he spoke, it was directly in her ear, the vibrations of the deep voice and the puffs of air as he spoke making her shiver, though from the heat of it and not the cold.

"I'm afraid we're just going to have to stay in bed until the house warms up."

He didn't sound too put out. "Oh yes?" Staying in bed with him until the house warmed up sounded wonderful.

"Yeah." He nuzzled her temple with his nose. "Might take hours." He sighed, his voice filled with regret as his hand touched her breast. She was somehow primed for this, because all he had to do was touch her, and the skin of her breast warmed. When his thumb glided over her nipple, she felt it, intensely, between her legs. She tightened around him, helplessly. His penis surged inside her, giving her a little electric shock.

Caroline smiled and lifted her arms back around his neck. His shoulders were so broad it was almost impossible for her to embrace him.

"Might," she answered. "Tough luck for us."

His mouth had moved to her neck, running his lips up and down the sensitive tendons. She arched her neck to give him better access. It was beyond delightful, feeling his mouth on her neck, giving her little biting kisses.

"So . . ." He started nibbling on her shoulder, delicate little nips. "What can we do in the meantime? Hmm? Talk?"

"I don't—" Caroline took in a sharp breath. He'd pulled out of her so far she could feel the huge bulbous head against the lips of her sex, then thrust slowly back into her. She laughed breathlessly. "I can't talk while you're doing that!"

"Doing what?" He pulled out again, slid slowly back in again. He was moving with ease. Caroline could feel the wetness of his semen and her own arousal.

In . . . Out . . .

"That," she gasped.

"Tell me about your family. What were they like?"

It took her a moment to realize what he'd said, she was so distracted by the feel of him sliding in and out of her, so slowly she could feel every inch of him.

But then she stiffened and pushed at his shoulders, a chill running through her. She couldn't talk about her family, not now. Not ever.

"No." She pushed at his shoulders again. It was like pushing against a steel wall.

He entered her again fully and stopped moving. "Talk to me." That deep voice was lulling, almost coaxing. "The cab driver coming in said that you lost your parents on Christmas Day five years ago."

"Six. Six years ago." Caroline's throat felt raw. She felt raw everywhere, all her emotions suddenly right there on the surface, horribly vulnerable. She didn't have her usual protection around her, he was demolishing it with kisses, slow runs of his fingers over her breasts. With sex.

"Talk to me, Caroline. It helps to talk. Tell me what they were like. Start with your dad. What was he like?"

"Funny. He was very funny, but he only allowed us to see it." The words were out before she could stop them. "Everyone thought he was this sober businessman, but he had a very ironic take on life. He hated hypocrisy and politicians. He did a wicked imitation of the governor, but only in the family and only when he'd had some whiskey. I knew exactly when to take things seriously and when not to, thanks to him. I could always count on him to put things in perspective when I was a girl. Once—"

She stopped, a tear trickling from the corner of her eye. She couldn't wipe it away herself, her hands were on his shoulders, so he did, with his thumb. "Once?" he asked quietly.

She sniffled a laugh. "Once this candidate for the Senate came to the house, trying to get Dad to become a fund-raiser for him. He was a businessman, real rah-rah, and dumb as a rock, only less interesting. He thought that since Dad was a businessman, all he'd care about was tax cuts and deregulating. So he and his horrible wife sat there smugly talking about incorporating in the Virgin Islands to avoid taxes, and how he'd raided his company's pension fund to pump up the stock price and how he'd eliminated five thousand jobs." She gave a little laugh, remembering. "So Dad met Mom's eyes and started talking about their plans to liquidate, give everything to charity and move to an ashram in India. The candidate and his awful wife were so horrified they didn't stay for dessert. Mom and Dad opened a bottle of champagne when they left and drank it all in front of the fire. I caught them necking and laughing."

She met his eyes. "I've never told that story to anyone. And now I'm the last person to remember that."

He wasn't smiling, the deep grooves bracketing his mouth

dug even deeper. "Why haven't you told anyone that story? It says a lot about your dad. It's the kind of story that automatically makes you like the guy. I think I would have liked him a lot. I like no-nonsense people."

"Maybe." It was an unusual thought. But who knew? Maybe they *would* have gotten along. Jack seemed the opposite of her father, who'd been a man who'd liked to live large, who'd liked his comforts and his pleasures, who'd enjoyed life with gusto, even better when it was first class.

He'd enjoyed elegant clothes, fine wine and cooking, expensive Cuban cigars, single-malt whiskeys. Her dad flew first class, always stayed in five-star hotels and always got the best seats in the house when they went to the theater.

Jack was a soldier, a hard man, a man used to living rough. He wore old clothes and down-at-heel boots, and had been so incredibly grateful for the meal, she was sure he didn't eat well on a regular basis. Not much in common there.

But her father had hated bullshitters and snobs and plastic people. He'd despised Sanders once he got to know him, though at first he'd tried to hide it.

Dad might have liked Jack, after all. Jack never pretended to be anything he wasn't, hadn't tried to impress her in any way.

"And your mom? What was she like?"

"She was wonderful. *Ah!*" He suddenly changed the angle of penetration, doing something with his body, his hips, so that he bore down on her clitoris with every slow stroke into and out of her. The pleasure was almost electric in its intensity. A couple of those honeyed, electrifying strokes, then he stopped.

"Tell me more. She was wonderful. What else?"

"Beautiful." Her body was so pleasured, she didn't have the energy to weigh her words. They came from somewhere deep inside her. "Mom was such a beautiful woman—inside and out."

He bent to nuzzle her neck. "I know," he whispered against her skin. "I saw the pictures. You look just like her."

Caroline smiled. She'd been told that often enough. It pleased her.

"Dad loved to show her off. He loved pampering her, buying her expensive gifts, it made him happy. And I think Mom loved making a nice home for him. Toby and I would catch them kissing when they thought we weren't looking. I'm glad they died together. That's what they would have wanted." She tightened her hands on Jack's biceps and looked deeply into his eyes. "You know, after—after the accident, no one would let me talk about my parents. No one wanted to hear me grieve, and no one wanted to hear me reminisce. I've heard every possible permutation of 'find some closure' that exists. It was as if talking about them was somehow . . . in bad taste. I could just see it in people's eyes, they'd listen impatiently, then change the subject as soon as they decently could. All I wanted to do was—was remember them, and no one would let me."

"And Toby? What was he like?"

This was without a doubt the weirdest conversation Caroline had ever had. He'd started moving in her again, the movements slow and heated. Her entire lower body was taken up with the sex. But then he was engaging her head, too. They were having two conversations at once. Heated sex below the waist, their bodies talking to each other loud and clear, and a deep conversation above the neck.

"Toby. Before the accident, Toby was a real little boy, you know? A scamp. He was always getting into trouble and getting out of it because he had this big wide grin, and you just melted. You forgave him everything, until his next trick. I even forgave him the frog in the bed that nearly gave me a heart attack." Caroline watched Jack's face as he listened to her. No one had ever listened to her so intently before, completely focused on her.

What had *he* been like as a boy? A scamp? Overactive and mischievous? Probably not. He'd probably been quiet and serious. Though there was something in his face, thinking about him as a boy, something almost . . . *familiar* about him, which was ridiculous.

"After the accident, he was in a coma for three months. He never walked again. And for six years, he never once complained, even when he was in excruciating pain. He loved company, but no one came. His school friends came for a while, then they stopped coming. Toby was in a wheelchair, he had seizures, and that frightened people. No one wanted to see Toby, be reminded that he was what could happen to them. My best friend from high school once said to me that she didn't understand why I didn't put Toby in a h-home."

Caroline looked up at the dark face an inch from hers, dark eyes boring into hers. While she'd been talking, he'd stepped up the tempo of the lovemaking, making the bed creak.

Caroline began the long free fall into climax, but somehow she couldn't stop talking.

"Toby was so incredibly brave." Tears filled her eyes as she watched him watching her. "He couldn't walk and, at the end, h-he could barely move, but he always kept his spirits up. He kept *my* spirits up. I think the past two years, he knew he was dying, but he never said anything. I was so p-proud of him, I thought he was braver than any soldier who ever won a medal, and—and every time I brought a friend home, or a date, they always behaved as if Toby weren't there. Or they'd talk too loud, as if he were brain-damaged. And always, they behaved as if I should be—sh-should be ash-ashamed of him when I—Oh God, Jack. *Oh!*"

Shaking wildly, Caroline started coming, in long liquid pulls, so strong even her stomach muscles clenched. It was as if the pleasure cracked her wide open. Even before her sheath stopped its convulsions, she buried her face against Jack's neck and burst into tears.

There was no stopping them, she couldn't fight them if her life depended on it. The hot sex and her climax had simply blown away any defenses she might have mustered and left her raw and vulnerable, open to her deepest sadness.

She wept until she could barely catch her breath, then wept some more. She wept out her grief and anger and fear. She wept for the long lonely nights in which she didn't dare weep because Toby would see her swollen face in the morning and know. She wept for three wonderful lives cut so tragically short, leaving her on the other side of the wall between life and death.

And she wept because, at times, it had felt like she wasn't

on the living side of that wall, but on the other side. How many times had she felt so dead inside, it was a surprise to remember that she hadn't died with them?

She wept until her throat was raw, until her chest ached with every shaking breath, until, finally, there were no more tears left to cry.

Throughout, Jack held her tightly, still inside her, but unmoving. He didn't try to talk to her, perhaps realizing she was beyond words. And she'd heard all the words, anyway.

You have to let go of your mourning. You must get on with your life, Caroline. Grieving is a process, and you're not processing your emotions at all.

It was true. At times, she felt mired in a deep black hole, a bottomless, airless well with only the faintest of lights at the top. The words other people spoke could barely reach her.

So he knew not to give her words. He gave her something better—the comfort of his body. With all the thousands and thousands of words her friends had offered, nobody had thought to hug her, to let her cry her fill in someone's arms, as Jack was doing.

Finally, the tears stopped, and she lay still under him, trying to catch her breath. Slowly and so gently she wanted to weep, he withdrew from her and, still holding her tightly, turned them over. Now she was lying in his warm, tight clasp, her head on his shoulder. His very wet shoulder. She couldn't control her muscles or her thoughts, as ravaged as if she'd been in a bad accident.

"I'm sorry," she said, dazed.

He wiped her face with something. "I know about loss," he said quietly. "Do you feel better?" He reached under her hair to massage her scalp.

"Yes, thank you," Caroline said politely in a waterlogged voice, then stopped. She *did* feel better. It felt as if the crying jag had coughed up a ball of black bile that had been poisoning her system for a long, long time.

He wiped her face again. She gave a half laugh. "I can't believe you came to bed with a handkerchief."

"It's not a handkerchief," he said matter-of-factly. "It's the sheet."

Caroline blinked, appalled. "I've been crying and blowing my nose into my *sheet?*"

"That's okay." Oh God, how she loved his voice. So deep, so calm. If only it could be bottled and sold as a tranquilizer. Better than Prozac. "We can change the sheets."

We. One small word and it meant so very much. *We can change the sheets.*

Caroline realized that it was the very first time since her parents' death that someone acknowledged that she wasn't alone with a problem. Friends and the occasional date—somehow they were always up for an evening out or a night at the theater, but she was always alone with her problems. This particular one was stupid and minor. She had plenty of sheets, but something in his voice told her he'd stand by her for more than sheets.

"You wouldn't have run away from Toby," she said. It wasn't a question.

"No." His hand tightened in her hair. "I wouldn't have."

She lifted her head away from his shoulder to examine his face. "I wish I'd known you earlier."

Something—some strong emotion—crossed his face. The grooves around his mouth deepened, and the skin across his cheekbones grew tight.

"I wish I'd been around earlier, too."

Brighton Beach

Brighton Beach, a community of 150,000, is part of Brooklyn. Its nickname is "Little Odessa" because most of its inhabitants are Russian immigrants.

Deaver appreciated the irony because he'd met the man he was going to see in Big Odessa—the real thing. He'd first met Viktor "Drake" Drakovich in the late eighties, when everyone on the ground, with two eyes in their heads and working brains, knew the Soviet Union was going belly up.

The CIA hadn't known—the CIA couldn't find its ass with two hands and a stick—but anyone stationed east of the Elbe had known.

Drake at the time was the biggest arms dealer in the world, operating out of a nondescript high-rise in Odessa, supplying arms to the mujehaddin in Afghanistan as fast as he could funnel them in. Deaver'd been a young Special Forces soldier and had been tasked with supplying money to Drake, in briefcases containing half a million dollars at a time. He'd once calculated that the U.S. government had poured at least $10 million into Drake's hands.

It was value for money, too. Drake was known for his quality goods. He had four former Russian soldiers who'd been armorers on his payroll, and when you bought weapons from Drake, you got exactly what you had paid for, in good working order, clean, oiled and ready to roll.

Drake's career stopped on 9/11. Actually, it stopped on September 10, when he got word that Shah Achmed Masood had been killed.

Deaver had been in Odessa that day, the day the shortwave radio gave the news, and he watched, astonished, as Drake immediately started packing up his gear, quietly, emotionlessly. "Bad things are coming," was his only answer when Deaver asked what was going on. "This business is over."

A day later, Deaver realized that Drake was right. And Drake was right to stop supplying the Taliban because the full weight of the U.S. government would have stepped in to crush him. Drake was smart, and he knew where to pick his battles. A month later, he was based in Ostende, Belgium, supplying arms to Ashad Fatoy, the Congolese rebel leader, where Deaver'd crossed his path again. When he could, he threw work Drake's way, and once he was able to warn him that agents of the Belgian Flemish state security agency, the Staatsveiligheid, were closing in on him.

Since the tenth of September, Deaver had kept tabs on Drake, knowing he would always land on his feet, knowing he'd need him one day. That day had come.

"Here," he told the cab driver, thrust what the meter showed and a five-dollar tip over the seat and got out. It was early in the afternoon, but the sky was so sullen with snow, it was as dark as evening. Inside a minute, Deaver had disappeared from the cab driver's sight.

Five minutes and two city blocks later, he was ringing a bell in an anonymous high-rise, not unlike the building Drake had lived in in Odessa.

It didn't matter what name was on the bell, he knew which button to press. The top one. Drake arranged little booby traps on the lower floors that would slow down any assault troops on their way up, and the roof was a helipad. It was his MO, and it hadn't changed, in Odessa, in Ostende, in Lagos and now in Brighton Beach.

A security camera swiveled on its pivot when he rang the bell and Deaver raised two fingers to his brow in ironic salute. Drake had three levels of security, and it took a quarter of an hour to pass through the scrutiny of two very large, very efficient guards in full combat gear outside the nondescript door on the tenth floor. Frisked quickly and impersonally, Deaver was ushered into a large foyer, where he waited for a few minutes, certain that he was being subjected to a full-body scan.

Drake had a lot of enemies and there had been at least five assassination attempts, that Deaver knew of. None of them had even come close. Drake was a very hard man to kill.

Deaver was okay with the security measures and the body scan—he was clean. He'd be crazy to come armed with anything larger than a toothpick into Drake's presence. So he waited patiently while whatever security protocol Drake had worked itself out.

Finally, another big, silent bodyguard motioned to him to

follow, and they walked down a long corridor, stopping outside another nondescript door. The bodyguard knocked, then ushered Deaver over the threshold.

"Dear friend," Drake's deep voice said from the darkness, "please enter." His English was excellent, as were his French, German, Dutch, Spanish and Arabic. Drake believed in doing his own negotiating, and to do that, he had to speak the lingo.

Dark-haired and dark-eyed, Drake was of average height, but he was immensely strong. He was a master of several martial arts, but more than that, he was an uncannily effective street fighter. His hands were the largest Deaver had ever seen, with knuckles the size of airplane bolts with a quarter of an inch of tough callus on the edges. His feet were lethal weapons, too, almost yellow from calluses. Deaver had seen him punch a man in the face with such ferocity that he did almost as much damage as a bullet would have. He'd seen Drake destroy a punching bag with one blow from his foot.

He was dangerous as hell, but he had his own crazy moral code. Drake had never been known to go back on his word, but by the same token you never went back on your word with him. If he became your enemy, you might as well start planning your funeral.

Drake was standing, pointing at a comfortable armchair.

The entire room was built for the comfort of a man. Despite the nondescript building and the barren walls and corridors, in here it was luxurious. Deep leather armchairs, thick luxurious carpets, a sideboard filled with bottles of expensive spirits, a humidor full of cigars.

Legend said that the cigars came in monthly shipments directly from Fidel himself, as a thank-you for something Drake would never talk about.

The room had the look, the smell and the feel of money and power.

Deaver sat, unzipping his jacket with a sigh, knowing he could relax completely for the first time since Obuja. He was definitely safe here. The layers of security, the quiet *whump* the door had made closing which meant it was blast proof, the deep, quiet luxury of the room—oh yes, he was in safe hands. They'd spent the better part of twenty years technically on opposites sides, but Deaver was on Drake's side now, and he liked what he saw.

A cut-crystal glass half-filled with an amber liquid was at his elbow. He sipped, appreciating the aged, single-malt whiskey.

"So," he said finally, putting the empty glass down on the side table and turning to Drake. "You're Stateside now. Is that going to be permanent?"

Drake shrugged. "Yes, I'm in the belly of the beast, now," he replied mildly. "We'll see how it works out. So far I have no complaints. What can I do for you?"

Deaver didn't presume that any more small talk would be appreciated. Drake looked relaxed, but he ran an empire worth more than many third-world countries and he was a hands-on manager. His time was very precious. Time to cut to the chase.

Deaver leaned forward. "First off, I need a laptop to do Internet research on. A used one will do, I'll have to throw it away. But make sure it's got a hard disk with enough RAM to do some serious searching. No fingerprints, and I guarantee I'll purge the search history before tossing it."

Drake nodded. "I have one here."

Okay, first problem over. "Second, I need a new identity that will keep me for a while, until I finish my business. It might take a week, it might take a month. But not much more than that. I'm tracking someone down, and when I find him, I'm relocating permanently OUTCONUS. To Monte Carlo, I was thinking. So I'll need a passport for later. Not U.S. And the identity has to be a little deeper. I'll need a birth certificate that will withstand at least a casual scrutiny."

Drake inclined his head gravely. "Consider it done. One of the guards will take you to my specialist. He has everything. He'll set you up with a new identity that will withstand a casual check, and more. And he'll get you a Maltese passport. Malta's a member of the EU. With the passport and enough money deposited in a Monte Carlo bank, you can get a permanent *permis de sejour*. Keep your nose clean for ten years, and you'll get citizenship."

Now Deaver knew where the passports had gone. The Maltese embassy in Zagreb had reported 190 blank passports stolen, a fortune's worth. So they'd gone into Drake's hands. It was good to know.

Now came the hard part. "That's not all. I'll need FBI credentials and a number and someone sitting at the other end of that number ready to verify that I'm a Special Agent."

Drake nodded. "For how long?"

Deaver's jaw muscles jumped. "For as long as it takes. And

I'm going to need some firepower, but I'll need it where I'm going. I want to fly clean."

Drake provided an essential service. He not only got you the weapons you wanted, "cold"—untraceable—and in perfect working order, but he could get them to you at a time and place of your choosing. Drake's network spanned the world, and he could provide just about any weapon short of a nuclear warhead more or less anywhere. It saved trying to smuggle weapons onto aircraft, and it saved trying to track down local suppliers, particularly if you wanted to hit the ground running.

Drake sipped his whiskey and spoke calmly. "Tell me what you need and where."

Deaver ticked them off. "A Beretta 92 with three clips and shoulder rig and a Kel-Tec P–32 for backup with three magazines, an M40 rifle with a 10X scope, carrying case and four boxes of ammo. They all need to be cold guns."

"Of course," Drake said, the even temper slightly ruffled. His reputation was on the line. "And where do you need them?"

The 20-million-dollar question. "I don't know yet. When I do, I'll let you know immediately. How much is this going to cost me?"

"Two hundred thousand dollars," Drake said promptly, and Deaver barely kept from wincing. It would almost wipe him out. Finding that fucker Prescott became urgent. And when he did find him, Deaver was going to make sure he died slowly and badly, for all the trouble he'd put him through.

"Done. Give me a bank account number and I'll e-mail the

request through immediately. The bank's open twenty-four/seven. You'll have your money within twenty-four hours."

"Oh, that's not a problem," Drake said, his voice gentle. "I trust you."

He could, too. Even though Deaver would be left with less than ten thousand dollars in his bank account, welshing on the deal didn't even cross his mind. The last person who'd cheated Drake had choked on his own dick, which had been cut off and encased in the intestines that had spilled out from his slashed-open gut. No, Drake could trust him.

And anyway, when Deaver found Prescott, he'd be rich. Not as rich as Drake, but almost.

"Is there anything else?"

Even if there were, Deaver couldn't afford it. "No, that's it."

"Then I think we're done here," Drake said, rising. "My men will accompany you to our ID facilities. It shouldn't take long. Someone will be manning a phone number you'll be given for a month, round the clock, ready to verify your identity as an FBI agent. If you require that service for longer than a month, it will cost you extra."

"No, a month should be fine." Deaver was a good tracker, the best. He'd find Prescott before the month was out.

"Then we have a deal." Drake offered his hand, and Deaver took it. The hand was cool, dry, the grip strong. "Let me know where you'll need your weapons."

Deaver nodded. There was no overt sign, no button pressed, but the steel door suddenly opened, two bodyguards at the other side ready to accompany him to where he'd get his ID.

"By the way," Drake said in his cool, precise voice when they were standing on the threshold. "When you recover your diamonds, bring them to me. I can get you a very good price."

The steel door closed on Deaver's astonished face.

Ten

Summerville

"Oh yeah, baby, give it to me," she purred. "Big and thick and hot."

"You got it, honey." Sanders McCullin obliged, holding the woman's skinny hips and bucking up into her. It was pleasant enough. She was very wet and was enthusiastically bouncing up and down on his dick.

Sanders couldn't remember her name. Karla—Kara—Karen. Something like that. They'd met last night at the Zig Zag. On Christmas Eve, the bar had been bouncing and loud. She had slid over to the empty barstool next to his after the girlfriend she'd been with dumped her for a guy.

They'd been fucking for the past twenty-four hours, breaking only to eat, shower and go to the bathroom. Not being sure of her name wasn't that hard. *Honey* did just fine.

Kara-Karen threw her head back, eyes closed, hips pumping.

Sanders guessed her age to be about thirty. Except for her breasts and nose, which were probably about four.

Women with breast implants shouldn't be on top. Everything wiggled except the breasts, which looked bolted to her chest. Fascinated, Sanders watched her breasts—big stiff things that didn't move, like water balloons under the chest wall. She was skinny everywhere except for the balloons on her chest—tits on a stick. And with her head back, he could see the signs of plastic surgery on her nose.

And . . . on her *face*? Jesus. He hadn't noticed that at the Zig Zag, and they'd been fucking in the dark ever since. So maybe she wasn't thirty after all.

After pumping energetically for a few minutes, she came with a great howl, cunt pulling hard on him, startling him into his own climax.

With a cat that ate the cream smile on her face, she settled back down on top of him, clearly intending to stay there, head on his shoulder.

"Wow," she purred. "That was fantastic."

He could smell the sex on them. *Ugh. Cleanup time.*

"Hey, honey, sorry. Nature's calling." Sanders nudged her off him and rolled from the bed, padding naked into the bathroom. As he walked past the dresser, he caught a glimpse of himself and stopped, pleased. Those hours at the gym sure paid off. He had a flat stomach and some good definition, except right now he looked . . . inelegant with the condom hanging off his dick. He pulled it off.

Not bad, he thought. *Still holding up*. The ladies sure weren't complaining.

In the bathroom, he threw the condom in the wastepaper basket—there were four of them on the bottom.

He loved his bathroom. He'd spent $30,000 remodeling and loved every inch of it. Next to the shower was a stand-alone bathtub carved from a single block of marble that weighed one ton. The floor had had to be specially reinforced before it could be winched into place.

Sanders stepped into the shower and felt his spirits lifting at the sight of the gleaming fixtures and pale cream Valentino tiles. It was a spa-quality steam shower with thirty shower jets, a foot massager, piped-in music and a hands-free phone system.

As he soaped up with his Clinique for Men shower gel, Sanders realized that he wished the woman in his bed would just disappear before he got out of the shower. He was all fucked out and didn't like her enough to spend time with her not fucking.

She wasn't the brightest tool in the woodshed and she had an annoying, screechy voice. She was good in bed and gave great head, though there'd been a shocked moment when he looked down at himself afterwards and seen a black cock, as if it had suddenly turned gangrenous. It was just Karla-Kara's trendy Goth black lipstick all over his dick, but he'd had an ugly moment there.

Karla-Kara worked at an advertising agency and talked about music he'd never heard of, films he'd never seen and bars he'd never been to. It was tedious.

He wanted her gone, so he could enjoy the big jar of contraband Crimean caviar and the bottle of two-hundred-dollar Dom Pérignon in the fridge. They would be totally wasted on Karla-Kara, whatever the fuck her name was. At the bar where he'd picked her up, she was drinking some sugary drink and eating a club sandwich.

Maybe if he took enough time in the shower, she'd get the hint, get dressed and leave.

Fat chance. She looked settled, there in his bed, as if she didn't ever want to leave. It was really annoying. He wished there were just a button he could press and hey presto!

No more Kara. Or Karla.

He was wishing that more and more often lately after sex.

She was okay in bed, but boring and vulgar outside of it. Sanders had had just about as much sex with her as he was willing to have. He looked down at himself, checking with his dick, seeing what happened at the thought of another round.

His dick stayed firmly down. So that was that.

The thought of more sex with her was actually just a little depressing.

Nope, Karla or Kara or whatever the fuck her name was, was shit out of luck.

He'd chosen the wrong woman with whom to spend Christmas Day.

He knew the right woman, though he'd have to wait until after Christmas to get her into his bed. *Back* into his bed. Back into his life.

Caroline Lake.

Their time had come, Sanders could feel it. He and Caroline had been dancing around each other since they were teenagers and the time had come to make it permanent. They'd broken up a few times, the first time in their teens. Well, he was going off to college back East, wasn't he? And he couldn't have a small-town girlfriend dragging him down, no matter how rich her family, no matter how pretty she was.

And then Caroline had come back East too, to Boston, an hour's train ride away. And she'd become even more beautiful. They'd had a couple of tumbles in the sheets and he was seriously thinking of an engagement ring when her parents died in a car crash.

It was impossible after that.

Robert Lake had been making some bad investments when he died, and what with the medical bills and her father's debts, Caroline had skated bankruptcy, surviving by a hair after opening that bookshop of hers. With that and her grotesque brother, there'd been no time for him.

When Sanders had returned to Summerville, he'd often thought about getting back together with Caroline, even though she didn't have any money.

There were a lot of advantages to Caroline. She was beautiful, cultivated, and you could take her anywhere. As Sanders's law practice grew, he often wished Caroline were by his side when talking with big clients. She had a magic touch with people that rubbed off on him by association. The few times he'd managed to convince her to accompany him to an important event, his stock went way up.

But she made it clear that her first, second and third loyalty was to Toby and that Sanders came in a miserable fourth.

Unacceptable.

It never failed to appall him—that she'd prefer a writhing pathetic cripple to *him*, and to the life he could offer her.

He knew she was struggling, but that was her own damned fault. She insisted on holding on to that ancient pile of bricks that was falling down around her head and simply wouldn't listen to reason, no matter how many times he told her to sell.

Sanders had quietly had Greenbriars appraised, and to his astonishment, though it was falling to pieces, it was worth over a million dollars. Something about the design. But still. Even more reason to sell it. It was at least seventy years old. She was sliding into genteel poverty, heading straight for ruin, and he could save her ass, give her the life she'd been used to, but she turned her pretty nose up at him and chose to stay with her crippled brother.

It still baffled him.

All she had to do was sell that damned house, put Toby in a home where he belonged and other people didn't have to see him. Then get together with him—get *back* together with him, he never let her forget that she lost her virginity to him—and all her troubles would be over. He'd made that clear every way he could.

Well, Toby was dead now, thank God. This huge drain on

her finances was over, not to mention the ick factor. Even now, the memory of Toby—crumpled in his wheelchair, face so scarred he looked like Freddie, hands slowly retracting into claws—was enough to make him sick.

Sanders had a very clear memory of the last date he and Caroline had had. He'd taken her to Chez Max, over in Bedford. Hundred bucks a head, worth every penny.

Caroline had been particularly beautiful that evening, dressed in a black Versace. Sanders had no idea how she'd been able to afford a Versace, but there it was. And it looked terrific on her. She turned heads.

They were getting on just fine, too. Sanders could tell that she enjoyed the elegant surroundings and the superb food. He ordered a two-hundred-dollar bottle of Chateauneuf du Pape, and they polished it off. Caroline was relaxed, so stunning he was finding it hard to keep his eyes off her.

This was where a woman like her belonged—and on the arm of a man like him.

She refused to come home with him afterwards, so he drove her home and accepted her invitation for a nightcap.

Her creepy brother was up, in the living room, watching TV. Caroline poured Sanders a drink, talking calmly, and poured her brother a glass of milk. She had to hold the glass to his mouth, and even then half of it was spewed down the front of his pajamas. He slurred badly—half his mouth was scar tissue—and Caroline waited patiently for him to finish whatever nonsense he had to say.

After, she put her hand over his, and the sight nearly made

Sanders gag. Her beautiful, slender hand over that monstrous . . . *thing.*

Sanders downed his whiskey without sitting down and left, fuming. She'd essentially ignored him since they walked into the house, in order to fawn over that pathetic excuse for a human being.

Well, fuck that. Toby was finally dead. And Caroline was free. And still poor.

"Hey, baby," Karla-Kara whined. "Momma's getting cold."

Sanders rolled his eyes.

It was entirely possible he was getting too old to play the field. Hell, most of the clients he met were married, some on their second or even third marriage. He was starting to get odd looks when he said he was single.

He needed a wife. Not some bimbo who was good in the sack until it got old, which it usually did, very fast, but a *wife*. Someone who looked good on his arm, someone who would keep house for him. Bear him children. Good-looking, healthy, bright children.

Put that way, there was only one woman who fit the bill. Caroline.

Last month, he'd been called to Seattle to meet with a couple of businessmen who were active in politics. After a couple of hours of talk, after probing him about his opinion on some controversial issues, they'd asked whether he'd like to stand for representative in the midterm elections next year. No answer necessary, just think about it.

Sanders was made for politics. He had looks, brains, money

and above all, he knew loads of people who had even more money than he did and who could be persuaded to back him. It wasn't hard at all to see himself climbing the ranks. State representative, governor, senator. Hell, maybe even all the way up to the top.

That was his destiny. Sanders could feel the power of it tingling in his fingertips.

He was too old now to keep fucking around. Openly, at least. That part of his life was over. He needed the stability of a home life, wife and kids. A politician's wife had to be photogenic and gracious and presentable. That was Caroline, in a nutshell.

Political wives needed stamina and loyalty. If Sanders was ever caught fucking an intern, he needed a wife who'd stand by him, cover for him. Well, if ever there was a woman who didn't abandon her responsibilities, who had loyalty bred in the bone, who was almost *too* loyal, it was Caroline.

Yes, she was perfect. She'd keep him a beautiful home, make a charming hostess, bear him beautiful children, put her family's interests before hers.

The time was finally right for them. It had taken them thirteen years to get to this point.

He'd steered clear of her over the Christmas holidays out of self-defense. Caroline got very glum and boring at Christmastime. And she'd probably be mourning Toby—though any sane person would be rejoicing at getting rid of such a burden.

So he'd let her get all that out of her system.

Monday he'd visit the shop and get the ball rolling. How

hard could it be? Caroline was alone now, and hurting for money. And probably a little lonely. People tended to avoid her. She didn't complain, but everyone knew what her situation was. Nobody liked people with problems.

He'd be the answer to her prayers. They'd be engaged by Easter, married by June. Just in time to test the political waters for his candidacy.

He needed to get rid of Karla-Kara. She was just white noise, and now that he'd made his decision she was distracting.

Sanders dug his personal cell phone out and called his business cell phone number. A few seconds later, it started ringing in the bedroom.

"Hey, baby—the phone!" Karla-Kara shrieked.

Gritting his teeth against her voice, like chalk on a blackboard, Sanders walked into the bedroom, flipped his phone open and put it to his ear, listening to the empty sound.

"Uh-huh," he said, listening with a frown. "When? . . . Does Bowers know about this yet? . . . Uh-huh . . . I guess so . . . It's Christmas, in case you haven't noticed . . . uh-huh . . . Oh, all right." This last was said in irritation. He flipped the phone closed and picked her clothes up from the floor.

"Sorry, honey," he told the pouting woman on his bed. "Business emergency. People are coming over in about half an hour, then we have to fly to Los Angeles." Her bra and panties were red silk, slightly dirty. He tossed them to her. "Hurry up, I'll call a cab."

He was actually looking forward to Monday.

It was time.

New York
Waldorf-Astoria

Deaver had a Christmas dinner brought up by room service from Peacock Alley. Maine lobster salad, prime grilled sirloin, dry-aged for twenty-eight days, with a wild mushroom side dish and a forty-dollar bottle of Valpolicella breathing on a sideboard—150 bucks, including tip, and worth every penny.

Axel continued with his generosity and Deaver lifted a cut-crystal glass in his honor.

When the waiters had finished setting the meal out on the huge, antique oak desk, and bowed themselves quietly out of the room, Deaver breathed in deeply and savored the moment.

It was all so perfect—the linen tablecloth and napkins, the fine bone china, the heavy silverware, the crystal glasses. The delicious smells of excellent food and clean table linen.

Deaver had grown up in a trailer park outside Midland, Texas. All his childhood, most of his food had been eaten cold, out of a can, and he had had to fight the cockroaches for it. He'd been eighteen, and in the Army, before he knew that forks came in different sizes.

But that was a long time ago, and he'd discovered that he had a taste for living large. *This* was how he was meant to live.

An hour later, Deaver wiped his mouth with the peach-colored oversized linen napkin and gave a little belch. Perfect. Perfect meal. The first of many.

The rest of his life was going to be like this. Exactly like this—luxurious surroundings, staff, superb food and wine—except he was going to have women around. Lots of them.

No women now. Now it was hunting time.

Wrapped up in the hotel's thick terry-cloth robe, he opened the laptop he'd bought from Drake. Again, whatever Drake delivered was excellent. It was clearly a laptop that had seen heavy use, but its hard disk had been wiped clean, and it powered up just fine. Deaver connected to the high-speed Internet access port, went to Google, then sat back to reflect, staring at the bright screen.

The Colonel had found Prescott in January of 1996, emaciated, half-dead and half-frozen behind a Dumpster. Deaver had been OUTCONUS most of that winter, freezing his butt off in Bosnia. By the time he got back to base, Prescott was a done deal. The Colonel had adopted him, he'd put on forty pounds of muscle and was studying for his GCE, intent on joining the Army.

Deaver had hated him on sight. The Colonel thought the sun shone out of his ass. Well, he would, considering his own son, the other Jack, had been a whiny wimp who'd started drinking at fifteen and managed to wreck a car he'd stolen for a joyride and got himself killed at the age of twenty, together with a family of four, before his new cocaine habit could do it for him later.

One thing you had to say for Jack—he was as straight as they come, and the Colonel had taken him like a second lease on life.

When the Colonel retired to found ENP Security, everyone had assumed that Deaver would be his second-in-command.

After all, he'd served under the Colonel for almost twenty years. It was his due, damn it.

Twenty years in the Army and he had fuck-all to show for it. Everyone else was making a bundle off Homeland Security, and it should have been Deaver's turn.

But the only thing the Colonel had offered *him* was a job—and a miserably paid one at that, even though it was double what he'd been making in the Army. Deaver was expecting a managerial position with stock, and he ended up being a glorified hired gun, sent immediately to Waziristan to guard a pipeline, then to Sierra Leone to guard fat mining executives.

And Jack Prescott quit the Rangers and was made executive vice president of ENP Security the next day.

It still burned.

But he couldn't dwell on that now. No emotion when planning a mission. Love, hatred, revenge—they could get you killed quicker than gunfire. No, Deaver had to think it through, logically and clearly, step by step.

Well, step number one was to be sure that Elvis had actually left the building.

Half an hour later, it looked like he had. Prescott had sold the company to a competitor and had sold his house to Rodney Strong, a CPA, and his wife Cathy Strong, lifestyle coach.

Prescott's phone had been disconnected, as had all the utilities. There was no record of sale of property, or utility contracts, in the name of Jack Prescott, either in town or in a fifty-mile radius.

Much as Deaver found it hard to believe, since Jack had inherited a big, expensive house and a thriving company—he'd sold everything and disappeared off the face of the earth. He'd even sold his car.

Just to torment himself, Deaver hacked into Prescott's bank account and stared at the screen, jaw muscles jumping.

On the nineteenth of December, just before leaving for Sierra Leone and fucking up Deaver's life, Jack Prescott had converted all his assets into a cashier's check for $8 million and change.

The fucker!

Deaver slammed his hand on the walnut desk, cracking it slightly. He stood up and walked the perimeter of the room, trying to calm himself down.

That son of a bitch had over 8 million plus *his* diamonds. Deaver was going to take the diamonds back, have Prescott wire all his money to Deaver's account in the Caymans, then break every single bone in the son of a bitch's body, before slitting his throat.

Then he'd kill the woman.

It took fifteen minutes before he could settle back down, but when he did, it was with a soldier's concentration. The beautiful surroundings, the staff on call, quivering to be of service, the lavish meal—they all disappeared as he focused like a laser beam on the mission.

There would be no more indulgences, no more forays into the good life, until Jack Prescott was found.

Turning to the computer, Deaver checked the car rental agencies in town and in the surrounding towns. Prescott hadn't rented a car. He wouldn't take a bus—what man with almost $30 million would? So he'd flown out of town, to . . . where?

Half an hour later, Deaver had the answer. A credit card corresponding to Jack Prescott had been used to buy a one-way ticket from Freetown to Seattle, via Paris, Atlanta and Chicago. He couldn't find any car rental agencies that had rented him a car.

So Deaver knew two things. One, Jack Prescott was in the Pacific Northwest, and two, he hadn't bothered hiding his tracks. He'd left a clear trail behind him, which meant he didn't know Deaver was on his trail.

If Jack hadn't wanted to be tracked, Deaver would have ended up playing with his dick forever. So Jack wasn't expecting anyone to follow him. Perfect. Surprise attacks worked best.

So, Deaver thought, leaning closer to the screen showing a detailed map of Washington state, where in Washington are you? Did you go up into Canada? His eyes tracked to the top of the screen, which cut off about a hundred miles north of Vancouver. He let the thought run through his mind, examining it from different directions.

Nah. He had a valid passport, and he wasn't on the run. If he wanted to go up into Canada, he would have gone straight there.

No, everything pointed to Prescott being a man on a mission and taking a beeline to get there. Just as soon as he humanly could, he liquidated his assets and made straight for . . .

Straight for the girl—now a woman. Find her, find Prescott. Deaver was sure of it.

Once more, Deaver placed the two photocopied photographs flat on the table and studied them, more intently this time. This time, they had to tell him where Prescott was, and fast.

It was entirely possible that Prescott would find a married woman with six kids, who over the past twelve years had gained fifty pounds and lost teeth and hair and didn't remember him.

If that was the case, Prescott would disappear and Deaver would never find him, or his diamonds, again.

So he studied the photographs the way soldiers going into battle studied a terrain map—carefully and thoroughly, because it all depended on knowing what you were going to face.

The photograph had to date back to 1995 at the latest. Prescott hadn't been linked to any particular woman since the Colonel found him. So this obsession he had was with someone he'd met in 1995 or earlier. The date on the newspaper clipping was October 15, 1995, so maybe the photograph was from that period.

He studied the high-school photo. Staged, like they all were. Deaver hadn't had one. The old man wouldn't spring for it, but he remembered everyone else's at the high school. For most of them, it was their first formal portrait, and they had fixed grins, or at least the ones whose teeth were good enough to show did. The girls had slapped on the makeup with a trowel, and the boys had worn dress shirts instead of tee shirts, some for the first time in their lives.

This girl's smile was natural, not stagy. Maybe she was

used to being photographed. She looked like a million other pretty teenagers, though prettier than most. Long, strawberry blonde hair with a little curl to it. Straight, even, white teeth. Some kind of pink sweater with a pearl necklace. No indication of what her body looked like, only a general impression of slenderness.

Deaver switched his attention to the photograph of her playing the piano, dressed in a sweater and a long skirt, showing off a great body, though the face was in profile.

He looked again at the newspaper heading. *ville Gazette*.

Well, he had a state to start with, Washington. Why would Prescott head straight for Seattle if what he wanted wasn't in Washington?

Deaver called up all the townships in Washington state. Seventeen cities, ninety-two townships. Four ending in –ville. None of them had a newspaper called the *Gazette*.

Deaver sat back, thinking furiously.

This whole exercise might be futile. Maybe he was barking up the wrong tree. Caroline Lake had been a pretty girl. If she'd grown into a beautiful woman, she'd be married by now. Hell, she might be on her second or third marriage, having changed names a couple of times. She could be Caroline Warner in Las Vegas, or Caroline Yoo in San Francisco or Caroline Steinberg in New York.

Fuck.

Maybe he should start looking for Jack, who wasn't bothering to hide his tracks. Maybe he should just hole up here for as long as Axel's credit card lasted until the next time Jack used *his* credit card.

Idly, Deaver Googled "newspaper + Gazette + Washington + 1995" and bingo! There it was. He leaned forward, surprised at the hit. Goddammit, bless the Internet because there it was in black and white, cursor blinking gently, just waiting for him to connect the dots. The *Summerville Gazette*, local rag for a small city called Summerville, defunct since 2002, but alive and well in 1995.

Eyes narrowed, Deaver leaned over the keyboard, Googling Caroline Lake + Summerville, Washington, and came up with ten hits, all concerning a Caroline Lake who ran a bookshop, gave prizes and played the piano in church. To be on the safe side, he clicked on *images* and gazed at about fifteen photographs of Caroline Lake. Prescott's Caroline Lake. Still beautiful, still unmarried.

Jack Prescott was there, right now. He'd bet his left nut on it.

Deaver started furiously looking for online sites to book a flight immediately to Seattle, cursing because there was no way he could get there before 9:00 P.M. tomorrow night. Most flights were booked solid till after the New Year. The flights he finally found would take him twelve hours from Newark to Atlanta to Chicago to Seattle. It was the best he could do.

Well, at least he'd be there on Monday morning.

He looked once again at the photos of Caroline Lake, a truly stunning woman.

Prescott would still be in Summerville on Monday. Oh yeah. He wasn't going anywhere.

Eleven

Summerville

They never did have that big Christmas meal Caroline had planned.

After the crying storm, Caroline had fallen into the deepest sleep of her life, almost a coma. When she woke up alone in her bed, it was pitch-black outside, and she had no idea how long she'd slept.

It was dark, the only light coming from the hallway outside. Caroline lay in bed, staring at the black ceiling, sorting through her feelings, so mixed it was impossible to know which was the strongest—shame, embarrassment or relief.

There was some shame, but not much. It was true, she should be feeling ashamed for crying like a baby on Jack's shoulder—a man she barely knew, even if they had had sex. And she did feel ashamed. Then there was embarrassment.

That wild crying jag after—not even *while* coming—wow, that was beyond embarrassing.

But there was also such a great sense of . . . peace. It was as if the tears had washed away something black and foul inside her, leaving her depleted, exhausted, empty—but not sad. The sadness was gone. Sadness had been her constant companion for years now, and she almost didn't recognize herself in its absence.

She felt rested, refreshed and . . . hungry. A quick trip to the bathroom to put a cold compress on her eyes, a quick shower, pulling on cherry red sweats, and she was out the door.

Caroline was halfway down the staircase when Jack appeared suddenly at the bottom of the stairs, though she hadn't seen him move.

When their eyes met, her heart gave a massive thump in her chest.

His dark eyes checked her over quickly, impersonally, like a soldier checking a comrade for wounds. Then his gaze turned warm.

"Hi." His deep voice was calm, quiet.

"Hi." Caroline's voice sounded breathless to her own ears.

He started up the stairs, taking them two at a time until he came to a stop on the step below hers. It put her face almost on a level with his.

His face was fascinating—so deeply unequivocally male. "How are you feeling?" His eyes searched hers.

"Better, believe it or not." She shook her head slightly. "Though a little embarrassed at bawling all over your shoulder."

"Anytime." That hard mouth lifted in a half smile. He took her right hand, lifted it to his mouth, placed it on his left shoulder. "Consider my shoulder yours."

It was an interesting notion. It was an interesting shoulder. Caroline kneaded the hard muscle under the soft cotton of his sweat suit. She'd held him in her arms a couple of times now, and it never failed to astonish her—the absolute iron feel of him, as if he were made of something harder than mere human skin and muscle.

Her hand danced lightly from his collarbone to the huge ball of his shoulder, and she remembered very vividly the feel of him naked under her hands. Without the softening effect of clothes, he was almost frightening in his power, the strongest-looking human she'd ever seen.

She watched his face as she smoothed her hand over the broad, deep muscles. It was a mystery how a man who wasn't handsome could be so attractive. He was wearing his long, black hair loose instead of tied back, and it framed that strong, narrow face, softening its harsh features. It was almost impossible to guess how old he was, though she suspected he was about her own age, but without the benefit of moisturizer, which she used religiously. The skin was weather-beaten, with faint white lines fanning out from the corners of his dark eyes.

He'd shaved this morning—she'd heard the electric razor buzzing—but he already had a five o'clock shadow. Had he grown a beard in Afghanistan? Many of the photographs of the men guarding the president showed them with beards.

What was his background? Jack Prescott—it was a perfectly

ordinary name for an unordinary man. His skin and eyes were so dark, there must have been Hispanic or—considering his high cheekbones—Native American blood somewhere in his ancestry.

She could stand here for hours, one step above him, looking at him. His face was so fascinating. She'd never met anyone even faintly like him, and yet she couldn't seem to shake the feeling of recognition each time she studied his face.

She could only imagine that it was the sex. They'd short-circuited the normal getting-to-know-you phase, and the hot sex had imprinted her with him, so that she felt as if she'd known him forever. Déjà vu sex.

"Let's go down," Jack said, placing a strong arm against her back. Caroline wondered what he thought about her standing and staring at him. She'd make dinner memorable, to compensate.

"What would you like for din—" Caroline cut herself off. Something was missing. They were walking down the stairs, and something was missing. Something should have—"The steps! You fixed the steps! Oh my gosh!" She turned and threw her arms around Jack's neck in a rush of gratitude. "Thank you thank you thank you!"

It was on her urgent to-do list. Item number 476 on her superurgent to-do list. *Call carpenter to fix stairs before someone breaks their neck.* But she knew she could get around to it only when she had some spare cash. Which meant never.

His arms had gone around her immediately, holding her tightly against him. "If I'd known I'd get this reaction, I'd have fixed all your stairs. They creak a little. I did, however, fix your shelves in the bathroom, repair the banister and fix the loose doorknob to the study. What do I get for that?"

He was teasing her. She had no idea that was in him. He actually had . . . well, not a smile exactly, but his eyes crinkled, and his hard mouth curled slightly upward.

"My hero," Caroline said, smiling, and reaching up on tiptoe, gave him a big wet smack on the mouth.

He tensed. She could feel his muscles becoming even harder under her hands, his big hand between her shoulder blades pressing her forward.

His mouth settled over hers.

This kiss was different from the other ones. Maybe he had a whole repertory of them? This was warm, possessive, right from the beginning. He didn't coax her mouth open with his to test her with little forays of his tongue. Her mouth was already open to him, to the slick feel of him licking inside her mouth. She was still on the step above his and it was wonderful being almost at the same level, so she didn't have to stretch up to kiss him. She slumped against him, heart beating wildly as he kissed her nearly senseless.

Every stroke of his tongue sent shooting darts of fire all through her, but particularly between her legs. He cupped the back of her head tightly and changed the angle of his mouth so he could delve more deeply inside her, and this time when his tongue touched hers, her vagina *fluttered*. Oh my God, he was making her vagina contract with his mouth alone!

She pulled back and gazed at him wordlessly, almost frightened at the power he seemed to exert over her body. Caroline had always been so slow to arouse, and here she was having the prelude to an orgasm with a mere kiss.

She had the same effect on him. Under the deep tan and his naturally dark skin, deep red slashes of red rode his high cheekbones and lower, she could definitely feel what she'd done. His penis lay like a column of marble against her belly.

Nervously, Caroline licked her lips. He followed the movements of her tongue closely, breathing hard. When she wet her lips again, his penis surged against her stomach.

Which growled.

Caroline lifted startled eyes to his, blushing furiously. "Sorry," she gasped, mortified. Her body was making parallel demands—for sex and food—and her head couldn't keep up. "I guess that's a sign for me to go cook our dinner."

"I have another idea." He bent to kiss the corner of her mouth. "Don't cook. Why don't you put some stuff on a tray and bring it into the living room? I'll light a fire, and we can have a Christmas picnic." He bent again to her, lightly brushing lips and teeth along the skin of her neck. "I don't want you spending hours in the kitchen cooking. I want you spending hours with me."

Oh God, when he did that, she melted. Caroline's neck arched, and she found herself smiling. How could anything so simple feel so good? He was barely touching her with his mouth, yet it sent pleasure zinging through her body. "Sounds wonderful, but I used up all the wood yesterday. If we want a fire, I'll have to—"

Jack frowned down at her. "*I'll* go to the garage and stack some wood. Then we stuff our faces." He took her hand and started back down the stairs. Caroline grasped the banister, which had been dangerously loose, and made a point of shaking it. She couldn't move it at all, it was solid. Jack watched her, smiling faintly.

"You did a good job."

He nodded his head. "Got an advanced degree in stair and banister repair. Aced the classes."

Maybe he did have a degree in stair and banister repair. Boiler repair, too.

She was almost certain he had a degree in something, he was surprisingly well-spoken and seemed somehow very knowledgeable about the world. Part of that was the travel, even if to places where sandbags and machine guns trumped museums. They did say that travel was broadening.

He had been an officer, she was almost sure he'd said that. And didn't officers have to have a college degree? And what was his degree in?

She was suddenly desperately curious about this man, who'd appeared out of nowhere to give her amazing sex and repair her house. "Where did you—" she began, but he was striding away.

"Hurry up with the food, I'm starving too." His deep voice floated in from the mudroom, and a second later she heard the door to the garage open.

Caroline started ferrying the food out on big trays—cheeses, whole wheat bread, corn bread, focaccia, leftover roast beef, slices of baked ham, butter, lavender honey, homemade chutney, a sliced tomato salad with a drizzle of olive oil, lettuce and arugula salad, carrot and celery sticks with a sour cream dip, a bowl of Greek olives and two slices of chocolate cake—one big and one small.

In the time it took her to bring out several trays of food, Jack had neatly stacked enough wood in the bin to keep the fireplace going for days. It was a job she hated, and she rarely lit the fire because of it, except, of course, when the boiler died. It was dirty, backbreaking work, and he'd done it in the blink of an eye.

It was hard to keep her eyes on what she was doing. Jack was kneeling in front of the fireplace, building a fire, massive thigh muscles straining his jeans, broad back outlined in red from the burgeoning flames, exactly like last night. With any luck, it was a sight she'd be seeing all winter—Jack stoking the flames, the firelight dancing across his strong features.

He moved easily, with grace. He knew what he was doing, too. In no time, a perfect fire was blazing.

Caroline stepped back and looked, pleased, at the spread on the big coffee table. She lit four red candles and placed them on the four corners, and thought it looked like a very festive Christmas meal.

The fire had already begun blazing merrily, the warmth seeping into her bones. Jack stood, brushing his hands, looked at the spread and turned to her. "Looks nice."

"It does, doesn't it? So I guess we're all set—oh! Wine. We finished the bottle last night, I'll go down to the cellar and get another one."

"I'll go. You relax on the couch. Any special bottle?"

Her father had always opened a Burgundy at Christmas. "Get a red, a Burgundy. You'll find a selection on the far wall. The cellar is—"

He had already disappeared, before she had a chance to tell him that the door to the cellar was next to the kitchen door.

It was completely dark outside. Christmas Day had passed, and it was already Christmas night. A day she'd dreaded since Toby's death was almost over.

There were no sounds at all outside. Usually, she could hear the sound of the odd car driving by, or a dog barking. Now, they could have been the last human beings on the face of the planet, it was so quiet.

Who knew what was happening out there?

She was feeling so good, maybe world peace had broken out. Wouldn't that be wonderful? Only one way to find out. Caroline clicked the remote control on to the local news channel and found snow. CBS, NBC, CNN . . . snow.

She began clicking through all the channels when suddenly the remote disappeared from her hand and the TV screen went black.

"I'm not ready for the outside world yet," Jack said, putting the remote down with one hand and wagging a bottle from side to side with the other. "I think we should be doing our celebrating without any interference from all the yahoos and creeps out there."

"Okay." He was perfectly right. "TV wasn't working anyway. We'll need a cork—"

Somehow, by some magic, he had the corkscrew already in his hand, and Caroline laughed. The cork came out with the cool little pop of a well-aged bottle, and Jack poured them half a glass each while Caroline filled their plates.

Both of them ate with enormous gusto. Sooner than she'd have thought possible, they'd polished everything off, including the cake crumbs. The bottle was almost finished. Caroline had forgotten to put water out, but who needed water when there was excellent wine? The Burgundy was liquid joy. It was exactly the bottle she would have chosen. He had a sophisticated wine sense, her soldier.

Caroline settled back with a happy sigh into Jack's arm, bare feet curled over the edge of the coffee table. The fire crackled and hissed merrily.

She had no idea what time it was and didn't care. All she knew was that soon Christmas would be over, and a day she had been dreading with all her heart had been wonderful in many different ways.

She tipped her head back over Jack's arm and looked up at him, at the man responsible for her wonderful day. "Where were you last Christmas? What were you doing? How did you celebrate?"

Jack finished his wine and put the glass down carefully on a side table. He ran the back of his forefinger along her neck, gently, up and down. "Last Christmas I was on duty all day in Afghanistan, where Christmas doesn't exist. And if it did, it sure wouldn't herald a day of peace. The warlords would have been delighted to nail Habib on a Christian holiday. So that was my Christmas and it was more or less par for the course, the same as the other 220 days before it. A tour of duty lasting twelve hours, a meal of stewed goat meat, which is what we ate every day, at the end of it, no wine because it's a dry country, and reruns of *Lost*." He leaned over and kissed her on the ear. "And you? Where were you last Christmas?"

"Here." Caroline sighed. "With Toby."

"What did you two do?"

"In the beginning, in the first couple of years after the accident, I tried inviting people over for Christmas. Both of us got depressed on Christmas Day, and I thought having people over would cheer us up." She stopped, remembering. Remembering how awkwardly people reacted to Toby. How no matter what Christmas feast she cooked up, they would start leaving right after the coffee was served.

It was such a painful contrast to before. To when Christmas at the Lakes' was a lavish celebration lasting days, often with houseguests, full of food and wine and music and laughter.

"And? Did it work?" He was watching her closely, as if her answer mattered to him.

"Sort of. In the beginning, anyway. Toby—Toby had some control over his movements in the first few years. But then as his physical condition deteriorated, our popularity . . . waned. The last few years, we just celebrated by ourselves. I always put up a tree, and played some carols, and we watched TV and played chess. Toby is—*was* a wicked chess player. He always beat the pants off me."

His hand suddenly tightened around her shoulder, and Caroline looked at him in surprise. The firelight danced in his dark eyes in tiny pinpricks of light. Of heat.

"I can't play chess worth a damn, but I'd sure like to learn how to, so I can beat the pants off you," he whispered in a low, purely male growl that had prickles running up and down her spine.

Just like that, desire surged up, like an electric shock she could feel down to her fingertips and toes. It was a miracle her hair didn't stand on end, like one of those cartoon characters sticking a finger in the electric socket. She'd thought the wine had created heat in her system, but there wasn't a Burgundy in the world that could stand up to the heat in Jack's eyes.

Warmth spread throughout her entire body, pooling in her breasts and sheath, which was already wet. He'd barely touched her, hadn't even kissed her, and her body was readying itself for him.

And he knew. Of course he knew. Those sharp dark eyes missed nothing.

"But then," he whispered, his arm curling her toward him, "maybe I don't need to lose at chess to get your pants off." She was brought up against him, and his mouth covered hers. The kiss was long and languid, his tongue deep in her mouth, stroking hers, in time with the big hand stroking her leg, from her hip down to her ankle, and back again.

On the third pass, his hand slipped under the elastic of her sweatpants to caress her bottom. Oh God, it was wildly exciting, feeling his big, warm hand on her skin, slowly stroking, reaching farther and farther down with his hand until he touched her most sensitive skin, entering her slightly with the tip of one finger. She was slick already, she knew he could feel her arousal. As she could feel his, huge and hot against her stomach. His finger pressed more deeply into her, just as his tongue delved more deeply into her mouth. She could hardly breathe with the excitement, but it didn't make any difference. Somehow he was breathing for her.

A long finger entered her, stroking the inside walls of her sheath in slow passes. His thumb passed over her clitoris.

Caroline gasped into his mouth and felt him stiffen. In an instant, her sweatpants and panties were off. She barely felt him strip her, she was so taken with his hands and his mouth. One moment she was wearing her soft sweatpants, the next moment, she felt the heat of the fire on her backside.

Somehow his sweat suit had come off, too, though she couldn't figure out how since he was always touching her.

"Make me go slow," he whispered into her mouth as he lifted her over him. In a moment, her legs were straddling him, the lips of her sex open over that long, thick hot column. "Put me in yourself."

"Okay," she whispered back.

He was so aroused she found it hard to pull his penis away from his stomach and had to lift herself up on her knees to position herself against the head. She slid along it, testing herself, and felt him exhale heavily into her mouth.

He disengaged his mouth and gently bumped his forehead against hers. She held his penis and swirled herself around the head, feeling him swell against her fingers and against the swollen tissues of her sex.

"Oh, God," he said, his voice shaky. "Do that again."

He was sweating lightly. A bead of sweat trailed from his temple down over the high cheekbone to the jaw, where it trembled lightly and disappeared into the thick mat of hair covering his chest.

It wasn't that hot. What had him trembling and sweating was the self-control he was using, letting her set the pace.

He was deliberately not touching her, his hands fisted on the couch, white-knuckled, as if he didn't trust himself to use his hands.

Caroline circled her hips, dipping slightly so that he entered her maybe an inch, then lifting away. He made a low sound deep in his throat, but didn't move. He was so hot she could almost see steam rise off him; he was breathing hard, so aroused the penis she was holding was like a bar of steel, but he was still letting her run the show.

Another dip into him, another whimper, and he let his head fall back over the couch, eyes closed.

The visible control he was exerting over himself was so exciting she could feel a rush of moisture well inside her. A drop ran down his penis, and he shuddered.

"Now. Please." His voice was low and guttural.

Yes. Now.

Holding him by the thick base, Caroline lowered herself slowly onto him, feeling him slide inside her, first the thick head, then the long column. When she stopped, he was fully embedded in her, and she felt his thick, wiry pubic hair against the sensitive skin of her inner thighs.

While feeling him slide slowly into her, she'd closed her eyes, to savor the feeling. Now she opened them to find his eyes fixed on her, burning bright. Watching them, she leaned forward and lay her lips lightly on his. Everything about his face was hard—the brutal slashes of his cheekbones, the rigid, well-defined jawline, the finely flared nostrils. Everything except his mouth, which looked so hard and yet felt so soft under hers.

Turning her head, she opened his mouth with hers, exploring him with her tongue. At the first touch of her tongue to his, he made a noise deep in his chest, and his penis leaped inside her, swelling impossibly bigger.

Oh, God, this was just so enticing!

Jack Prescott was the strongest man she'd ever met, ever *seen*. He carried an aura of power with him, strong and durable. She was no match for him in any physical way and yet right now, she felt much more powerful than him.

She felt like the Queen of the World, with a warrior to command, that powerful body humming under hers, ready to do her bidding.

She stroked his tongue again, and when he moved inside her, she bore down on him, so that it was like a stroke. His breath came out in a soundless explosion.

"Do you like that?" Caroline slid her hands into his black hair, curling her fingers a little to tug it. Not enough to hurt him but enough for him to feel the bite of it.

It always surprised her to feel how warm his hair was since it was the color of midnight.

"God, yeah," he muttered, the tone guttural.

"And this?" She rose a little on her knees, pulling him slightly out of her, then slid back down, using all her weight. "Do you like this?"

"Yeah. Oh yeah." He was panting and sweating, jaws tightly clenched at an effort to maintain self-control.

Caroline intended to torture him a little, explore these feelings of power over him that were so enticing, even though she knew quite well it was power he willingly ceded. Still, it was heady.

But her plan was starting to backfire. Little tremors were running along the insides of her thighs, her vagina clenched once, twice. The free fall into orgasm was beginning, and she hadn't even begun to enjoy this feeling of dominance.

No matter, her body was taking over.

She slid up, then down, and felt his trembling. She was trembling herself. "And that?" she whispered, watching him watching her. She felt like she was falling into the dark depths of his eyes.

"Caroline, I can't—I'm sorry, I have to—"

The hands that had been fisted on the couch came up and fitted themselves on her hips, holding her still as he thrust up inside her, hard.

She winced, and he stopped, panting. His big hands opened, letting her go.

"Can't touch you now," he gasped. "Don't want to hurt you."

She was going to have to do it herself.

Caroline leaned forward, clasping her hands behind his neck for leverage, and began a slow dance on him, long, lazy strokes as she nipped lightly with her teeth at his earlobe.

The trembling increased, she was so close . . .

Jack turned his head and caught her mouth with his, moving his hips just enough to match her rhythm. In and out . . .

He speeded up the strokes, and she met him, rising and falling on him, a flash of heat, then another and suddenly she was coming, milking him hard, sharp contractions so intense they were almost painful.

With a strong jolt, he came, too, the jets of semen so strong they prolonged the climax. They groaned into each other's mouths, and Caroline felt like she was breathing through him.

It took her a long time finally to settle down, but when the tension finally left her body, she curled forward, nestling her head on his shoulder.

As always, he was still hard inside her, even after his climax. She lay still. Any movement with him inside her would abrade her supersensitive skin, on the razor's edge of an arousal so strong it was painful.

He somehow understood. He didn't move, didn't try to press up inside her, didn't try to start making love again. The only thing he did was reach for the afghan thrown across the back of the couch and fold it gently around her, then wrap his arms around her back.

She settled more deeply against him, lax and warm.

Though Caroline was boneless with pleasure, she was keenly aware of everything. The sharp smells of sex mingling with the rich smell of woodsmoke. Her breasts and belly rubbing against the hair-roughened hard muscles of his chest and stomach each time they breathed. His soft hair tickling her cheek. The taste of salt on her lips.

Above all, she was aware of some giant emotion swelling inside her, big and bright and new.

It took her several minutes before she realized it was happiness.

Twelve

Summerville

It had taken him all day Sunday to cross the fucking continent, and when he finally landed in Seattle in the middle of a snowstorm, Deaver had only taken the first step toward getting his diamonds back.

He had two new identities—Frank Dawson, farm machinery sales rep out of Iowa and Darrell Butler, FBI Special Agent. Both of them were shallow identities, but Deaver wasn't expecting to use either one for more than a week, two tops.

It was Dawson's passport that would get him to the Caymans. Once he got his diamonds back, he'd drive down to Tijuana, ditch the rental SUV, then fly one way to Grand Cayman Airport. Even after paying Drake, he still had enough to lie low for a while. And once he had his diamonds in his hands, he would contemplate Drake's offer.

It had stunned him, that he knew about the diamonds, but then Drake wasn't a millionaire many times over because he was stupid. He was a dealer, sure, but his main commodity wasn't guns or fake ID, though he did a thriving trade in them. No, the main thing he sold was information, and it flowed to him, wherever he was, like a river to the sea.

That system of information extended to a network that crisscrossed the States. Half an hour after landing, Deaver was at a warehouse outside Seattle, the meeting having been set up by Drake. Deaver got every single thing he'd paid for, in excellent working condition and with extra ammo thrown in for goodwill.

Three hours after that, he was pulling into Summerville. He'd called ahead for a room at a Holiday Inn in Darrell Butler's name and said he was arriving late. He had something to do before checking in.

A downloaded map of Summerville lying on the passenger seat helped him to find Caroline Lake's house. It was in the rich part of town, old stone-and-brick mansions set on ample grounds.

He drove by slowly, carefully studying the house. It was one of the nicest ones in this part of town—large but graceful. There was no wall, just an upward slope of what might have been lawn but now was an expanse of snow, split by a walkway. Someone had shoveled the snow off the walkway and the drive.

Ten minutes later, he drove by again, trying to see whether there was an external security system, but the light from the streetlamps wasn't enough to be able to tell whether the windows were alarmed or what kind of lock was on the front door. That would require close scrutiny, and he'd have to leave tracks in the snow. If Prescott was in there, he'd notice immediately.

The only thing he could tell with certainly was that there were no security cameras.

So maybe the beautiful Miss Lake was the trusting sort.

It was a thought. Jack Prescott was a tough man to break. Trusting little Caroline Lake was going to be the hammer that would smash him.

This was good. A plan was forming.

Satisfied that he had done all he could for the moment, Deaver drove off to his hotel.

Tomorrow the endgame began.

On Monday morning, Caroline peered out at the sky, trying to gauge what to expect. It wasn't snowing at the moment, but the sky was a sullen dark gray, even though it was eight in the morning.

Would it snow today? She hadn't been able to listen to the forecasts because the TV and the radio were both still on the blink. She could check the Internet, but her computer was up in her room and by the time she powered it up and Googled the weather, she'd be running late.

Whether it snowed or not was out of her control. She needed to drive to work, and that was that. Plus, Jack wanted to get going on whatever it was he needed to do today. He was already in his denim jacket, ready to go.

Caroline pasted a smile on her face. Monday mornings were always hard, but this one was harder yet.

If she could, she'd press rewind and live yesterday all over again. They'd done absolutely nothing but eat and make love all day. Well, *she'd* done nothing but eat and make love all day. Jack had managed to fix her leaky washing machine, repair the bookshelves in her bedroom, oil the hinges of the garage door and shovel another bazillion tons of snow off the driveway. All the while insisting she sit in front of the fire with a book, a glass of wine and a blanket.

He didn't take no for an answer. The only thing he let Caroline do was cook, then wolfed down whatever she put in front of him. They'd made love in front of the fire, in the shower and several times in her bed and she'd slept like a log afterwards.

It felt as if she and Jack had been living in a delightful little Christmas bubble, cut off from the outside world and its cares. But now the outside world loomed, and she had to face it, starting with driving them into town over icy roads with bald tires and no spare.

"Weather looks bad." She sighed.

"Yeah." He glanced at his watch with a frown. The doorbell rang. "About time," Jack muttered, and went to the front door.

Someone was standing there with a form and a set of keys. Behind him, on the street, was a big black Explorer. Jack signed the form and took the keys. When the door closed behind him, he dangled the keys in front of her, and said, "Wheels."

He bent and gave her a quick kiss.

"What?"

Jack pointed to the Explorer outside. "I rented that for a week, until I can find something to buy. It's no weather to be driving around with bald tires. I'll drive you in and drive you back until the weather clears up."

A couple of days ago, Caroline would have objected, out of pride if nothing else. But she'd almost got them killed Friday night, so she said nothing.

He helped her into her coat and put on his denim jacket.

Caroline fingered his jacket. "You need warmer clothes."

"Yeah. I'll buy some today."

"The cheapest place in town is Posy's, and the Christmas sales have already begun, so you should get some good deals. Or you could maybe try The Clothes Factory on State Street. They have used clothes, sometimes very good ones. I shop there a lot. I hate thinking of you going out in this weather with only this jacket."

He looked down at her, eyes dark and unfathomable. "I'll be okay," he said softly. "Don't worry about me."

Don't worry. Caroline nearly sighed. Worry had been her middle name for so many years now that she'd forgotten what it was like not to worry.

She looked up at him, hand still on his jacket. She was stalling and she knew why. "I don't want to go out," she whispered.

He picked her hand up and brought it to his mouth. "No," he said simply.

Outside was cold and bleak, another country. A country of problems and hardships. Inside was warm and safe, where nothing could touch her.

Except Jack, of course.

Caroline stepped forward and put her arms around his lean waist and burrowed in. His arms went around her immediately. There was one thing to be said for dressing lightly, she could hear his heartbeat, strong and steady. Just like him.

She had a sudden panicky intuition that this weekend had been a mirage. Maybe she'd invented a Jack Prescott out of her loneliness and depression. He'd done nothing but give, filled her with warmth, shown her a sensuality she had no idea existed.

"I can't tell you what this weekend has meant to me," she whispered, holding him tightly. The happiness she'd felt seemed to her like smoke, already dissipating in the air. The more closely she tried to clutch it, the more quickly it vanished.

Walking outside her front door scared her, like leaving an enchanted castle to face lions and tigers.

She felt a kiss on the top of her head, and Jack stepped back. His eyes were like dark flames. "We either go now," he said, "or we go back to bed. Your call."

Put like that, well . . . Did she want to spend the day in the bookshop, with maybe three customers all morning if she was lucky, go over her accounts—which always made her wince—longing for the day to be finally over, or did she want to spend the day in bed with Jack, being pampered with fabulous sex?

Tough call.

But she was hardwired for duty, and she had a lunch date with Jenna, so she sighed, and said, "Go now."

Jack opened the door and ushered her out with a hand to her back. "Spend the day thinking about what you're going to cook for me for dinner."

He laughed and evaded her elbow.

Jack was doing one of the hardest things he'd ever done in a lifetime of hard things. He didn't dump a massive amount of money into Caroline's bank account. Did not did not did *not*. He had to grit his teeth to keep from doing it, but he managed.

He was at a Summerville bank. It didn't matter which one—he'd chosen it because it was next door to a Starbucks, so he could go to the bank and get a good cup of coffee at the same time. The important thing was that it wasn't Caroline's bank.

He knew which bank she kept an account in. He also knew how much money was in that account, and he knew how big her debt was. She banked at the Central Savings & Loan, she had less than $1,000 in her checking account—almost $2,000 with his month's rent and deposit—and she was $354,759 in the red.

Caroline was entirely too trusting. Her bank records were kept right out on her desk for all the world to see.

Knowing she had essentially nothing except debts, he deliberately chose another bank, any other bank, because if he went to hers, the temptation would be overwhelming simply to shift money from his account to hers.

A million, two. Hell, even three, what did he care? He had more than enough for his needs for the rest of his life, and it would be worth every penny to see those slight frown lines caused by money worries disappear.

Well, all in due time. It would happen, just not today. Caroline was no dummy, and it wouldn't be hard for her to connect him appearing in her life together with a large sum of money showing up in her bank account.

His turn up at the window. There was a perky brunette, who made no attempt to hide her interest.

"Yes, sir? May I help you?"

He'd take care of diversifying in stocks and bonds later. For now, he just wanted to dump the money in an account.

"Yes, I want to open a bank account and get a safe-deposit box."

The smile was frankly flirtatious now. "Yes, sir. Please fill out this form. We'll need your address and telephone number. Will you be making a cash deposit or check?"

"Cashier's check."

Jack filled the form out quickly, putting Caroline's address and phone number down. He slid it across the counter together with the cashier's check for $8 million and change.

The teller turned it around, running a quick, experienced eye down the form, then glanced at the check and did a double take. A quick look at him, smile gone, and with a murmured, "I'll be right back, sir," she disappeared.

Jack was prepared to wait for as long as it took, but she came back immediately with a short man who was going to fat. Clearly the branch manager.

"If you'll just step this way, sir," the man said, pointing to a door. Jack entered first. It shouldn't take long for the bank to check with his own bank in North Carolina. A couple of calls later, the money was deposited, and Jack had put the diamonds in a safe-deposit box.

Putting the cloth bag into the flat box gave him a huge sense of relief. Even through the cloth, they felt hard, even hostile. Cold lumps of pure evil. He'd taken them from Deaver because he couldn't stand even the thought of someone profiting from the massacre he'd been helpless to stop and because there'd been no one left alive in the village to give them to. And turning them over to the Sierra Leone authorities . . . Jack had rarely seen a more vile or corrupt group of men. No, they were going to stay in the safe-deposit box until he could get them where they needed to go.

When he'd finished his bank business, he stood outside, the gelid wind whipping at his clothes. So this was a Summerville winter.

He turned his jacket collar up against the icy wind trying to drive needles of sleet into his neck and entered the Starbucks. He needed winter clothes, but he needed another infusion of hot coffee more.

Jenna came into First Page in a whirl of sleet and the scent of pine. "My God, the weather's awful!" she exclaimed as she rushed in, kissed Caroline on the cheek and handed her a pine wreath.

Caroline smiled and turned the sign around to CLOSED, which is what she usually did when Jenna showed up for their Monday lunches. Tuesday to Saturday, she stayed open over the lunch hour, hoping for a few extra sales.

No hope of that. Jenna was the first person to come into the bookstore today, and Caroline had a sinking feeling she'd be the last.

She turned the small wreath around in her hand. "It's lovely," she said. And it was—finely made of pine branches with a red silk ribbon braided through it. She brought it to her nose and drew in the marvelous fresh scent of pine. "Thank you."

"Don't thank me." Jenna was removing layers of clothes, dumping them on the armchair. She hated the cold and always said that when her ship came in or she found a millionaire to marry, she'd move to the Bahamas. "Thank Cindy. She made it for you. I'm so proud of her. She found the instructions in a magazine and spent an entire evening on it." She eyed the wreath proudly. "Not too shabby for a nine-year-old, eh?"

"No, indeed." Caroline carefully placed it on a side table, next to a pile of Christmas-themed books. "She's coming along well. I'm glad to hear it."

"Thanks to you," Jenna replied. "I'm so grateful to you, I don't have words to tell you."

Caroline waved that off with a smile.

Jenna had been her best friend all through high school. She'd married her high-school sweetheart instead of going to college, and had had two kids in quick succession—Mark, now twelve and Cindy, nine. Jenna had reveled in marriage and motherhood and had cut herself off from the outside world in a little haze of domesticity. When Caroline's parents died, and Toby was left so damaged, Jenna had proved completely unable to cope with the idea of tragedy. She hadn't come to the funeral, and she didn't answer Caroline's phone calls.

It had been such a common reaction that Caroline didn't even hold it against her. Lots of people somehow felt that bad luck could be contagious, and for a while after Toby's funeral, Caroline noticed people crossing the street to avoid having to offer their condolences. Nobody likes bad news.

Then last year, in the space of a week, Jenna's husband left her for his secretary, and her father left her mother, who had just been diagnosed with Alzheimer's.

Jenna was left with two small children, a sick mother, no money and no job. She fell to pieces, leaning heavily on Caroline. For a while, Mark and Cindy had come to stay with Caroline while Jenna made arrangements for care for her mother and found herself a job as a bank teller. Mark and Cindy had been two shocked and scared kids when they'd arrived, their world having fallen apart. If there was one thing Caroline and Toby knew, it was your world falling down around you.

Jenna placed a big bag on Caroline's desk and started pulling out cartons. It was her week to buy.

"God that smells good," Caroline said eagerly, opening one and picking up the dim sum with her chopsticks, rolling her eyes in delight, "and tastes even better."

"Here," Jenna held her carton out. "Try the beef in black bean sauce, it's great. And it's definitely not going onto my hips because I used up at least ten thousand calories walking here in the cold."

They dug in happily, the delicious warm food raising their spirits. "Ah, food, glorious food," Jenna said, leaning back, excavating the last shred of chicken from the bottom of the carton, the chopsticks making a grating sound. "Better than sex."

Caroline smiled secretively. No, it wasn't. Good as the food was, she'd just discovered that sex could be a whole order of magnitude better.

"Speaking of which," Jenna pointed the chopsticks at her. "Talk to me. I can't believe you've got this gorgeous guy living with you and you *never told me.*"

Caroline's eyes rounded.

Oh my God, what was this? Did Jenna have some kind of radar? Was Caroline somehow moving differently? *I want you to feel me inside you all day*, Jack had whispered in his deep dark voice while making love this morning, and she did. Every time she moved, she could almost feel his presence inside her, against her slightly swollen tissues. Her nipples rasped against her sweater, constantly reminding her how he'd suckled them hard.

In an instant, her body had a flashback to that morning, spread-eagled out on the bed, like a sacrificial virgin in an ancient religion, watching him thrusting in and out of her . . .

Caroline tried to control her breathing, her shaking hands. Oh God, she was in trouble if just the thought of him hurled her halfway to an orgasm. She had to calm herself down. She drew in a deep breath. "If you're referring to my new boarder, um—"

"Jack Prescott," Jenna interrupted, a smug smile on her face. "Age thirty-one, former Army officer, and most important of all, tall, dark and handsome." She wrinkled her nose. "Well . . . not handsome so much as sexy. *And*"—she rapped the chopstick on the table—"currently residing at 12 Maple Lane which just happens to be—*ta da!*—Greenbriars. So talk. Tell all. Where did you two meet? I mean it must have been since last Monday because surely you would have told me you'd started going out with someone? My God, that was quick! You haven't even known him for a week, and you're already living together. I mean, at warp speeds like that, can wedding bells be far behind? And let me tell you, couldn't happen to a nicer girl."

"Whoa!" Caroline laughed, shaking her head. "It's not—it's not what you think." She tried to sound prim and disinterested, but she knew that she was blushing beet red.

And Jenna was no fool. Except for her husband, whose affair came as a total shock, she had excellent sexual radar. She'd been the first person to notice that the mayor and Amanda Riesenthal were having an affair.

"I mean we—" Caroline bit her lip. She had no idea if Jack wanted to make public their—what was it? An affair? A weekend tumble? She hoped it was more than that, but until she knew what he thought, better not to advertise that they'd become lovers. So she tried to put it on safe ground. "He's my new boarder. He showed up on Christmas Eve, and was I ever grateful. The Kippings left, I never had a chance to tell you, and I was stuck without the extra rent money. So Jack—Mr. Prescott—showing up and needing a room was a very lucky chance for me."

Jenna was listening, dark brown eyes wide open in surprise. She frowned. "He's a *boarder*? Your boarder? That's insane. What does he want with a room with you?"

Caroline bristled a little. "Well, I know Greenbriars is a little uncomfortable, but I don't think he could find a much better room at the price. He'd just arrived and needed a place to stay."

"Well, well why didn't he go to the Carlton?" Jenna asked. "Or the Victoria?" The Carlton was Summerville's oldest hotel, a turn-of-the-century building recently restored. The Victoria was a modern five-star hotel, with a Jacuzzi in every room.

That was rich, coming from Jenna, who barely made it to the end of the month on her salary. "The Carlton costs $190 a night and the Victoria costs $170. Why do *you* think he wanted a room?"

"I have no idea." Jenna shook her head, puzzled. "Unless he wanted to move in with you."

Caroline made an exasperated sound, picking up florets of stir-fried broccoli. "We'd never met before. How on earth could he want to move in with me if he didn't know me?"

"I have no idea. It just sounds weird to me, wanting to rent a room when he could go to a comfortable hotel. No offense, Caroline, but beautiful as Greenbriars is, it's no match for the service and comfort at the Carlton. Or the luxuries at the Victoria."

Was Jenna being deliberately obtuse? "How could he afford to stay at the Carlton? Do you know what it would cost? Almost six thousand dollars a month. And he's a former soldier. How could he afford that?"

"Jesus," Jenna whispered, wide-eyed. "You don't know. You really don't know."

"Know what?" Jenna didn't answer. "Jenna, you're scaring me. Know what? What should I know?"

"I—I can't talk."

Caroline was getting scared. Jenna was looking stricken, as if she had knowledge that Jack Prescott was really Jack the Ripper but had taken an oath not to reveal it. "Jenna—you've got to talk. What's wrong with him? What's wrong with Jack? He's living in my home, Jenna. I have to know if there's something wrong."

Jenna stared for a moment, face somber. Finally, she gave a little nod, as if coming to a secret decision. "Okay." She swallowed and lay a hand over Caroline's. "Okay, I'll tell you, but you have to keep it a secret." Her hand tightened. "You have to promise me."

Wide-eyed, throat tight, Caroline nodded.

Jenna was leaning forward, watching Caroline's eyes, looking so troubled that Caroline felt her heart clench.

"I'd lose my job if you let slip to anyone that I told you. Particularly him, Jack Prescott. It's against every rule in the book, talking to you about a client. Are we clear on that?" Caroline nodded. "Okay—here it is. I have no idea why Jack Prescott wants to rent a room from you if he's never met you before. And if you think he's just a simple soldier, think again. He doesn't need to rent a room with you. He could buy the Carlton, the Victoria *and* Greenbriars and never feel the pinch." She put her hand over Caroline's. "He came in this morning, opened an account and rented a safe-deposit box." She stopped.

"And?" Caroline prodded. "That's not a crime. He wants to

settle down here, he's going to be needing a bank account."

"Yes, he sure will. Honey . . ." Jenna said softly, a small frown between her black eyebrows, "he deposited over eight million dollars in my bank today."

Thirteen

Deaver parked about a mile away and walked to Caroline Lake's home. He'd studied the satellite photos and maps carefully, and made his way mainly through back streets and service alleys.

He needn't have bothered, really. The weather was so bad there wasn't anyone around. Those who worked had already left, and the others were at home, sheltered from the icy sleet. It was a residential neighborhood and under normal circumstances at any given moment you could count on someone walking the dog or going for a jog, but not in this weather.

It made his job easy. So easy, he was even able to go in through the front door.

The front door lock was a joke, and once he got through it, he could understand why. Though the house was big, there was very little furniture, no artwork on the walls, no fancy home-entertainment systems or stereos, very little silver and no expensive knickknacks. Basically, there wasn't anything to steal.

Except, of course, for $20 million in diamonds.

Deaver went through the house carefully, room by room, making sure he put everything back the way it was. It went fast because the rooms were fairly empty. He saw no sign that anyone other than a woman lived there until he hit the upstairs master bedroom.

There was a big black duffel bag and a suitcase on the bedroom floor with men's clothes, size huge. Bingo. So Jack had made it to the pretty lady and into her pants pronto.

Good going, ace, he thought. You've just made my job easier. Get the woman, get a gun to her head and Jack was going to sing. Oh, yes.

Deaver went through Jack's bag very thoroughly. No weapons and no diamonds. That meant that Prescott was carrying, and he'd hidden the diamonds somewhere.

Deaver stood, blood pounding in his ears, fists clenched. He was so close, so goddamned *close*! He banged his fist on the dresser, then ran his hand over his short-cropped hair.

He had ten thousand dollars left, and if he didn't get his diamonds back, how the fuck was he supposed to live?

It was entirely possible that Jack had hidden the diamonds somewhere in the house, but Jack was a thorough man. If he'd hidden them somewhere here, Deaver would have to tear the house apart. It would take time, and Prescott might come in while he was searching. And in any case, Prescott would know someone was after him.

Deaver thought it through. Would Prescott leave a fucking

fortune in diamonds in this woman's house? Yeah, so sure, he was banging her, but he hadn't seen her in years. How could he know she wouldn't make off with them? And how could he know the house well enough to find a good place to stash them?

No, it wouldn't make sense for him to keep them here. So he'd stashed them somewhere else, somewhere only he could have access to, like a safe-deposit box in a bank or a warehouse rental unit.

Smart boy, Deaver thought. *But not smart enough*.

He let himself out quietly and got back into his rental Tahoe.

Time to check out Caroline Lake.

The bad thing about not having any customers is that it gives one way too much time to think.

Caroline walked around in a daze after Jenna left, absently straightening books and dusting shelves.

Finding out a man you were dating—or whatever it was they were doing—was rich wasn't necessarily a bad thing. Especially when he was filthy rich, as Jack apparently was. Eight million dollars. She could hardly get her mind around the thought. And she found it impossible to square it with Jack Prescott.

Rich men were vain, they liked the good life, they somehow felt they were blessed and better than others. Like Sanders, for example. Caroline tried to imagine Sanders dressed in tattered jeans, ancient boots, a denim jacket in the dead of winter.

Impossible.

Rich men hired other people to do their scut work for them. Caroline could hardly imagine a rich man wrestling with her boiler, making all the repairs that Jack had made, shoveling her drive. A rich man would have automatically picked up the phone and hired someone to shovel snow instead of taking a couple of hours to do a dirty, exhausting job.

She tried to imagine Sanders shoveling snow and snorted. Caroline entertained herself with an image of Sanders, in his Calvin Klein winterwear and cashmere-lined gloves, shoveling snow, ruining his manicure. The image was so enticing she actually smiled at Sanders as he walked into the bookshop, thinking him a figment of her imagination.

He clasped his glove-clad hands together and beamed when he saw her smile. "Caroline, my dear, how good to see you!" He clasped her shoulders and bent down to kiss her. She averted her face at the last minute, and he bussed her cheek instead of her mouth.

Oh my God, it *was* Sanders—in the flesh!

The last time she'd seen him had been for a disastrous nightcap at Greenbriars after a very nice dinner in October. The dinner had been so nice, and she'd been so grateful for the respite, that she'd asked him in for a whiskey only to have him behave badly toward Toby.

"What are you doing here?" she asked bluntly.

He took off his jacket and gloves leisurely, looking around the bookshop. Caroline had no idea what he thought of First Page. Sanders liked sleek and modern, which First Page certainly was not. He turned and focused his gaze on her. "I thought I'd stop by and see you. I haven't had a chance to offer my condolences for the death of your brother yet."

Uh-huh. He'd obviously been *amazingly* busy the past two months not to be able to drop in or pick up the phone or pen a note.

But Caroline had been brought up by her parents to be polite. She often thought of it as a handicap.

"Thanks, Sanders." She drummed up another smile for him. "That's very thoughtful of you. I appreciate it."

He nodded, clearly unable to process her ironic tone. He looked around again, then back at her, waiting.

Caroline suppressed a sigh. She couldn't even plead that she was busy. The shop was deserted, as was the street outside. It was entirely possible that the whole city was deserted, everyone in it just staying home.

"Do please sit down, Sanders. Can I make you a cup of tea?" Maybe he'd been passing by and wanted something warm. Maybe if she offered him tea, he'd leave. Caroline didn't think he'd stopped by for a book. In all the years she'd known him, she'd never known him to read a book. He read reviews, so he could sound knowledgeable, but he'd never read the actual book, that she could tell.

He gave her an alarmingly warm smile and placed his hand over hers. "I'd love a cup of tea, thanks."

Thank God for her little secondhand microwave oven in the office. In three minutes, she was back with two mugs of vanilla tea, berating herself for her unkindness.

It wasn't Sanders's fault he was an ass. And his visit did break the monotony of an endless afternoon in her empty shop, waiting for Jack to come pick her up. And it did distract her from endless speculation about Jack's money and where it came from.

So she leaned forward with genuine warmth to hand him the cup and was startled when he grabbed her other hand and kissed it. He held it for a long moment between his hands.

"Uh, Sanders?"

"Yes, darling?" He smiled at her.

"I need my hand back, so I can drink my tea. Please."

"Of course." He released her hand and sat back, sipping, completely at ease. "So . . . how was your Christmas?"

Don't blush, Caroline told herself furiously and managed by dint of sheer willpower to keep her color down. Oh God, she couldn't possibly tell Sanders what her Christmas had been like. Even if she wanted to confide in him—which she most certainly did not—she had no idea if Jack wanted to trumpet their affair, or whatever it was they were having, from the rooftops. Telling Sanders was the equivalent of taking out an ad in the local newspaper.

What could she say? If she said she'd been with someone, he'd immediately want to know who. And she was an atrocious liar. What could she say that wasn't a lie but didn't convey the truth?

"It was . . . quiet," she said finally.

He nodded, as if that was the answer he expected. "I didn't call because I thought you might want to be alone over the holidays. I know that Christmases have always been hard for you. But you know, Caroline, the grieving process must come to an end. You're still a young woman, and now Toby—well,

Toby has gone on to a better place, and you can start thinking of yourself. There are stages to grieving, you know . . ."

Caroline zoned out. It was a speech she'd heard thousands of times before from Sanders.

He was sitting directly under the overhead lamp, turning his perfectly styled hair a pure gold. He was definitely a handsome man, and he definitely knew it. Caroline watched him as he gave his little sermon, listening to one word out of ten.

The light also reflected off the top of his head. She peered a little, carefully disguising her interest. Was that his scalp she was seeing through the blond strands? Yes, that was definitely skin, not hair at his temples. His *receding* temples. Was Sanders going *bald*?

He wouldn't like that. Caroline imagined that he was using every expensive hair-care product on earth and that eventually, if he trod the tragic path of male-pattern baldness, he'd have a transplant. Jenna was absolutely certain that he'd already had a little nip and tuck around the eyes, but however carefully Caroline looked, she couldn't see any signs. But then, what would she know? She wasn't exactly an expert.

"—what do you say? I think it would be fantastic, and I think it would cheer you up. I just know you'd have a wonderful time."

He'd come to the end of his little spiel, and she hadn't even listened. Oh hell, he'd said something that required an answer. *Yes* was definitely out, if she didn't know what she was agreeing to. And *no*—well Sanders wasn't too big on no's.

She patted his hand and lied. "I'm so sorry, Sanders. I was listening for a deliveryman who is supposed to bring me the new weekly arrivals. He's new, so he doesn't know how to park out back. I thought I heard his van outside, but it wasn't him after all. However, I'm afraid I missed what you were saying. Would you mind repeating?"

His blond eyebrows drew together in annoyance and he gave a little sigh. "I *said*, I have tickets to *La Traviata* next Saturday in Seattle. Box seats. So I thought we might just make a weekend of it. I'll clear my calendar Friday afternoon and you can close up early. I've booked us a room at the Fairmont Olympic. I know you love that hotel, and it's been years since you've been there, right? We'll just relax and have a good time. Be together. Then on Sunday, there are some people I'd like you to meet." He put his hand over hers. "Be just like old times, eh?"

Caroline just stared at him. This was beyond alarming. He'd gone ahead and started up another round of their relationship without her! Except she had no intention of following along. She had bigger and better things to do.

"Sanders—you've already *booked* the room? That's crazy! I can't go to Seattle with you next weekend."

His head reared back in surprise at her reaction. "But I've got the tickets! They were almost impossible to find. Caroline, read my lips. *La Traviata*. And the Fairmont. How can you say no?"

This was going way too far, even for him. "Sanders, do you mean to tell me that you bought expensive tickets to the opera and booked a room at the Fairmont and you didn't think to ask me if I wanted to go?"

Sanders looked absolutely blank. "Well, why wouldn't you want to go? I mean it's not as if—" *It's not as if you have anything better to do.*

The words hung there in the room. Sanders's mouth had snapped shut, which was a good thing because if he said one more word, she was going to smack him.

Well, enough was enough. Caroline stood and, startled, Sanders stood, too. "I'm sorry I can't accept your invitation, Sanders." Not that it had been an invitation. It had been more like a summons. "But I'm afraid I'm busy next weekend." And the weekend after that, and the weekend after that. "And next time you want to invite a woman out, you might want to ask her first before making all the arrangements. Now, if you'll excuse me."

"Wait! Caroline, wait." He grabbed her by her upper arms. She looked at her arms and then up at him. "I'm sorry if that came out all wrong. Listen, I think we need to get our relationship back on an even footing. And I thought that a romantic getaway for a weekend would be a fabulous way to do that. Don't you think so?" He smiled down at her, his usual charming smile that wasn't working at all. "Come on, you know you've been having a hard time. I want to treat you to some luxury living. You know we're meant to be together."

Caroline tried to wrench herself away, but his grip was strong. He worked out a lot at the gym. "Sanders, I hate to break this to you, but we have no relationship. If anything, you've got a relationship with that brunette I saw you with last week." Considering he'd had his hand up her skirt and his tongue down her throat. Caroline had seen them outside a trendy Italian eatery, Patrizio's, as she was driving home after a late night in the shop shelving new books.

"Oh-ho." His face cleared. "You're jealous. That's it. Oh, sweetheart, I promise you, you have nothing to be jealous about. That woman doesn't mean anything to me. You're the one I care for. Always have. Always will. Now's our time, Caroline. Finally."

To her horror, he pulled her close and kissed her. It wasn't a first-date kiss either. They'd been to bed together so he presumed he had the right to go for full-frontal, tongue-in-mouth kissing.

Caroline tried to pull away, but he was holding the back of her head, hard, his fingers twisted in her hair. He was hurting her. Clutching her so tightly to him, it felt like her ribs were cracking. And—horribly—he was grinding against her and she could feel the beginnings of an erection against her mound.

That galvanized her. She did *not* want to feel his penis against her. Ack. She started pushing against him in earnest, trying to tell him to cut it out, but his mouth absorbed her words. She ended up making mewling sounds of protest, beating her fists against his chest.

He rubbed even harder against her, and she felt him surge into a full erection. God, this was awful! His eyes were closed, as if this were a romantic moment between two lovers, and not an act of force.

His tongue moved in her mouth like a warm wet slug, and it sickened her. She struggled harder, trying to kick him, managing mostly to bruise her toes. His hand tightened in her hair, pulling at it so hard it brought tears to her eyes.

Ouch! You're hurting me! The words were there, in her throat, but she couldn't say them, she could only make horrified noises. She finally landed a kick, but it only made him hold her head more tightly to him. He was in a frenzy now, his teeth clashing against hers as he changed the kiss to delve more deeply into her mouth, hips rubbing against hers. Horrible noises were coming out of his throat, and she could feel his penis swell even further.

He bit her lip, drawing blood. She could taste her blood, and so could he. His penis rippled with arousal, and he groaned as he ground himself against her. Her blood excited him.

Oh God, this had never even occurred to her. The couple of times they'd made love, it had been perfectly bland. Pleasant but not overly so. Totally unmemorable.

But right now, it looked like Sanders had a cruel streak she had never suspected. He got off on pain. He was definitely turned on by the taste of her blood and her pain.

She was fighting in earnest now, kicking, screaming into his mouth, trying to punch him, though it was almost impossible while he was holding her so close to him.

She was shaking with rage, trying vainly to free herself when all of a sudden she was free, staggering to catch her balance, staring.

Jack was holding Sanders's arm wrenched behind his back, so hard Sanders was on the balls of his feet, wheezing with pain.

He was white-faced, blond strands of hair falling over his forehead, eyes unfocused, a little stripe of blood at the corner of his mouth. Her blood.

His eyes were wild, so wide open she could see white all around his irises.

Though Sanders was writhing wildly to get out of Jack's grasp, it was impossible. Jack was standing utterly still, feet braced apart, touching Sanders only with his hand on his wrist, but it was as if Sanders were shackled in steel restraints.

"Touch her again, you fucker, and I will break your arm. Right after I break your fucking neck." Jack's voice was low, vicious. Sanders's eyes widened, then he cried out as Jack tightened his grip.

"Let me go! Who the hell are you? Caroline! Tell this maniac to let me go! Ahhh!" His voice rose in panic as Jack lifted his hand. Sanders was standing completely on the tips of his toes now, and if he dropped to his heels, he'd break his own arm against Jack's steady, relentless hold. Sanders was sweating, face completely bloodless. "Caroline, tell him to let me *go*!"

Jack lifted his hand another inch, and Sanders screamed in pain, writhing, out of control.

Jack wasn't out of control at all. He was utterly still, he wasn't even breathing hard, but something cold and feral in his eyes made her step forward and touch him on the arm. Later, she would mull over the fact that she felt no fear of him even in the middle of an act of violence.

She'd just been mauled by Sanders, a puppy dog compared to Jack, who looked utterly capable of terrifying violence, but not for a second did she fear him. Instinctively, the knowledge welling up from a place deep inside herself, a quiet, deep place she trusted, she knew he wouldn't hurt her.

He wrenched Sanders's wrist an inch higher, and Sanders screamed.

Satisfying as it was to watch, she couldn't stand by and watch Jack break Sanders's arm. "Jack," she whispered, putting her hand on his arm. "Don't. That's enough."

His dark eyes were narrowed into slits, a violent light in them. Still holding the writhing Sanders with ease, he reached out with his other hand to touch the corner of her mouth, wiping away the streak of blood.

"I could kill him for this alone," he said. There was something in his voice that had Sanders's eyes opening wide in panic.

"No." If there was one thing Caroline knew, it was that she didn't want any more violence. She already felt sick to her stomach after her struggle with Sanders, ashamed that she'd never seen beneath his surface. Her stomach was knotted with tension. "Let him go, Jack."

He looked at her, hard, jaw muscles jumping. His entire body language was screaming that he wanted revenge. He could take it, too. Sanders was something of a gym rat, but he was absolutely no match for Jack, who had an entirely different order of strength and knowledge of martial arts. He had subdued Sanders with ridiculous ease, and Caroline had no doubt he could have wiped the floor with him.

There was a shadow of extreme violence hovering in the room, visible in the tight lines around Jack's eyes, in the hot light of rage in his eyes, in his stance. Caroline was certain as certain could be that Jack was capable of killing Sanders. He was physically capable, and he could do it without remorse.

He was a soldier, after all, and that's what soldiers did. Killed their enemies.

"Let him go. Now, Jack," she whispered, and it was enough. Jack abruptly let go of him and Sanders lurched to keep his balance. He rubbed the ball of his shoulder, glaring at Jack, then at her, as if he'd been wronged. His hair was mussed, and he was sweating heavily.

"You son of a bitch, you're going to live to regret this," Sanders swore, slurring the words. It was a sign of how upset he was. Sanders's normal speaking voice was deliberate, almost a drawl, but now he was gulping in great gasps of air, the words pouring out of him. "I'm a lawyer, you asshole and you better believe I'm going to sue your sorry ass for so much money it will take you ten fucking lifetimes to get out of debt!"

The instant Jack released Sanders, he'd turned to Caroline, wiping away the little streak of blood at her mouth, tucking a lock of hair behind her ear. But at Sanders's words, he turned his head and looked back at Sanders.

He didn't do anything at all, just looked. Caroline couldn't see his expression, but whatever it was, it sure scared Sanders. His face had turned red with rage, but at Jack's glare, he turned white again, backing away, hands out in front of him.

It occurred to Caroline that if she hadn't been there to stop him, Jack would have used more violence than he had. He hadn't needed to issue threats, because every line of his big, strong body was a threat, and not an idle one at that.

Five seconds after Jack released his arm, Sanders had

grabbed his hat and coat and was out the door so fast that the bell over the door was still ringing by the time he'd turned the corner and disappeared from sight.

Suddenly, the adrenaline of her fight with Sanders and the violence that had swirled in the room swooshed out of her system, leaving her shaking and weak. She shivered and swayed a little on her feet, a chill at her core draining all energy. Sparks flew in front of her eyes . . .

A second later, she was sitting down, a strong, gentle hand pressing on her neck until she put her head between her knees. Jack's hand kept her there for a moment, then lifted. "Stay like that for a minute and breathe deeply. I'll be right back."

She breathed deeply, eyes closed, thinking of nothing at all, until she heard his voice. "Here, honey." He placed a steaming cup of tea in front of her. "Drink that up as fast as you can."

Caroline reached for it and sipped, wincing as the heat filled her mouth and as she struggled against a sugar fit. She raised her eyes to his. "How much sugar did you put in it? It's more sugar than tea."

He didn't answer immediately, only placed his hand under hers and lifted so that she was forced to take another sip. "You're a little shocked so you need heat, liquid and sugar. If you were a soldier on a battlefield, it wouldn't be tea with lots of sugar, it would be a glucose IV. I know it's not to your taste, but drink up. You'll feel better afterwards, trust me."

She did trust him, instinctively. Caroline tried to smile, a little ashamed of her reaction. "I'm not a soldier who's fallen in battle. I feel foolish even needing the cup of tea."

"Don't be." His voice was quiet as he watched her drinking. "It must have been a shock. I imagine you weren't expecting him to turn violent."

It was a question. "No, not at all. I never would have even believed Sanders was capable of behaving like that. I've known him for ages." Time to get a little unpalatable truth out there, too. "We've even . . . dated, now and again. We've had an on-again, off-again relationship for a long time."

Jack's dark eyes sharpened. "Since your teens?"

Caroline stared at him over the cup. "Why yes, how did you know that?"

He just shrugged. "Lucky guess. You feeling better?"

The icy feeling, the tremors—they were gone. "Yes, I do, actually. Though I'm also feeling stupid and a wimp. I'd like to think that Sanders caught me totally by surprise, but the truth is that I didn't defend myself very well." The least she could have done was bite Sanders's tongue and kick him roundly in the shins. "When you set up your self-defense school, I'm going to be your first customer. I want to learn to kick butt in a major way."

"Yeah?" The tension in his big body had gone, and he looked at her with a half smile.

"Absolutely."

"Well, you're going to get as many free lessons as you want."

"Can you teach me the knee-in-the-balls thing?"

He nodded. "Count on it. And the thumb on the carotid thing, too. Done right, it makes your opponent drop like a stunned ox."

"Sounds great." It did, too. "I don't ever want to be in that position again. Helpless, unable to defend myself."

"No," he said soberly. "Never again. It took years off my life coming in and seeing you being hurt. We're going to get you to a point where you can at least whip the ass of a softie like this guy—what was his name?"

"Sanders. Sanders McCullin."

"Stupid name." Jack shook his head. "Name like that, you should be able to learn to take him down in ten lessons. Next time he gets near you, you can toss him on his back."

Caroline smiled. It was a nice thought. She was feeling very much herself again, thanks to the thought of learning some basic self-defense—which would be good exercise, too—and thanks to the massive sugar infusion.

Jack was watching her closely.

"You're feeling better. Good." He looked out the window at the sleety afternoon. Nobody in the past half hour had even appeared on the street. He put his hand over hers, and gripped her hand warmly. "What would you say to knocking off now and going home?" He lifted her hand to his mouth. "We could have an early dinner, then fool around a little. I'll let you throw me. What do you say?"

Jack Prescott sitting on his chair looked like an immovable force of the universe. No way could she ever in a million years throw him, but it was nice of him to offer.

It was so wonderful sitting here with him, his hand on hers, looking forward to the evening and then—*God!*—the night. It had been a long long time since she'd looked forward to things, and he'd given her this gift.

"Thanks," she said softly.

He'd been scanning the street outside, but he turned his head at that, with a frown. "For what?"

"Oh, for taking care of Sanders without breaking his arm, even though you were dying to, I could tell. For stopping by to pick me up. For just—being around."

She leaned forward and pressed her lips to his. He took the kiss over immediately, hand to the back of her head.

It was exactly the gesture Sanders had used, but oh the difference. Jack wasn't using his strength to control her, though he was probably ten times stronger than Sanders. It occurred to Caroline that every time Jack had touched her, he did so carefully, careful never to hurt her.

A quick meeting of lips and he pulled back, his eyes searching hers. "Let's go home, warrior princess," he whispered.

Vincent Deaver slumped deeply in the booth at the diner across the street, head curved over the cup of coffee he'd been nursing for a couple of hours, and watched Jack Prescott leave First Page with his arm around Caroline Lake's waist.

He needn't have worried about being detected. He had on a watch cap and heavy dark nonprescription horn rim glasses. Prescott wasn't expecting him, and anyway, all his attention was on the redhead with him. He'd scanned the street out of habit, but he wouldn't be expecting trouble from someone in the diner. The street was empty, Prescott'd checked up and down, then his attention was riveted once more on the woman.

Interesting.

Deaver'd learned a lot since he'd watched a tall, handsome and elegant blond man in a cashmere coat just like the one Deaver was going to buy once he got his diamonds back walk into First Page. The woman—Caroline Lake—had greeted him as a friend. They'd talked, the woman keeping her body language neutral, then they'd started fighting and Cashmere Coat guy grabbed her and started shoving his tongue down her throat. The woman had fought but wasn't getting anywhere.

Deaver watched as Prescott came around a corner, saw what was happening through the shop window, and broke into a dead run.

Cashmere Coat was soft.

He came out of the shop at a run and got into a black Porsche. He put it into gear and took off fast, the back sliding on the icy roads.

Deaver got the tag number. He'd be easy to track down.

Blond Cashmere Coat was really lucky that the woman exerted some influence on Prescott and was able to stop him, because Prescott was a mean fighter, knew all the tricks. He also undoubtedly had a combat knife on him somewhere, and Cashmere Coat was lucky he hadn't been gutted.

Deaver had never seen Prescott lose a fight or back down from one. But all the woman had had to do to stop him was touch Prescott on the arm and say a few words, and it was as if she'd waved a magic wand.

Prescott, standing down. *That* was something Deaver had never seen.

Deaver watched Prescott and Caroline Lake disappear

around the corner and clenched his fists. The urge to get up right now, run after that fucker Prescott and shoot him dead was almost overwhelming. Deaver would make sure to kill the woman first, just to make Prescott suffer, then a double tap to the head, and Prescott would be down forever.

Deaver could see it, feel it, nearly smell it, and the temptation was so strong he broke out in a sweat.

But much as he'd love to nail Prescott and his woman right now, he needed his diamonds back first.

Then he could have his fun.

Fourteen

Jack nearly missed it.

He was so intent on getting Caroline safely home, relaxed and curled up before the fire, that he'd tunnel-visioned, just like in battle. All he'd seen was Caroline, all he could think about was Caroline, taking up every ounce of space in his head.

He was still battle-primed, adrenaline still coursing through his system, without a proper outlet. The proper outlet would have been to smash that fucker Sanders's face in, then haul him into the closest police station for assault and battery.

If he lived to be a million years old, he'd never forget glancing through the big glass panes of Caroline's bookshop and seeing her struggling against a man.

He'd broken his own land-speed record getting in there and getting that man's hands off Caroline.

She'd been in shock, though she'd come out of it with humor and grace. Still, all he wanted was to get her bundled up and into the house as fast as possible.

Jack had excellent situational awareness. Even with one goal in mind, he paid attention to what was around him. Only Caroline could mess with his head so much that he actually had the key in the lock and was turning it before seeing the faint scratches on the lock. Scratches that hadn't been there that morning.

In an instant his Glock was in his hand, and he was rushing Caroline back to his rented SUV. He bundled her into the driver's seat, made sure she had the keys and slammed the door shut.

"Jack!" Her voice was muffled through the closed door. Her eyes dropped to his weapon, then back to him. She looked shocked. "What's going on?"

There wasn't time to explain or reassure. Whoever had broken into the house could still be there, and Jack had to get in there, fast.

"Stay there and don't move!" he mouthed, tapping on the window. Caroline nodded, face white, silver-gray eyes huge in her face.

Good girl.

Jack loped back to the front door and entered silently with the key, weapon out, in a stance guaranteed to cover a 180-degree field of fire in two seconds.

Entry, clear. Living room, clear. Kitchen, clear.

Moving fast, moving silently, he went methodically through every room in the house, basement to attic.

Out of habit, he'd left telltales in the bedroom and there

were clear signs that someone had rifled through his things, Caroline's closet and the dresser. Someone—or several someones—had gone through their personal possessions. It was harder to tell in the rest of the house, where he hadn't left telltales.

As far as Jack could tell, nothing had been stolen. The TV and stereo were there, no artwork was gone from the walls, certainly nothing of his had been stolen, though there wasn't much beyond dirty socks and underwear. Everything of value he had was in his new bank account and the bank vault.

Of course, Caroline's TV and stereo set were at least ten years old and worth zero on the resale market. Though he didn't know anything about art, he suspected that what was left on the walls wasn't worth stealing. More or less everything of value in the house had already been sold, and not even the best thief in the world could steal walls and a roof.

When Jack was absolutely certain the house was empty, he pushed his gun into the waistband of his jeans and went out to get Caroline.

He hustled her up the steps.

"What was it, Jack? Is there someone in the house? Has the house been robbed?"

Damn, but he hated that white, pinched, anxious look on her face. If he had the fucker or fuckers who'd broken into Caroline's home, he'd break their hands, finger by finger, to ensure that they never picked another lock again for the rest of their natural lives.

Not that Caroline's locks were hard to pick. They weren't, a two-year-old could get through them. They were worth shit.

He could pick them blindfolded, with his hands in casts.

He closed the front door behind them, turned up the heat and folded her in his arms.

Too much stuff happening, all of it bad. He needed the feel of her in his arms like he needed his next breath.

"Jack?" Her voice was muffled in his jacket, shiny locks of red-gold hair escaping her wool cap to curl along his jacket. Jack bent to kiss her lightly, hand along the softness of her neck. His thumb grazed the pulse in her neck, beating a light, fast tattoo.

Feeling her safe in his arms, heart beating, calmed him a little.

"Jack." Caroline's voice was stronger and she pushed at him a little. Jack opened his arms, and she stepped back to look him in the face. "Tell me what's going on." She looked around carefully, then brought her gaze back to him. "I don't see any damage."

"No, no damage. Whatever it is they were looking for, it wasn't here. What they usually look for is plasma TVs, high-end electronics. Expensive artwork. Meltable silver."

"All gone," she said. "A long time ago." Her eyebrows drew together as she looked up at him. "Jack . . . when you got to the door you pulled out a gun. You had a *gun*. Where on earth did you get that?"

Uh-oh. Jack had to be careful here.

Caroline had just entered his world.

He wanted her to become security-conscious without being afraid of him. Jack was perfectly aware of the fact that most people considered men like him to be paranoid. If you've lived your life in safety and comfort, and you haven't traveled to the places he'd been, where humanity was at its rawest, most cruel, and where greed and lust were unbridled, then you looked at the precautions Jack took as a matter of course to be the result of a sick mind.

"I'm always armed," he said gently. The heavy weight of his Glock in the small of his back felt good and right. "Or I know how to get my hands on a weapon pretty damn quick."

"You mean, all this time we've been"—she waved a pink-tipped finger between them—"you've been *armed*?"

"Yes." He let the word drop like a stone between them. This was part of him, an integral part. She had to learn to deal with it. Jack was willing to compromise, but not on this.

Caroline blinked and gave a half laugh. "I don't believe this."

"Believe it. I'm fully licensed to carry a concealed weapon, and I know how to use it, don't worry about that."

She was staring at him. "To tell you the truth, that hadn't even occurred to me. I'm still trying to come to grips with the fact that someone I'm"— she swallowed—"someone I'm seeing runs around with a *gun* on his person. I don't think I've ever even met someone who owns a gun, besides the sheriff. Not that I know of, anyway."

"It's a bad world out there, Caroline," he said gently. "You have to be prepared."

Fuck, but that was true. He'd seen it, he'd lived it. In the shelters he'd grown up in, a beauty like Caroline would have been raped the instant she'd reached puberty, probably even before. In Afghanistan, she'd have been dressed in a head-to-toe burqa and beaten if a man could hear her footsteps. There, too, she would have been raped, with the added pleasure of being sentenced to death for fornication.

In Sierra Leone—Jack's back teeth ground together. He'd seen the shattered remains of the women who'd fallen into the hands of the Revolutionary Army. Death for them had been a release.

He knew what the world was like. Being armed, willing and able to defend the things he cared about, was deeply embedded in his bones, in his very DNA. And right now, Caroline topped the list of things he'd defend to the death.

"One last thing, honey." Jack clasped her shoulders. Through the thick down he could feel her shoulder bones, delicate, fragile. Everything about her was delicate and fragile, in a world that hated beauty and delicacy. He could lose her at any time to the scumbags of the world. He had to remember that. "Do you have a safe?"

Caroline nodded, eyes big, fixed on his face. "Yes, it's—"

"No." He lay a long forefinger across her lips. "Don't tell me. I don't need to know. I want you to go check your safe to see if everything's there that should be. Will you do that for me?"

Without another word, she disappeared upstairs, while Jack went over the living room again, more carefully this time. He still didn't see anything missing, and he had a good visual memory.

It never failed to astonish him that most people kept their valuables in the living room or the bedroom. In his own house back in North Carolina, his wall safe had been behind the toilet.

Caroline came back down the stairs.

"Anything gone?"

"No." She shook her head, looking troubled. "Everything is where it should be. In the bedroom, as well." A quick glance around the living room was enough for her. She was familiar with her own space. "And nothing is missing here. There isn't actually that much to steal. Are you *sure* the house was broken into?"

One picture was worth a thousand words. Jack simply took her hand and walked her to the front door. He opened it and took her hand to rub it over the shiny brass lock. "Feel that? Feel the slight scratches and abrasions?"

She nodded, finger moving gently over the brass and steel. "Maybe they were always there. How can you tell?"

"They weren't here this morning, trust me on that. Those scratches come from lockpicks, and it would have taken the thief about a minute and a half, tops, to get in."

"How would you know? And how come you noticed something as small as a few scratches?"

He had his own set of lockpicks in his duffel bag, though he thought it best not to mention that. She was spooked enough as it was. "We're trained to pick locks in the Army, so I know what a picked lock looks like. And the first thing a soldier does is establish a secure perimeter and be aware of what's inside that perimeter. I notice these things because I was trained to. Just about the first thing I noticed when I got here was that you have the flimsiest locks I've ever seen. A child could get through them, let alone a half-competent burglar."

Her eyes widened, and a little color came into her cheeks.

"Well, I'm sorry if my locks aren't up to par, but it's what I have, so deal with it."

She was angry. Great. He loved seeing that lost, pale expression chased from her face. "Tomorrow, first thing, I'm getting a decent security system in place. Maybe a Pressley or a—"

"Whoa, Jack." There were red flags now on her cheeks. She held up her hands in time-out sign. "I'm sorry, I realize that you're security-conscious, but I simply can't afford a security system, not the kind with electronic codes and alarmed windows and doors. I'm not entirely certain I could afford new locks for all the doors. So that is something that is simply going to have to wait."

Something clenched in his chest. "I'm not expecting you to pay for it, Caroline. I'm perfectly willing to buy the system. And I could probably get a good professional discount if I use my father's company's name."

"I can't accept that." She shook her head, her beautiful mouth set in a stubborn line. "I can't afford to knock it off the rent, and I certainly can't accept an expensive security system from you. So, I'm sorry, but the new security system won't be coming anytime soon. We'll just have to hope that the burglars don't come back. Maybe there's this burglar underworld, and the word has spread that there is nothing at all to steal at Greenbriars except for some mismatched silver, odd porcelain plates and my mother's watercolors."

Jack wished he could fast-forward to the next few weeks, or however long it took for them to become engaged, so that this nonsense about not accepting money from him could stop.

Instead, he ran the back of his forefinger along her neck, down to the delicate collarbones. She'd taken her coat off when she went upstairs to check on the safe—which was in her bedroom, he'd bet his left nut on it. Under the coat, she had a pretty turquoise V-neck sweater that turned her eyes a brilliant blue.

He watched her for a moment, running his finger under the collar of the sweater, loving the feel of her skin, like warm satin. "Do you know what I'd love to do?"

She shook her head.

He lowered his voice to a whisper as he lowered his eyes to her neck. "I would love to buy you a pearl necklace. The perfect pearl necklace. Your skin is made for pearls. I'd buy the slightly rosy-colored kind, I'm sure there's a name for that—"

"Overtone." She was smiling slightly.

"Pink overtone, then. I'd buy you strands of them, you'd look so beautiful, and it would give me so much pleasure. But you know what?"

Caroline shook her head again, watching his eyes.

"I'm betting that you already have a pearl necklace. Am I right?"

"Several. And very beautiful ones. They belonged to my mother."

"Uh-huh. My point exactly. I'll bet your father just loved buying them for your mother. You said he liked spoiling her. I can just imagine how much enjoyment he got out of his wife looking so beautiful in pearls he'd chosen for her."

The memory of something made Caroline smile. This was working. Jack wasn't used to convincing anyone to do something by coaxing. In the Army you gave orders, and they were obeyed. This was an entirely new field for him. He was going to have to get good at this skill, fast. Caroline had her own ideas about things, and she was no pushover.

"Well, the thing is this. Much as I'd love to buy you a pearl necklace, I know fu—damn all about the things. I'd get the wrong kind or the wrong size or the wrong number or something. Botch it up somehow. Just thinking about walking into a jewelry store makes me break out in a sweat. Pearl necklaces have not figured much in my life up to this point, and in all my training, they never came up once, so I'd be treading in very unfamiliar waters. But if there's one thing I *do* know, it's security. And you would be doing me an enormous favor in letting me set up your security system for you because it would save me going out of my freaking mind with worry that a burglar can just waltz in here, only next time he might have a knife or a gun and catch you alone and hurt you if I'm not here. So could you consider it the equivalent of a pearl necklace from a suitor? And a huge personal favor to me?"

His hand was warming her skin up, releasing that faint scent of roses that always went straight to his dick. Jack wanted nothing more than to carry her upstairs, lay her on her bed, get on top of her, get in her, just as soon as was humanly possible. But she was upset. First that fucker McCullin, then her house being broken into—he needed to get her fed and relaxed before they could fuck.

No. Before they could make love.

Wow. It was the first time he'd ever called it that in his head. It was also the first time he'd wanted a willing woman and decided to put sex off because she might not be psychologically ready.

"I hate it that someone was in my house, going through my things," she whispered.

"Yes," he said simply.

"And you'll set up a system no one can get through?"

He'd set up a system not even *he* could get through. He nodded.

"Well, I guess you convinced me." Caroline took in a deep breath, and Jack heroically kept his eyes on her face, though he had excellent peripheral vision and could see her breasts swelling a little under the sweater. "I'll accept your gift with thanks, and I guess I'll give *you* a little gift in return. Dinner."

She raised herself up on tiptoe to kiss him awkwardly on the side of his mouth. Jack was so surprised, he simply stood there like a dork. By the time he thought to kiss her back, she'd disappeared into the kitchen.

He stood there for a long time, listening to her rattle pans and run water in the kitchen, remembering the sharp burst of feeling in his chest when she'd kissed him.

He rubbed his hand over his chest, where it hurt.

Sanders sat behind his desk, teeth grinding. He'd combed his hair and straightened his clothes in his car before coming back to his office, but there must have been something else visible enough to set off alarms—the rage coming off him like steam, maybe—because his secretary had given him a startled look as he strode by.

Caroline was lost. Doubly lost. It was true, maybe he

shouldn't have pushed her so hard. But damn, walking into her shop, he'd been taken by a sudden surge of lust. He'd forgotten how beautiful she was, how perfect for him. So when she stood there, in her dinky little one-room bookshop that probably barely paid the rent and told him—*him*!—that no, she didn't want to go to the most fabulous hotel in Washington state and no she didn't want box tickets to the opera, he'd lost it.

Maybe he shouldn't have pushed it, but goddammit, when she said no, something snapped.

Caroline had never been great in the sack, but when she fought him, he could feel her fire, and it excited him. He shouldn't have pushed it as hard as he did, but damn, he'd been turned on.

And then it turned out that Caroline wasn't free after all. She was fucking someone else, and that someone else was territorial and violent.

In all these years, in the back of his mind, Sanders had taken it for granted that when he finally decided to settle down, it would be with Caroline, and she would fall into his arms with gratitude. After all, he was offering to give her back the life she'd been born to and had lost with her parents' death.

He'd always expected that she'd be free for him. But she'd hooked up with that son of a bitch who'd nearly broken his arm, and now she wasn't free anymore.

Something would have to be done and soon. Now that he'd made up his mind about Caroline, he wasn't going to let some violent asshole dressed like a bum steal his woman.

The intercom buzzed. "Mr. McCullin you have a visitor."

Sanders pushed the button. "I don't want to see anyone, Lori. Hold off all calls this afternoon."

"Ah . . . Mr. McCullin, you might want to see . . . this person. Wait!" her voice squawked through the speaker. "You can't go in there without permission! Hey, mister—"

The door to Sanders's office opened and a man walked in, holding out a badge at chest height. Not too tall, sandy hair, black horn rim glasses, cheap shiny black suit. "Mr. McCullin? Mr. Sanders McCullin?"

Sanders couldn't make the badge out. "Yes. Yes, I am. As I told my secretary to tell you, however, I'm very busy this after—"

"Mr. McCullin, my name is Darrell Butler. Special Agent Darrell Butler, of the New York FBI office. I understand you know a certain Ms. Caroline Lake. We're making inquiries about a man she's seeing, who is currently going by the name Jack Prescott. He is a very dangerous criminal. We have reason to believe that this man has committed war crimes and that he has stolen a fortune in diamonds in Africa."

Sanders sat back down, staring at the man, feeling hope unfurl in his chest once again. "Please," he said to the FBI agent. "Have a seat."

Jack was feeling rattled, so he went to tighten the pipes under the downstairs bathroom sink while Caroline cooked. The pipes were leaking, dripping water all over the place and, all in all, he thought her bathroom sink was a pretty good metaphor for his life. He was dripping too, leaking emotions all over the place.

Jack hardly recognized himself, it was like he was losing bits of himself by the wayside.

Caroline was messing with his head and tripping up his heart. In all these years, while dreaming of her and—in the most private recesses of his head—dreaming of bedding her, it never occurred to him that being with Caroline was going to change him in any fundamental way.

Jack knew himself and was very comfortable with who he was. He'd had a hard life, and it had taught him self-reliance and coolness and a great deal of emotional detachment in whatever he did.

Caroline had blown all that right out of the water.

His head had nearly exploded when he'd seen that fucker McCullin manhandling her. It was a good thing he hadn't known that he was the handsome blond boy Ben had seen through the windows that Christmas Eve long ago. He'd spent the past twelve years hating that boy, wondering whether he was the man Caroline would marry and have children with.

Even without knowing who he was, Jack had gone haywire inside. Another minute and he'd have shattered the guy's arm. The rage in his head had been so loud he knew he was capable of killing the man, which would have landed him in jail. Once in the slammer, he could kiss Caroline good-bye, literally, not to mention spending the next twenty-five years of his life behind bars.

It was only Caroline's hand on his arm that had pulled him back from the brink.

And just now, coming in. If he'd been paying attention, he'd have seen the tampering around the lock from the driveway. Instead, he almost missed it. That *never* happened. He was always security-conscious and had a sixth and even seventh sense for breaches of security.

So he lay on his back under the sink in Caroline's chilly little downstairs bathroom, feeling good about stopping the leaky sink, tightening the bolts fastening the toilet bowl to the floor and repairing the showerhead, all the while wishing he could fix himself, get himself back to the way he'd been BC—before Caroline—cold, businesslike, detached.

Caroline stuck her beautiful head into the doorway and smiled at him. It was like being struck by lightning.

"Dinner's ready, Jack," she said, and walked back to the kitchen. His eyes tracked her every step of the way, watching the way her shiny hair bounced on her shoulders, how her hips swayed slightly, listening to the light sound of her heels on the marble floor echoing the beat of his heart.

A faint scent of roses hung in the air.

Jack rubbed his chest again, where it hurt. Fuck, maybe he should see a cardiologist.

After the FBI agent left, Sanders sat very still at his desk, staring at his hands.

The office was quiet. He employed an administrative secretary, two legal secretaries and two interns. Everyone had long since gone, knocking off early due to the bad weather. He was alone in his office and with his thoughts.

Sanders was very aware that he'd just been handed a second chance with Caroline, but the next few steps had to be handled very carefully.

The FBI Special Agent had his own agenda and his own priorities and they had nothing whatsoever to do with getting Caroline Lake back together with Sanders McCullin.

Special Agent Butler had been very clear on that. He'd also been clear that he didn't want interference from Sanders. Butler had wanted some information and had warned Sanders to keep away, something Sanders had no intention of doing, not when it was a question of getting Caroline back.

When the fuck did she start going out with this guy—this Jack Prescott or whatever his name was? It must have been a very recent affair because just last week Sanders had seen Jenna, and she hadn't said anything about Caroline going out with someone.

It just went to show that Caroline didn't know how to manage her life. She didn't listen to him when he'd told her to put Toby in a home, she didn't listen to him when he told her to sell Greenbriars and now she'd hooked up with a criminal.

Instinctively, Sanders knew that this would be wonderful ammunition when they got married. Whenever she questioned his judgment, he had big howitzers full of ammo to pull out. *Yeah? And who fucked a mass murderer?*

She'd shut up and do what he said, guaranteed.

The past twenty-four hours had given him some startling revelations about himself. He'd been dancing around Caroline for years. He'd fucked other women, sure, hell—he was a man, wasn't he? But she'd always been in the back of his mind, and he knew he'd been waiting for just the right moment to come. That moment was now, without any interference from her family.

He'd also discovered that he very much liked having the upper hand with her. It was an aspect of himself that had never come to the fore with other women. His women were savvy and good fucks. He'd never wanted much more from them than a good time in bed and maybe some networking for his job. By the time he might start caring about them obeying him, he'd moved on.

But it turned out he liked dominance, a lot.

Dominance.

Caroline needed dominance. She needed a strong hand. And to his amazement and enjoyment, when she resisted, it turned him on, powerfully. So when they were married, he could look forward to an obedient wife, dependent on him for money and reluctant to cross him because she'd fucked the wrong guy. Sanders would never let her forget it.

Sanders looked at the visiting card Special Agent Butler had left and at the number on the bottom.

Sanders was a careful lawyer, used to checking all his facts. He rarely lost arguments, and he rarely lost cases because of that aspect of his character.

He picked up the phone and punched in the number. The phone was picked up on the second ring. "New York FBI Field Office, how may I help you?" a female voice with a heavy Hispanic accent said.

"Yes, I'd like to speak with Special Agent Darrell Butler please."

"I'm sorry sir, but Special Agent Butler is out of the office. Can I take a message?"

"No, thank you."

Sanders put the receiver down gently in its cradle, smiling.

Yes, things had taken a wonderful turn.

Fifteen

"Eat." Jack frowned at Caroline's plate, where she'd been picking at the same slice of chicken for the past half hour, looking more and more worried.

She'd prepared a fabulous dinner. Lentil soup, sourdough bread, chicken whosis—an Italian name like terrazzo only different—a four-bean salad and apple crumble. She'd cooked enough for four people, and he'd eaten for three and a half. The other half was on her plate, and she was pushing pieces around listlessly.

Caroline looked up from where she'd been watching her fork tines make interesting little patterns in the chicken breast. "Do you—do you think he went into the kitchen, too?"

Jack didn't have to ask who "he" was. "He" was the shithead who'd invaded her home and made her pale and shaky. "Probably not. Kitchens aren't usually where people keep valuables, though they should. Precisely because burglars don't check kitchens. Why?"

Caroline shrugged, the tines now making patterns on the plate with the beans. "I don't know. It's just—" She watched her fork shift a green bean from one side of the plate to the other. "Ever since I've been taking boarders, I'm sort of used to the idea of sharing my space. But the bedroom and the kitchen are *mine*, and I hate the thought of someone pawing through my things."

Jack speared a good bite of the chicken and held it in front of her mouth. "Well, then, it's a good thing that after tomorrow no one else is going to break into here. Now open wide."

He slipped the bite into her mouth and waited for her to chew. By the time she'd swallowed, he had another square of chicken at the end of his fork. "Another one."

She grimaced, but ate it. The third time she turned her head. "I'm really not hungry, Jack."

Frustrated, he put his fork down. He wanted to make her eat, but he found he couldn't use any form of force with her.

Caroline was looking down at the tabletop, a long lock of shiny hair falling forward over her face. Jack pushed the lock back with his forefinger, then lifted her chin so that she had to look at him.

"That's not all that's bothering you, is it?"

She shook her head, the movement enough to send a faint fragrance of roses over to him, rising over the sharp smells of the food. "No."

"This is about your—friend, isn't it? You were in shock this afternoon. You weren't expecting that, were you?"

"God, no." Caroline looked up at him, chin quivering. Her eyes welled, but she blinked back tears furiously. His heart gave a tight little squeeze at how she willed the tears back. He suspected she'd done a lot of that over the years. "I've known Sanders for . . . heavens, forever. I think I told you we dated in our teens. I thought I knew him inside out. He's got his good points. He's intelligent and good at his job. He knows a lot about art and design. He's a decent dinner companion, and he's fun if you want a relaxing night out. He's got excellent taste in films and theater. You just can't expect too much from him. He's vain and selfish, and he'll always look out for Sanders McCullin first, but then there's his charming side to make up for that. That's okay because I know him well enough not to expect more than he can give. Today just—" She shook her head. "I had no idea."

Jack placed his hand over hers. She needed to talk it out, and he was more than willing to give her the space to do it in. "Tell me," he said quietly.

Caroline looked him full in the face, eyes wide. "He liked it when I fought him." She shook her head, slowly, clearly still stunned at the idea. "It excited him. It was . . . God, it was unmistakable. At first, when he tried to kiss me, I thought all I had to do was push him away, so I did. Or tried to. He just held me closer. It's not—" She shook her head again. "Most women have experiences like that. Someone you don't want wants you. And usually it doesn't take that much to make them back down once you make it clear you're not interested. And I thought it would be like that with Sanders—just push away, and he'd stop. But he didn't. And when I started fighting back hard . . ." She drew a deep breath. "He got an erection. It was *horrible.*"

Son of a bitch. Maybe Jack had been wrong. Maybe he *should* have killed the fucker.

McCullin had punched a hole in Caroline's self-confidence, in her sense of herself as a woman. Jack wanted to give a measure of control back to her, repair the torn fabric.

"I know guys like that," he said, as he held Caroline's hand. "It's like there's something fundamentally wrong inside them, like there's something broken. Because, honey, a normal man does *not* get excited at the idea or the feel of a woman who's frightened or in pain. Trust me on this one. The military attracts a lot of guys like that fu—like McCullin. They like the idea of the power trip and of being trained to dominate physically.

"Luckily, the military also has ways to screen men like that out, and they do that because they never work out as soldiers. Those kinds of men are broken inside in other ways, too, not just sexually. They don't know how to work in teams, which is what a good Army is all about. They don't take orders well, and they often have an inflated idea of their own abilities, which can be disastrous in combat. So a lot of them get weeded out. Not all of them, but most of them." He held her chin and bent and kissed her softly, just a touch of his lips to hers. "The guy's a sick fuck, and he's not worth an instant of your time or your worry."

Caroline gave a soft laugh. "Actually, *you're* the one who should be worrying. Didn't he threaten to sue you? I warn you, Sanders is a really good lawyer. I hope you won't have any trouble because of me."

She'd been manhandled by someone she considered a friend, had had her home broken into, and she was worried about *him*. "Let me worry about that." He reached out with his thumb and erased the little frown line between her brows. "He doesn't scare me, believe me."

"No, I imagine he doesn't. And I never thanked you for showing up right in the nick of time, did I? Just like in the movies. Jack Prescott to the rescue. Thanks."

"You're welcome." Jack's voice was suddenly hoarse, and he had to clear his throat to get the words out.

She was holding the stem of her wineglass, twirling it, watching the deep red wine climb the walls of the crystal, lost in thought.

The hand holding the stem was delicate, as was her wrist. He could see the tendons working as she twirled the stem. Everything about her was delicate, even fragile. Tonight she didn't have her usual rose under ivory color—she was pale and looked tired.

Much as she tried to build little havens for herself from the outside world in her home and her shop, the sharp-toothed outside world had come roaring in to take a big bite out of her in both her havens.

The world was not kind to the kindhearted.

Jack's heart simply rolled over in his chest.

It was almost as if he were seeing her for the very first time. Caroline had been in his head for most of his life, it seemed. A mysterious, otherworldly beauty, unreachable, unapproachable. Someone to fantasize about while jerking off in lonely places. A unicorn. A myth.

But this—this woman was *real*. This woman with the gallant, warm heart wasn't a myth, but a real flesh-and-blood woman. Strong, yet vulnerable. Steadfast, yet fragile.

She was also the bravest person he'd ever known.

If you'd asked him, Jack would have said he was brave. Christ, he was a soldier. He'd been in more firefights than he could count. He went into battle each and every time fully prepared to die. He didn't back down from anything, man or beast.

Didn't mean jack shit. When the Colonel had fallen ill, *that* was when his courage had been tested. It had been three weeks of utter and total hell. He'd spent all the time he could at the hospital, wishing he could escape each and every second. Watching the Colonel die, inch by inch, watching him become weaker, day by day, had taxed his courage to the maximum.

Jack had gone home every evening, gone down to the basement and worked out at the punching bag for an hour a night, and it barely took the edge off his desperation.

At the end, he could barely look at the Colonel. He was ashamed of it still, but he couldn't stand to see that emaciated face, the skin paper-thin and almost bloodless. The tubes running in and out, the gasps for breath.

When the nurses came to change his bed linen or give him his medication, Jack took the excuse to escape, if only down to the canteen for a cup of what they laughingly called coffee. And each time he came back, he stood outside the door of the Colonel's hospital room, sweaty hand flat against the door, willing himself to push it open. It sometimes took him half an hour finally to get the courage to go back in and help his adoptive father die.

It had nearly killed him, and it had lasted three weeks.

Caroline had done that for her brother for six fucking *years*, while laboring under a terrible financial burden.

She deserved the Congressional Medal of Honor.

She was a woman in a million.

Caroline could be hurt at any time, be taken from him at any moment. The world is a big, cold and cruel place. No one knew that better than Jack. No one knew better than he how brutal and savage life could be. One swipe of the reptilian hand of fate, and Caroline could be wiped off the face of the earth in an instant, shattered and forever gone to him.

The beauty and goodness in her could vanish as quickly as a candle being snuffed out.

This woman was incredibly precious, light in darkness, grace in sorrow.

At that moment, Jack realized, with a sense of truth that went deep as bone, strong as blood, that Caroline held his heart forever, and that his mission in life was to keep her safe and happy, bring a smile to her face and the rose blush back to her cheeks.

As long as he drew breath, he would make sure no harm came to her that he could prevent. But even more than protecting her, he wanted her to be her truest self. Nothing could take her back to the carefree, privileged girl she'd been, but by God, he wanted the woman he'd caught glimpses of during the weekend back. A charmer, good-natured, secure in her beauty without being run by it. Well-read, with a good sense of humor, even earthy. That woman was Caroline, the essence of Caroline, when life wasn't beating her down with a big stick.

Jack couldn't go back in time and undo today, but he sure as hell could drown her in pleasure at the end of it.

"Come," he said suddenly, standing up.

She looked puzzled when Jack placed two clean stem glasses and the half-empty bottle of excellent wine they'd been having for dinner in her hands, then yelped as he scooped her up in his arms.

"Where—" she began, then held her tongue. Where they were going was very clear as he headed up the stairs.

"I thought we'd have a nightcap up here." Jack smiled in her eyes as he carried her along the upper-story landing to her bedroom. *Their* bedroom now.

He didn't switch on the light in the bedroom, but the light on the landing filtered in. It was just enough to wrap them in the intimacy of darkness, yet let him see her. He needed to be able to watch her as he loved her. He knew her body well enough by now to know that he could tell by touch what was happening to her, but he wanted to see it, too.

Nothing in the world was as exciting as watching Caroline's eyelids drooping with arousal, as if keeping her eyes open was too great an effort. Or watching her skin turn an even deeper rose where he touched her, or the barely perceptible beat of her speeded-up heart over her left breast.

God, it all turned him on. Everything about her was designed to make his cock swell, his heart beat faster, his blood rise. The sight of her, the sound of her, the feel of her, the smell of her—everything kept him in a state of semiarousal whenever he was near her or even just thought of her.

He wasn't in semiarousal now, it was the full-blown deal. Jesus, good thing he'd bought himself another pair of tight jeans because he needed to keep it in his pants for a while.

Tonight was a night for romance, and romance meant foreplay, though it wasn't what he was good at. Once he got a woman naked, sex was only a few minutes away. He wasn't used to pacing himself or holding back.

Tonight would be a crash course in control because tonight was about her.

Jack sat her on the side of the bed, poured her half a glass of wine and put it in her hand. He poured himself a glass and clinked it to hers. The pure ring of crystal blossomed in the room.

"To us." He drank, watching her over the glass.

"To us." Caroline smiled, swirled the wine around, sniffed deeply, then sipped. *That's my girl,* he thought. It's all about the senses tonight.

Enjoy.

He sure intended to.

Jack dropped to a crouch, wincing a little as his cock rubbed up against his jeans. Fuck, it hurt. Maybe he should just go naked around Caroline, spare himself the pain.

He slowly slipped her right shoe off, then the left, getting a kick out of looking at her pretty feet and her toenail polish gleaming creamy pink through the stockings.

In the quiet room, he undressed her, slowly, like unwrapping a wonderful Christmas present to himself. Stockings, skirt, sweater, panties, bra and there she was, naked, just for him.

His cock pulsed painfully. His heart pulsed painfully.

Her ankles were slender, he was easily able to encircle her ankles with his hands. "You have such beautiful feet," he whispered, raising his eyes to hers.

They were silver in this light, rimmed by a darker blue. "Thank you," she whispered back.

He leaned forward, running his hands from her ankles up the outside of her thighs, over her hips, nuzzling her soft little belly.

He leaned forward a little, his shoulders forcing her knees apart.

"Lie down, honey," he said, his voice a little hoarse. "This will take a while."

That brought a smile to her lips. She ran a hand over his hair, then slowly lay down, one arm covering her eyes.

Fine. She didn't need to see. She only had to feel.

She was so heart-stoppingly beautiful naked, hips sharply outlined, belly concave, legs dangling over the edge of the bed, completely open to him.

Jack rarely went down. He didn't have any objections to it, but he wasn't wild for it, either.

Right now, though, his head was filled with the thought of kissing her there—right where his cock would go, but later. A gentle movement of his hands, and she opened her thighs wider, and Jack simply couldn't tear his eyes from her. Pale pink, perfect flesh surrounded by a soft thatch of red-gold hair.

To give her a sense of intimacy, he hadn't turned on the light; but he had excellent night vision. He could see everything, perfectly. The long, pearly, silky slide of her thighs, gently rounded hips, small firm breasts.

He parted her with his thumbs, like unfurling a flower. He'd done this before, but it felt like the first time. It had never been Caroline whose legs he held apart, whose delicate flesh he caressed, warm and wet.

He kissed her, exactly as he would her mouth. She tasted like the sea, spicy and warm. She was panting lightly, the sound loud in the quiet room, a little moan with each pass of his tongue. Jack closed his eyes a moment and concentrated on her—on the moisture welling out of her, on the way her thighs shook slightly, on the way her stomach muscles clenched when he entered her with his tongue.

"Jack," she murmured, drawing in a sharp breath when he licked her more deeply. He angled for a deeper taste of her and felt the walls of her little cunt move, a sharp contraction.

Oh, yes.

Silky soft, wet. Tasting of the sea, smelling like roses and sex. He lapped and licked and completely lost all sense of himself, kneeling before her, like a supplicant kneeling before his goddess.

When she came, it was with strong little tugs of her cunt against his tongue, the most amazing feeling.

"Jack." There was need there in her voice.

Caroline needing something . . . he was programmed to respond. Though part of him wanted to spend the next ten thousand years kneeling by the bed, loving her with his mouth, the rest of him needed to be in her.

A second later, he'd entered her in one long stroke, both of them moaning with relief. He bent to kiss her, and the rest of her moans were lost in his mouth.

The strokes were long, deep, lazy, the entire world reduced to the woman under him and to where they were joined.

There were no thoughts possible in this enchanted land of Caroline—just sensations. The warmth and softness of her, the wet welcome he could feel along every inch of his cock, her arms and legs holding him tightly.

Strong as he was, he could never break her hold on him.

For the first time in his life, Jack lost all sense of himself. He felt like he'd entered her skin, her head, pulling out exactly what she wanted. When she came, he prolonged it, changing the angle of his thrusts, until her head fell back over his arm and her arms and legs fell back on the bed.

That was when he took his own pleasure, hard and fast. She was wet and soft enough to take him fully and—oh my God—when he came, he exploded with his entire body, from his toes to the top of his head.

He collapsed on her, wrung out, a completely different man, Caroline filling his head. She'd been violated today, but he'd make it better, and from this moment on, nothing would ever touch her.

He nuzzled against her ear, head lying on her hair, the scent of roses rising sharply in his nostrils.

"After the security system goes up, we'll do some decorating together. Paint the kitchen and the bedroom. And we can paint the dining room yellow again. You'd like that, wouldn't you? You won't recognize the house when we're done." His voice was slurred with sleepiness and the aftereffects of sex.

He kissed her temple and went out like a light.

Caroline lay on her back, muscles lax with pleasure, inner muscles still so hypersensitive from the powerful orgasm that she couldn't move her thighs without feeling a jolt of pleasure-pain.

Her body was sending a huge packet of powerful messages of joy to her head, but it was like feeling something happening far away. Her face was numb with shock. Jack tried to move her into his arms, but she turned herself into a deadweight, as if fast-asleep, and could feel his decision to let her be, to let her have her rest. He pulled the blanket up over her shoulders and settled down himself, so close she could feel his heat, but without touching her, asleep in an instant.

If he touched her again, she didn't know what she would do. Run maybe. Scream. Her jaw muscles tightened.

The meal and the wine lay curdled in her roiling stomach. She had to swallow heavily against the bile rising up her throat.

Her instinct told her to get up out of bed and run—but run where?

Her head ached as she stared dry-eyed up at the dark ceiling, wondering whether some answers lay up there in the shadows, knowing there were no answers at all. Knowing that either she was insane or Jack had been lying to her all along.

Somehow the huge man lying next to her, who'd made love

to her for hours, who had been inside her body, who'd given her such mind-blowing pleasure, somehow he wasn't who he said he was.

It would be wonderful to forget what he'd said. She'd found herself a magnificent lover, sexy as hell, who'd done nothing but help her since he'd arrived. Courteous, gorgeous, fantastic in bed, focused completely on her.

Rich, too, unless Jenna had played a trick on her.

Total dreamboat, Jenna would have said in high school.

But his words ran round and round in her head, in an endless refrain, mocking her. Words that shifted the ground beneath her feet and made her doubt her own senses. Words that made no sense at all coming out of his mouth. Out of the mouth of a man she'd met for the first time four days ago.

We can paint the dining room yellow again, he'd said. *You'd like that, wouldn't you?*

Yes, of course she'd like that. A nice canary yellow instead of puke green. Who wouldn't?

It was very thoughtful of him to think of it.

Except, of course, the last time the dining room had been painted yellow was over six years ago.

Sixteen

When Sanders walked into First Page, a very bad day suddenly turned worse.

Very few customers had showed up all morning and those few were, she suspected, dying from the cold instead of dying for a good read. By eleven o'clock she'd racked up a grand total of $27.15 in sales, her second-worst day. The worst had been Friday, with a grand sales total of zero.

Still, maybe it wasn't a bad thing that the weather was still so bad people would rather reread their old books than drop by First Page. She found it hard to pay attention to the few people who actually ventured inside the shop. They'd talk, and she'd suddenly zone out, then have to scurry to apologize when it was clear she hadn't been listening. So, all in all, it was a good thing she was mostly alone with her thoughts.

Except for the fact that she *was* alone with her thoughts.

No matter which way she looked at it—upside down, inside out—Caroline couldn't figure out how Jack could know that the dining room had been painted yellow six years ago.

As if it were the first trickle from a cracked dam, now she felt the cold floodwaters of doubt rise in her mind, sickening her. Besides the color of the dining room, she now realized with hindsight that he seemed to have an uncanny knowledge of Greenbriars. That first night, he hadn't even wanted to be accompanied up to his room. He seemed to know where the tools were kept, where the wine cellar was, even—that first night—where her bedroom was. He'd said he recognized it by her smell, but it didn't ring true.

He'd known.

How had he known?

And, most horrible of all, how could he at times look faintly familiar to her?

She hadn't slept all night, had simply stared at the ceiling, mind whirling restlessly and uselessly, until the black outside her window had slowly turned steely gray.

Jack realized that something was wrong. There was no way she could hide her upset from those perceptive dark eyes, and she'd had to pretend the onset of flu to distract him. And then she'd had to stop him from bundling her back into bed with hot tea and seven hundred blankets.

They'd fought about her coming in to work, but she'd been adamant, threatening to drive herself in if he wouldn't. That had shut him up, and he'd driven her in, tight-lipped and silent.

Fine. Let him be angry. His anger allowed her space and

time. She needed to know who he really was. Tonight. They had to talk tonight.

Maybe he'd been too good to be true. Maybe, in her loneliness and grief, she'd conjured the perfect lover out of thin air. Simply invented him.

The bell rang over the door. Another customer. She should be happy, but right now all she wanted was to be alone with her thoughts. Still, customers meant money, so she pasted a smile on her face and walked toward the door.

"Oh." Caroline stopped when she saw Sanders. He was with another man, who was standing slightly behind him. "Sanders," she said coolly. What did he want? To apologize? Today was *not* a good day for him to show up. "I don't think this is a good idea. I think perhaps you'd better leave."

"Now, Caroline, don't be like that. You haven't heard what I have to say."

Something had happened to him. The crushed, beaten Sanders had disappeared, and he was back to his old assured self—elegant and in control. He even had that slight smile that looked like a smirk. It did not endear him to her.

"I'm sorry, Sanders, I'm very busy. Maybe some other time."

He held his expensive gloves in one hand and looked slowly around the bookshop. The very empty bookshop. He took his time and finally brought his gaze around to her.

"I think you're going to want to hear what I have to say. Or rather, what this gentleman has to say." He stepped to the side, and Caroline saw the other man clearly now.

He was of medium height, with short sandy hair, big oversized, unfashionable glasses. Whippy rather than thin. Shiny, black, ill-fitting polyester suit, white shirt, shiny black tie. Completely nondescript, except for his eyes. They were light blue, flat, cold.

"Ma'am," he said, and flipped a leather holder open to reveal a brass badge. "Special Agent Darrell Butler. FBI. New York Field Office."

FBI?

Was this Sanders's idea of a joke? Or had he actually called in the FBI because Jack had thrown him out of the shop yesterday? That was going way too far, even for Sanders.

And shame on the FBI for even giving Sanders the time of day. Didn't they have anything better to do? Crazed terrorists were plotting day and night to blow people and buildings up, and what do they do? Fly across the country because Sanders had had his hair mussed and his feelings hurt.

Caroline rounded on Sanders. "Listen, I know you said you'd sue, but calling in the FBI is just insane. You should know better than that. It's a totally overblown reaction to what happened yesterday. This is—"

"Ma'am," the FBI Agent—*Special* Agent—interrupted. "I think you need to sit down. This isn't about Mr. McCullin." He shot Sanders a hostile glance. "Actually, Mr. McCullin shouldn't even be here. But never mind. We need to talk somewhere, Ms. Lake."

He wants to talk to me? Bewildered, Caroline led the Special Agent to her desk at the back of the room, separated from the rest of the bookshop by a counter stacked with books.

Caroline sat behind the desk, and the Special Agent sat across from her. There were only two chairs in her office, but Sanders went and dragged another chair from out front.

The FBI agent ignored him totally. He placed his briefcase on his knees and took out a folder. He didn't open it, just set it on his lap and placed his hand over it, as if protecting it.

"Ms. Lake. I understand you know someone who calls himself Jack Prescott. How long have you known him?"

"Why, I just met—" She stopped suddenly, frowning. "What do you mean—*calls himself* Jack Prescott? Isn't that his name?"

Butler opened his briefcase and slid a photograph over her desktop, facing her. It was an enlarged snapshot of Jack in uniform, full face, the kind used as military ID. He looked younger, with a buzz cut and some kind of beret.

"Is *that* the man you know as Jack Prescott, ma'am?" He thumped the photograph with a rough forefinger.

Caroline swallowed and looked up into cold pale blue eyes. "I have no reason to think that he is anyone else. What is this about? How can this possibly be your business?"

"Just answer the question," he snapped. "Is that the man you know as Jack Prescott or is he not?"

"Yes."

"And when did you meet him?"

He'd left his badge open, and the brass reflected the ceiling light. It sat there with the weight of the U.S. government behind it, the shiniest thing in the room. Caroline watched it, as if it could yield up answers.

"Ms. Lake." He didn't say anything else. He didn't have to.

Her throat felt tight. "I met Jack—Mr. Prescott last Friday. He'd just got into town and needed a place to stay. I take in boarders."

"If he just got into town, how did he know that you have rooms to let?"

"The cab driver told him, on the way in from the airport."

"What time did he arrive in your shop?"

"Around four, I think. I was thinking of closing up early because the weather was so bad. Nobody had come in all afternoon. He was actually the only person who came into the shop that afternoon."

"What did he have with him?"

"I beg your pardon?"

"What did he have? What was he carrying?"

"Oh. Well, he had a duffel bag and a suitcase."

"Were they heavy?"

"I have no idea. He carried them in and carried them out."

"Was he armed?"

Caroline's mouth closed with a snap. Yes, he'd been armed, though at the time, she hadn't known it. She would never have taken an armed man into her home. The silence stretched out.

"Ms. Lake. Answer the question."

"Is Jack being accused of something?"

"Just answer the question. You can do it here, or in Seattle. Your choice."

It felt like a betrayal—of a man she wasn't sure she trusted anymore. Still, Caroline found it hard to tell the truth. "Yes," she said finally. "He was armed. I didn't know that at the time."

"What kind of weapon was he carrying?"

She stared at him. "Are you joking?"

He stared back, gaze flat, utterly impersonal. No, he wasn't joking.

"Mr.—Special Agent Butler, I know absolutely nothing about guns. It was big and black, that's all I can say."

"How do you know he was armed?"

"Someone broke into my house yesterday." Or rather, Jack told her someone had broken into her house. Caroline *hated* this, hated second-guessing herself, second-guessing and doubting him. Hated the feeling that she'd been making love—and falling in love—with a fraud. "I found out then that he was—was carrying a weapon. Until then, I had no idea."

"See, Caroline," Sanders said suddenly. "You should have known better. You've never been a good judge of people. This should teach you a lesson in trusting perfect strangers."

Butler didn't turn his head. "Mr. McCullin, one more word out of you and I will have you arrested for obstruction of justice, is that clear?"

"Sorry." Sanders tried to look chastened, but it wasn't working very well. He sat back in his chair and crossed his arms.

"Now, Ms. Lake. Did he say where he'd come from?"

Caroline was starting to realize how very little Jack had said about himself. "Well, he said he'd been in Afghanistan. And he said that his father had died very recently, in North Carolina. I don't know whether he flew in all the way from

Afghanistan or whether he'd stopped off in North Carolina."

"Our records show him as flying in from Africa. From Freetown."

"The capital of Sierra Leone?" Caroline asked. "What on earth was he doing there? He didn't say anything about Africa."

"No? That's probably understandable, seeing as how he and three other mercenaries massacred a village of women and children."

"That's a lie!" The words came from deep inside her. She stood up suddenly. "I refuse to listen—"

The Special Agent didn't raise his voice, but then he didn't have to. "Sit down, Ms. Lake, or I will haul *you* in for obstruction of justice. Sit!"

She sat and folded her hands on the table to keep them from trembling. "There is no way Jack Prescott could do something like that."

He didn't even answer, simply stared at her out of his cold eyes.

"Have you been watching the news over the weekend?"

What she'd been doing over the weekend was no business of his. "I fail to see—"

"Answer the question, Ms. Lake," he interrupted in a hard voice, "or I will take you in to the Seattle office and have you questioned there, which would be much less pleasant for you. Would you like that? Your choice."

"I—no, um, to answer your question, I haven't been watching the news over the Christmas holiday." She'd been too busy with Jack and besides—now that she thought of it—both her radio and her TV set had been on the blink. It was only then that it occurred to her how unusual it was for both the radio and the TV to die on the same weekend. "I don't really see what that has to do with anything."

"It's been all over TV," Sanders said, leaning forward. "I don't know how you could have missed it."

The FBI agent shot Sanders a look that had Sanders lifting his hands—*sorry*—and sitting back. The agent turned back to her. Caroline kept herself from shivering by force of will. The man had the coldest eyes she'd ever seen.

"Ms. Lake, it appears you are unaware of the fact that six days ago, four U.S. military contractors who worked for a U.S. private security company called ENP Security massacred a village of women and children in Sierra Leone and made off with a fortune in uncut diamonds. Sierra Leonean soldiers appeared at the end and killed three of the military contractors. One escaped with the diamonds."

What a horrible story. Maybe her TV and the radio had died out of compassion, deciding to spare her this news. "I'm sorry. What does that have to do with me?"

"The man who escaped was Vincent Deaver, the leader of the military contractors. You know him as Jack Prescott. He's a very dangerous man, and we need your help in bringing him in."

A sudden gust of gelid air burst into the shop as a customer walked in. Caroline heard the ping of the bell as if from a great distance. Laurel Holly, the mayor's wife. She had to do something, get up, go to Laurel, get away from this terrible man. She placed her hands flat on the table, but somehow she couldn't. Something was wrong with her legs.

Sanders got up immediately and went to Laurel. Caroline heard them murmuring, then Laurel left and Sanders turned the OPEN sign around to CLOSED and walked back, never taking his eyes from her face. "No one will bother us now."

He had the most awful look—triumphant and self-satisfied. Happy. Happy at the thought that she might have been sleeping with a mass murderer.

If there had been a tiny little something inside her, a little softness for Sanders, for old times' sake, it died right then and there. He wanted Jack to be a monster, a war criminal. It made him happy.

Well, too bad, because she didn't believe it, not for a moment.

Jack—a mass murderer? *Jack?* A man who'd kill for diamonds? It wasn't possible. She refused to believe it. Her body didn't.

The man who'd held her so gently, so self-controlled he constantly reined himself in so he wouldn't hurt her, not even inadvertently, in the throes of passion. That man wasn't a murderer.

Of course, he was a soldier. Undoubtedly he'd killed, time and time again, in the line of duty.

Caroline shivered violently, as if her heart had suddenly frozen. The taste of the breakfast she'd choked down this morning was in her mouth. She clamped her jaw shut as bile tickled her throat.

Never mind that she'd had her doubts about Jack. They'd been more along the lines of how he knew her home so well, not whether he might be a monster.

She looked the Special Agent straight in the face. "That's insane. Jack's not a mass murderer! And he wasn't in Africa, he was in Afghanistan this winter. You've got the wrong man."

Agent Butler slid another photograph across the table. Caroline crossed her arms, body language rejecting what she was seeing in the photograph, and stared straight ahead. The agent was a good starer, better than she was. His gaze was steady and unrelenting, and with a shudder and a sigh, Caroline gave in and dropped her eyes to the photograph. Just a flicker of a gaze, but it was enough.

The photograph was very clear.

A slightly leaner Jack, with several days' growth of beard, in camouflage, holding a big black gun. Dense, blindingly green foliage in the background, a line of wooden huts with tin roofs, African children playing in the dust, African soldiers standing guard.

There was a time stamp in white at the bottom. 11:21 A.M., December 21.

"That's not Afghanistan," the FBI agent said.

"No," Caroline whispered. "It's not."

She wanted to pull the photograph closer for a better look, but she couldn't. She was hugging herself, deeply chilled in the core of her being.

"That was shot by a UNOMSIL soldier in Freetown, seven days ago, just before Deaver headed into the hinterland for a village called Obuja, where there were rumors swirling around about a sackful of diamonds. He caught a pirogue going upriver to Obuja. Twenty-four hours after that photograph was taken, everyone in Obuja was dead, and he had found the diamonds. The UN is still looking for him there, but we'd got word that he'd flown back to the States."

Caroline had to cough to loosen her throat. She licked dry lips as she counted the days. "But—but that would mean that he flew from Africa directly here." She stopped, her throat hurting. "But . . . *why*. Why come *here*? It's halfway around the world. It doesn't make sense. Why here?"

"To see you," Agent Butler said.

The quiet words seemed to fill the room, bounce around the walls, echo in her head. It took her several minutes to process the words. He didn't hurry her, just watched her closely.

The tea she'd just had threatened to come up, and Caroline swallowed heavily.

"I—I'm afraid I don't understand. He flew straight back from Africa to see *me*? Jack Prescott didn't know me. I met him for the first time on Christmas Eve. He can't possibly have flown something like ten thousand miles for me."

This time there were two photocopies slid across the table. Caroline didn't look at them. Didn't want to look at them. Special Agent Butler tapped first one, then the other.

"He knew you all right. These photographs were found in his backpack, which he abandoned at the village. They were faxed to me by a UNOMSIL sergeant. Look at them, please, Ms. Lake. He came here for you."

Caroline held his eyes, completely unable to read them. Finally, with a feeling that nothing would ever be the same, she looked down, then looked away immediately. A cold fist gripped her heart and squeezed.

"You found those in *Africa*?"

"Yes, ma'am."

Caroline hugged herself more tightly—cold, miserable, stomach roiling. She heard a vague whistling sound in her ears and wondered whether she was going to faint.

"Do you recognize these photographs, Ms. Lake?"

Caroline couldn't speak. She could barely breathe.

"Ms. Lake?"

Sanders leaned forward. "Caroline, that's your high-school photo, don't you recognize it? And the other one—"

Special Agent Butler spoke without turning his head or taking his eyes from hers.

"Shut up. Sir." His gaze was fierce and unblinking, focused tightly on her. "Ms. Lake, I'm asking you for the second time—do you recognize those photographs? And don't even try lying because I can drag you to the Seattle office and make you swear all of this under oath, and you know what the penalty for lying under oath is."

Caroline nodded jerkily. "Yes," she whispered. "I do."

"So what are those photographs of?"

"Me." Her voice came out thin and reedy, almost a wheeze. "One is my sophomore high-school portrait. The other is—is a photograph cut out of a local newspaper. Of me at a piano recital. I must have been—what? Sixteen? How on earth could those photographs be in Jack Prescott's possession?"

"That's precisely what I want to know from you," he said grimly. "Maybe the two of you were in it together?"

"What?" Caroline whispered, shocked.

Special Agent Butler nodded. "You could be a great alibi. Deaver couldn't have killed the villagers, stolen the diamonds, because he was with his lady love over the Christmas holidays. It makes a crazy kind of sense, because he traveled under a fake name. If we didn't have that photograph and the time stamp, well then, he could just say that he was curled up in his love nest, and who'd be the wiser?"

"Damn right," Sanders said. "Caroline, you barely escaped. Why when I think of what could have happened to you if the FBI hadn't been on this guy's trail . . . God knows he's violent enough to really hurt you. Even murder you, if he had to." He didn't look unhappy at that notion. The darker the picture of Jack, the brighter his star shone.

Caroline looked from Sanders's smug face to the bleak, cold features of the FBI agent. She felt trapped, as if the walls of her shop were closing in on her. Cold sweat beaded on her forehead, her head swirled, her chest felt tight.

A younger, happier her looked up at her from the tabletop, a mocking reminder of life's cruelties. She reached out a shaking finger to touch first Jack's photograph then the photocopy of her high-school portrait, trying to make the connection between the sunny high schooler and the dark, dangerous-looking man in the jungle fatigues.

Sanders laid his hand over hers and squeezed. She whisked her hand out from under his.

It was the last straw.

Don't touch me! The words were there in her throat, and she had to clamp her jaw closed to keep them in.

Suddenly, Caroline couldn't stay in the same room with the two men, with the photographs and with the doubts about the man she'd made love to all weekend. The man she'd fallen in love with. Was half in love with, still. If she stayed in this room one second more, she'd vomit her misery all over the floor. She shivered violently, stood up and rushed out the door.

Jack parked on the other side of Hamilton Park just as it started to snow. Didn't make any difference. He didn't mind the cold, and he needed to stretch his legs after the long day spent in his SUV driving around offices. He needed the walk across the park on the way to Caroline's shop, to clear his head.

Something was very wrong with Caroline. Jack could feel it in his bones. All day, as he'd gone about his business, he'd had the tickle of unease as a background noise in his head.

Pity, because otherwise it had been a good day, no doubt about it. An airtight security system was going up at Greenbriars tomorrow. Cost him the better part of $5,000, but it was worth it. Caroline didn't have to know how much it cost.

A fabulous property in a busy downtown building which would be just perfect for his business was for sale at a very reasonable price, and he had an appointment the day after tomorrow with the Realtor. With luck, he could incorporate and start his new business by mid-January.

His day had ended with a visit to an estate lawyer, something that had been preying on his mind. No matter what happened to him, if he dropped dead this instant, from this day on, Caroline would be taken care of. She was his sole heir, and she could live in ease from the proceeds of his estate.

Very satisfying all in all, but he couldn't relax until he cleared up what was eating Caroline. She'd been pale and silent over breakfast, looking worried and wan.

He hated that. He hated to see that look on her face. It was probably a mix of money worries, someone she considered a friend attacking her and that fucking son of a bitch breaking into her home.

Well, *that* wasn't ever going to happen again. The new security system was airtight. The only way to break into Greenbriars as of tomorrow would be to blow up the door with Semtex or fire an RPG through the living room window of Caroline's home.

His home. Soon.

The last thing he'd done in his busy day was price diamond rings. It hadn't been fun making the rounds of jewelers, but it had to be done. His head swirled with technical data. Carats, clarity, hue. He didn't give a fuck. All he knew was that he wanted something big and his on her ring finger. Big and bright and shiny enough so that it screamed *back off!* to every male who came within a hundred-foot radius of her.

He'd seen at least twenty rings that would do. Tomorrow he'd swing by again and bag one.

The irony of shopping for a diamond ring when he had a fortune in uncut diamonds in a safe-deposit box wasn't lost on him.

Not for a second, though, was he tempted to use one of

the diamonds in the cloth bag. They were tainted with blood, heartbreak and suffering. He'd never let one of them even near her. The stones would have to go as soon as he could arrange it. He wanted them out of his life and Caroline's. There was a perfect way to wipe out the bad karma, and he was sure Caroline would approve.

That idea was for later, for when she'd accepted that they were together. Were meant to be together for a lifetime.

When could he give her the engagement ring? Not today—today she was upset, tired, worried. He was going to have to work overtime at loving her tonight, not that it would be a hardship.

Maybe he'd give it a week. A week of sex and food and rest, fixing up her house, making it safe and comfortable. Put the roses back on her cheeks, wipe the worry off her face.

Yes, this time next week, he'd find out what the nicest restaurant in the area was, take her out and propose. Or take her to Seattle. Or—hell—to Aruba. That sounded about right. Some luxury resort, days in the sun, nights making love. A candlelight dinner, the ring and the promise to love her all the rest of his days.

And he'd have Caroline for the rest of his life.

The idea wouldn't leave his head once he'd planted the seed of it. Caroline—his forever. They'd have children, and he'd grow old with her by his side. It was the one thing he'd never even dared to dream, all those lonely nights thinking of her, and here he was, close enough to touch the dream.

The image filled his head so much he could see her, right before him . . .

Jack frowned. That wasn't a vision—it was Caroline, running right into the park in the middle of the fucking snowstorm. His jaws clenched. Shit, she was without a coat and had on a pair of those fancy shoes that might be good in a heated shop but were ridiculous in the snow.

His frown deepened. She was going to catch pneumonia. Right after she slipped and broke her fucking neck.

"Caroline!" he roared. "Get back in the shop before you catch your death of cold!"

She looked up, saw him and froze, panic and fear etched on her face. Then she whirled and disappeared into the shrubbery lining the path. In a second, the only thing on the path was falling snowflakes.

A sudden gust of raw easterly wind parted the snow. Jack could see all the way across the park and the street to Caroline's shop. He had only a glimpse before the snow curtain closed again, but it was enough.

Standing in the doorway was Vince Deaver.

The shock of seeing a man he'd left in custody ten thousand miles away sent him reeling.

His hands shook as he drew his weapon and checked it for ammo. It was second nature. He always had a full magazine. But he was operating on half his wits right now because the other half was scared shitless.

Vince Deaver, a man he'd watched blow kids' heads apart, was here, gunning for him, and Caroline was caught right in the middle.

Weapon in hand, crouching, Jack started circling toward Caroline.

* * *

She'd taken him completely by surprise; otherwise, she'd never have left the shop. Not alive, anyway.

Deaver raced after Caroline Lake, but a curtain of snow drifted down and enveloped her before he could get out of the shop. She could have bolted in any direction.

Deaver stood in the doorway, senses wide open. He couldn't let Caroline Lake get away. She was the key to the diamonds, and she was what would get him his revenge.

"Caroline!" a deep voice shouted from across the street. "Get back in the shop before you catch your death of cold!"

Jack Prescott! Deaver would recognize that voice anywhere. He was here! It was impossible to tell how far away he was, the snow muffled sound, but by God, he was here, Caroline Lake was here, and Deaver was so close to the diamonds he could almost smell them.

He reached into his jacket and pulled out the Beretta 92 Drake had acquired for him. The snick of the safety coming off sounded loud in the room. As did the sudden intake of breath behind him.

Fuck, he'd completely forgotten about McCullin.

"Hey!" McCullin said. "You can't fire that thing. What if you hit Caroline? Aren't there rules for you guys about using your weapon?"

"Shut up," he growled. This guy yapping in the background was distracting him. He needed to figure out where Prescott was and where the Lake woman was so he could grab her without getting shot. Prescott was damned good with his weapon.

Well, fuck, so was he.

The snow was drifting in through the open door, melting onto the shop's hardwood floor. Ordinarily, this was a bad position to be in for a firefight. No one stood in a lit doorway. But the weather was so severe, it didn't make any difference. Deaver sighted down his weapon, tracking in quarters. First quarter, blink to black, second quarter . . .

McCullin tapped him on the shoulder, hard. Hard enough to make him miss the shot if he'd been about to take it. "Put that gun away, someone might get hurt." He had the petulant voice of the rich. *Don't pull a gun, you might hurt someone.* Another sharp tap. "Did you hear me?"

There he was! There was a break in the snow, and Deaver could see Prescott. He was dressed in black and contrasted with the snow. It had been just a glimpse, but Deaver had been able to make out his outline. Deaver didn't see a weapon, but that didn't mean Prescott wasn't armed. Still, if he knew Caroline Lake was in the vicinity, it wasn't likely he'd start shooting until he knew what the situation was.

Deaver had a little window of opportunity here. He didn't want to kill Prescott—not yet at any rate. He wanted to wing him, disable him, and use the Lake woman as leverage.

Good thing he'd done some zone recon yesterday. Across the street from the bookshop was a little park. It didn't offer much coverage—just some shrubbery and a little gazebo in the middle. It was perfect. Prescott would be afraid to use his weapon, and the Lake woman would have huddled up in the center.

There he was again! Up against the big oak in the center

of the park, trying to get his bearings. Deaver bent his knees and brought his weapon up two-handed, at an angle to present as small a target as possible, ready for the next break in the snow. A heavy dump of it came, then the wind parted one of the sheets. Deaver was breathing regularly, feeling his heartbeat, waiting for the moment from one beat to the next, though at this range, he could hardly miss.

Now! A slight break in the snow. Deaver sighted . . .

A thump on his back broke his concentration just as he was gently squeezing the trigger. By the time he was able to focus again, the snow had come down like a curtain across a stage. He'd lost sight of Prescott.

Deaver twirled around, staring into McCullin's arrogant, angry face.

McCullin had a finger up, pointed at him. "Listen, I won't have you firing g—"

Without changing expression, Deaver grabbed the fuckhead by the shoulder to steady him, brought the muzzle of his Beretta up against McCullin's chest, and fired right through the heart. That petulant voice stopped instantly, the arrogant expression going blank in the space of a heartbeat.

Deaver had turned back around before the body hit the floor.

He scanned the area outside the open door. The snow was so thick he couldn't see farther than the lampposts, but he knew Prescott was out there. He wasn't going anywhere, not with Caroline Lake in the park. But where the fuck had he gone? Deaver waited in vain for another break in the snow, but it didn't come.

This wasn't working. He'd have to go straight into the kill zone.

He loped across the street, invisible in the snow, stopping behind a huge elm, listening and waiting. This was it. If he played his cards right, he'd be leaving this godforsaken frozen burg soon with $20 million and a dead enemy.

"Ms. Lake, for God's sake, come back in here! That's a murderer out there! Get away from there, for your own safety!"

Caroline heard the words, muffled by the snow, but it took her a second to realize that the FBI Agent was talking about Jack. He meant that Jack, a murderer, was in the park. That Jack could kill her.

Wasn't that precisely why she was hiding behind the gazebo? She hadn't even thought it out. She'd seen Jack's broad, dark outline and without thinking she'd darted into the bushes.

"Ms. Lake!" the agent called. "For your own safety, I must ask you to come back inside."

Yes, of course. She was out in the open with a mass murderer. A man who, moreover, had boasted that he was always armed. Actually, he hadn't boasted, he'd just said it matter-of-factly, but still. She had no doubt that he was armed right now.

For your own safety, the agent had said. *Get away.*

Jack was armed, Jack could hurt her. However painful that thought was, it was the truth. Wasn't it?

An FBI agent, ready and willing to protect her, was right there, outside her shop. All she had to do was run to him.

So why was she hunkering down behind the gazebo, cheek pressed against the splintery wooden base, hands turning blue from the cold?

The cold was so intense, it was a wonder Special Agent Butler and Jack couldn't hear her chattering teeth. She was in her shop shoes—pretty black pumps that were pathetic in this weather. They were waterlogged and stiff with the cold. The snow was already halfway up her shins, her feet lost in the cold, wet slush. She could barely feel them. If she was going to make a run for it, now was the time, before her feet froze, and she had to be carried out of the park.

She held on to the brass railing ringing the base of the circular gazebo, heart thudding. She had to run, she had to . . .

"Caroline!" Jack shouted. "Come to me!" Oh God. Caroline closed her eyes at the sound of his voice. So deep, so reassuring. She huddled more deeply into the snow. Her cheeks were wet and cold with melted snow and tears.

"Ms. Lake!" Special Agent Butler sounded closer. The voice was muffled, but by snow and not distance. "Remember what I said about Deaver! He's a killer. He'll use you as a hostage to get away. Run toward me, and I'll cover you."

"Jesus, Caroline!" Jack's deep voice cracked. "Don't believe him! *He*'s Vince Deaver. He'll kill you the way you squash a bug, and with just as much remorse. I saw him kill women and children in Africa. Stay put! I'm coming toward you."

"No!" she screamed, standing up, ready to run if he came for her. The wind was whipping ice particles in her eyes, and she had to swipe at them to be able to see for even a moment. Her hands were so cold they were clumsy as they batted at

her eyes. "Don't come near me." She sobbed the words out, tears streaming down her cheeks. "Don't come, Jack. Stay where you are."

Silence. The only sound was the wind in the trees, muffled by the snow and her own thundering heart.

Fuck!

Jack didn't dare go after Caroline. He could barely see her, behind a big round bandstand, hunkered down. But he didn't have to see her face to know that she was crying, the tears had been in her voice.

She was scared and disoriented, her head filled with Deaver's lies. None of it made any difference, what was important now was keeping her away from Deaver. If he was here, it was to use Caroline as bait for the diamonds.

Jack had no idea how Deaver had escaped from the UN soldiers and tracked Caroline down, or known enough about her to know that he'd travel to her, but here he was. Ready, willing and able to hurt Caroline or—God!—kill her.

He wouldn't kill her right away, he was too smart for that. He'd put a bullet through her kneecap or through an elbow, make her suffer.

If Jack had thought it through, he'd never have taken the fucking diamonds. He didn't want them. The diamonds weren't worth one hair on Caroline's head. If he could, he'd go straight to the bank, open the safe-deposit box and hurl them at Deaver's head. He couldn't though. If he didn't play this right, Caroline would get hurt. Maybe killed.

Jack grew cold and detached in combat. His heart rate actually slowed during firefights. He could strategize with bullets flying overhead. Not now, though. Right now he was sweaty and panicked and terrorized. Caroline was forty feet away from him and just might flee into the hands of a stone killer.

How could he think? How could he plan, make the right moves, when his head was filled with horrific visions of Caroline shot, her lifeblood seeping away into the snow? Screaming in pain with a bullet in her gut.

Jack had seen Deaver take careful aim and blow a woman's arm off at the shoulder. If he closed his eyes, he could see that on the inside of his lids, only it was Caroline in the line of fire, and it drove him crazy. His heart beat high and wild in his chest, and his weapon slipped in his fist. His hands were sweating. He was sweating all over.

What could he do? If he ran toward Caroline, she would bolt, straight into Deaver. If he didn't make a move, Deaver would. Either way he was fucked.

"Ms. Lake!" Deaver called. "Run now, before it's too late! I've got agents coming, we'll keep you safe. We've got to get you back to your shop. Make a run for it, and I'll cover you!"

Deaver's voice was stronger. He was edging closer to Caroline. Soon, he'd be able to take a bead on her even if she didn't bolt.

"Don't believe him, honey." Jack kept his voice low, hoping it wasn't carrying to Deaver. "He's lying."

"How—how can he be lying?" Caroline's voice quavered. "He's an FBI agent."

"No, he's not." In two long strides, Jack came several feet closer to Caroline, finding cover behind another big oak.

"He's not an FBI agent. He's a war criminal. He's responsible for a—"

"Massacre in an African village. Stealing diamonds. I know." Caroline was keeping her voice low. "He told me. Only he said it was you. That *you* were a war criminal with a fortune in stolen diamonds. And he showed me a photograph of you, Jack. You said you came from Afghanistan, but the snapshot showed you in Africa. The time stamp said it was taken on the twenty-first of December. And Jenna Johnson said that you deposited eight million dollars in a bank account. How can I believe you?"

Oh, Jesus.

He didn't have time to explain, convince. Deaver was going to pounce any minute. Jack would gladly take a bullet for her, but she wouldn't let him get close enough.

The sweat was pouring down his back, falling into his eyes. He felt sick with fear.

He could see the lampposts along the street—the snowstorm was easing up slightly. Deaver was out there, moving from cover to cover, and inside a few minutes, he'd reach Caroline. Deaver didn't need for her to bolt. All he had to do was sneak up behind her, snake an arm around her neck, and call for Jack to put down his weapon.

Jack would do it, too. Even knowing that certain death would follow, he'd do it to save Caroline. Only he wouldn't save her. She'd be next.

Jack swallowed the surge of bile in his throat, the taste of defeat.

There! Something flitted between the trees, a ghost of movement. Deaver. Coming closer.

Caroline couldn't stay there, she'd be dead inside of five minutes. And Deaver had filled her head with so many lies, she wouldn't run to him.

She had to get away, *now!*

Jack dug into his jeans pocket and tossed a mass of metal toward Caroline. Even in the dusk and in the snow, he had an excellent aim. It fell at her feet, sinking instantly into the snow.

She bent and picked it up, turning it over in his hand. He could see her clearly now. She raised her eyes and saw him. His heart clenched at the expression on her face—sorrow and fear and grief.

"Caroline," he said urgently. "Those are the keys to the Explorer. It's parked on Harrison. Get in and drive, just as fast as you can. Head for Seattle or Spokane. There's a couple of thousand dollars in the glove compartment, use that. Just get yourself away from here. If something—if something happens to me, get in contact with Philip Napier. He's an estate lawyer on Hewitt. I've left my will with him. You'll inherit everything I own. Have him wire you the money and disappear. Don't ever come back here. Deaver will kill you if you do."

She stared into his eyes. "Where did the money come from?" she whispered.

Another glimpse of a shape, barely visible, taking refuge behind the concrete walls of the public toilets before Jack could aim. He was moving toward the bandstand. Jack could see the barrel of Deaver's gun jutting out from the right-hand corner of the wall. Caroline was on the other side of the bandstand. He'd figure it out in a moment and rush her. She had only minutes left.

"Listen carefully, sweetheart. The money didn't come from the diamonds, I swear. I sold my father's company and my house. Use it and stay far away from here. Promise me you'll go. I need to know you're safe."

"You had photographs of me." Tears were rolling down her cheeks. "You know Greenbriars inside out. Who *are* you?"

He had to get her away, *now*. Only the truth would work.

"Ben."

"What?"

"I'm Ben, sweetheart. Do you remember the boy in the homeless shelter? Twelve years ago? You brought me food and books."

Her eyes were wide, fixed on his. He could see her very clearly. The snow had almost stopped. Fifty feet away, Deaver stepped out from behind the concrete wall and assumed the stance.

"Ben? You're Ben?"

Jack brought his weapon up, aimed. Time had run out.

"Run, Caroline! Run!" he screamed.

Caroline bolted and ran. But not toward his vehicle. She ran straight toward him.

Deaver stepped out from behind the concrete wall, tracking her . . . finger on the trigger . . .

Jack caught Caroline with one arm, lifting his weapon with his other, going for the one shot certain to kill instantly—putting a round right on the bridge of Deaver's nose. Deaver fell backwards, the spray of blood bright on the pristine white snow.

And that was all Jack saw as he wrapped his arms around Caroline, safe now, safe forever, and buried his face in her hair, tears bright and cold on his face.

Headquarters of The Children's Shelter
Chicago
Two weeks later

Sister Mary Michael smiled at the envelope on her desk. Over the course of the past ten years, there had been many of them—all the same. They had all been addressed to her, care of the nondenominational charity she headed. The Children's Shelter, dedicated to providing an education to the lost children in homeless shelters.

Each envelope was written in black ink in a bold, strong hand. Each envelope held the same return address—a foundation incorporated in the Bahamas. The JP Foundation, Box 1341, Freeport, Grand Bahama. Each envelope had held a check.

There was no way to know whether the person writing was a man or a woman, but Sister Mary Michael just knew it was a man. Something about the strong strokes of the pen, the spacing, the evenness of the letters . . . over the years she'd even built up an image in her mind. A tall, strong man, who didn't want gratitude.

She'd tried to thank him. Oh, how she'd tried. After the first few checks had arrived, she'd asked Tom Pinto for help. Tom had learned to read at the age of twelve thanks to the Shelter, and he had become one of the finest private investigators in the country. She asked him to track down the person or persons behind the JP Foundation. Tom was very good at his job, but he never managed to crack the infinite layers of protection screening the Foundation's backers. Finally, Tom had told her gently to let it be, and she had.

The Foundation was clearly an example of God's will, shining through.

Sister Mary Michael laid the envelope down on the desk before her, touching it with the tips of her fingers and said a prayer for the immortal soul of the sender, knowing that God's grace shone particularly strong in him. The Shelter would have long since had to close its doors if it hadn't been for her mysterious and generous benefactor.

Sister Mary Michael picked up a wooden letter opener that had been carved for her by one of her lost children, lost no more, now a second-year surgical resident in Boston, and slit the envelope open.

The checks had started out small. A thousand dollars, a couple of times a year, at first. As the years went by, the checks increased in size as her benefactor, bless his soul, grew wealthy.

The last check had been for thirty thousand dollars.

Smiling, Sister Mary Michael slid the check out and looked at the figures. Two thousand dollars. Well, maybe business hadn't been . . .

No, she'd read it wrong. Twenty thousand—no. Sister Mary Michael caught her breath and blinked, staring at the words written in black ink in that familiar strong hand.

Twenty million dollars.

Lisa Marie Rice

LISA MARIE RICE is eternally thirty years old and will never age. She is tall and willowy and beautiful. Men drop at her feet like ripe pears. She has won every major book prize in the world. She is a black belt with advanced degrees in archaeology, nuclear physics and Tibetan literature. She is a concert pianist. Did I mention the Nobel?

Of course, Lisa Marie Rice is a virtual woman and exists only at the keyboard when writing erotic romance. She disappears when the monitor winks off.

Lisa Marie welcomes reader fan mail at *lisamarierice@hotmail.com*.